THE
GAME

D0833411

THE
GAME

KRYSTYNA KUHN

Translated from German by
Helena Ragg-Kirkby

www.atombooks.net

For Christiane and Christiane

ATOM

First published in Germany in 2010 by Arena Verlag GmbH
First published in Great Britain in 2011 by Atom

Copyright © 2010 by Krystyna Kuhn

Translated from German by Helena Ragg-Kirkby

The moral right of the author has been asserted.

A CIP catalogue record for this book
is available from the British Library.

ISBN 978-1-907410-56-7

Typeset in Melior by M Rules
Printed and bound in Great Britain by
Clays Ltd, St Ives plc

Atom
An imprint of
Little, Brown Book Group
100 Victoria Embankment
London EC4Y 0DY

An Hachette UK Company
www.hachette.co.uk

www.atombooks.net

CHAPTER 1

Six and a half thousand feet up, Julia was wrenched from a half-sleep by the brakes squealing. The heavily laden jeep seemed to be groaning aloud as it rounded every new bend. No wonder. The Land Rover had spent more than an hour heaving its way up the steep serpentine roads. It was evidently past its prime.

Last one out turns off the light!

That's what her mum had always said as she left the house. And it now seemed to Julia as if someone had in fact switched off the sun as soon as they'd left Fields, a godforsaken little dump in the Rocky Mountains.

Julia stared through the dusty car window. She could see only a tiny bit of the road that snaked its way ahead of them and up the mountain: the grey asphalt gleamed wet in the dim headlights. High above them, she could make out the silhouettes of the pine trees which bordered the road to left and right.

Julia had never seen such tall trees. The tops of them rose menacingly into the dark sky, allowing only a tiny glimpse of the stars. They made a spooky welcome party, standing there for one reason alone: to protect the valley from intruders.

Intruders like Julia?

Or was it the birds who circled above the trees, ready to pounce on one another or to plunge down on to the car that was disturbing the peace and quiet of their hunting ground?

The car headlights briefly illuminated a sign at the edge of the road.

Caution: Falling Rocks.

Shortly afterwards, the forest cleared to her left. A steep cliff rose up, momentarily blocking her view of the road ahead. The Land Rover turned a corner, then crossed a bridge across a gaping ravine. Julia's body was pressed into the seat as the vehicle rumbled over the unsteady surface, evidently wooden planks. In front of her, Robert's head bumped against the headrest of the passenger seat, but her brother didn't wake up.

Julia sighed, realising her leg had gone to sleep. It felt as if it wasn't there any more. She moved it cautiously, and knocked against something soft. The colossal black dog at her feet stared up at her. Even in the dark, she could sense the dog's aggressive eyes. His name was Ike. Ike growled softly.

'Sorry,' she whispered in an attempt to placate him.

Julia wasn't a country girl. She belonged in the city. But she couldn't dwell on that.

Not now.

Never again.

For the past two days, Julia Frost and her brother Robert, a year her junior, had been en route to Grace College, which lay in Grace Valley, high up in the Rocky Mountains. They had taken several detours; rather than flying straight to

Calgary, they had flown first to New York and then on to Seattle. There, they had finally boarded a plane to Calgary. From Calgary, they had carried on to Banff and Lake Louise, one of the most famous parts of the Rockies, where a tiny propeller aircraft had been waiting to take them to the Yoho National Park.

Julia shut her eyes. It still felt like a dream to her. Maybe it was all happening in one of the parallel universes that Robert was always on about. It was always the same thoughtful expression behind the round glasses that he'd found in the flea market. They made him look so earnest, it was as if you were talking to the youngest Nobel Prize winner of all time: Robert Frost, international expert in extraterrestrial phenomena.

Right in the middle of a song Julia's iPod gave up the ghost. She looked at the display: the battery was dead.

'Robert?' She could just make out his silhouette in front of her. 'Robert, can I have your iPod?'

No answer.

Alex, their driver, looked across at Julia's brother sleeping in the passenger seat and grinned. Alex was a senior at Grace College – or just Grace, as he called it – and was their student mentor. At Grace College, an elite college for highly talented students, it was a tradition for the fourth-year students to mentor the freshers. Grace put particular emphasis on fostering good relationships between the students, Alex had explained right at the start of their journey.

Alex had met Julia and Robert at the little airstrip in Fields with such a beaming smile that Julia had relaxed for the first time following their long, tortuous journey. And now, too, as he cast a brief, amused look at Robert, he seemed kind. He looked over his right shoulder at her and gave her a cheerful wink.

Julia returned the smile almost automatically. She was, after all, a nice girl. Little Miss Perfect. The girl whose sunny personality ensured that everyone got on with one another. That's what it had said in her last report: *Her cheerful disposition rubs off on all the other students.*

'Your brother's sleeping like a log! He's not on drugs, is he?'

'No!' Julia replied, feeling her smile freeze. That was all they needed, people saying that kind of thing about Robert before they'd even arrived. Attracting attention was the very last thing they wanted to do.

'Hey, chill out.' Alex's eyes appeared in the rear-view mirror. 'It was just a joke. Believe me, I know how it feels after a mammoth journey like that. But before I came to collect you, I made sure that they'd have a hot meal waiting for you at the college. The Grace kitchen isn't exactly a five-star restaurant, but it's not bad. And you can take it gently with the classes tomorrow.'

Alex sounded genuinely concerned. There was no doubt about it, he was one of those 'Mr Sunshine' types of guy. And he was extremely good-looking. The kind of guy who was probably conceived on the beach and born with a surfboard tucked under his arm.

Julia stared at the immaculately ironed collar of his sky-blue shirt. He would surely be more at home in Florida than in this grubby, rickety Land Rover. And he was presumably a girl-magnet.

Her foot bumped against the dog once more, who was now taking up the entire foot-well. He growled menacingly.

'Shh, Ike, stop showing off,' said Alex, adding: 'Don't worry: he's all bark and no bite. He's no danger when he's quiet, but he's no use when there's danger around either.'

'Is he your dog?' asked Julia.

'Ike? No! He really belongs to Professor Brandon, one of the college's philosophy lecturers. But he really belongs to anyone who likes him.'

'I like him!' Robert gave an enormous yawn, stretched, and looked out of the window. 'Aren't we there yet?'

No. They seeemed to be even further away than ever.

The steep rock faces were by now behind them. Instead, the forest had closed around them once more like a giant living thing. The road was still heading steeply upwards: Julia could feel the incline, and she briefly wondered what would happen if the groaning engine were to pack up here in the middle of nowhere.

Wasn't that how horror films always began?

Julia could feel the hairs on her arm stand on end. Oh, for goodness sake, she told herself. Stop being such a baby. How many times have you been alone on the Underground at night? That's a thousand times more dangerous. I mean, this is just a forest!

And yet – she suddenly found it hard to breathe. Maybe it was because the pine trees were closing in on one another more and more. She couldn't see a single gap.

And, God, they had spent hours now driving up through the mountains. They should surely have reached the end of the trees by now!

Julia clenched her fists, and her fingernails dug into her delicate palms. She'd known that the college was isolated – that was, after all, the real reason why she'd chosen it. But she'd had no idea what such isolation meant in practice: even in her worst nightmares she hadn't imagined it to be quite so desolate.

'It makes you feel a bit uneasy at first, just driving through endless forest, doesn't it?' said Alex. He evidently sensed what was going through Julia's mind. 'But you get used to it. And Grace is really cool – really different from other schools. Did you know that it's the highest college in the whole of North America?' A strand of longish blond hair fell across his right eye. 'And if it makes you feel any better, we're nearly at the pass – and then we go down into the valley.'

'How high's the pass?' Robert was a numbers geek. He couldn't survive without precise information.

'More than 8,000 feet. It's called White Escape, though that isn't an invitation to go AWOL!' Alex's laugh was infectious. Robert joined in, as Julia looked out of the window again.

White Escape.

Oh great!

'Wow! So presumably skiing is compulsory here?' Robert said, turning to Alex.

'Compulsory? No! Skiing in these mountains is ...' Alex shook his head, and his face suddenly closed up. Or was

Julia just imagining it? 'And in any case, summer's on the way. Most kids go swimming instead. The college has a huge swimming complex. Our team is really successful.'

'And what about the lake?'

Alex shook his head regretfully. 'Swimming's only allowed in one particular part of Mirror Lake. I'll tell you now that all the warning signs aren't there just for decoration. So if you see any signs saying *Danger of Death*, stay away!'

'You don't need to worry about Julia. She's like a world champion diver. She's won loads of prizes, haven't you Julia?' Robert said proudly.

Julia didn't reply.

Alex whistled admiringly and looked at Robert. 'And what about you?'

'I'm allergic to water.'

'In that case you and Ike have something in common.'

'How do we get to town?' Julia asked. It was a deliberate interruption. Under no circumstances did she want Robert to say anything else. Sometimes you couldn't get a single word out of him, and other times he talked non-stop, as if he had an irreparable defect in his language control centre.

'Most students here don't have a car. The journey is just too long. But there's a bus into town once a week if you want a dose of civilisation. Although – well, you've seen Fields!'

'Civilisation?' said Julia, grinning. 'That dump felt as if the first settlers were still living there.'

'Don't worry – if you need anything at all, there's a supermarket, two cafés and a cinema on campus. And you can order whatever you like over the internet. You don't have to leave the valley. You can survive quite well up here.'

Just a few weeks ago, Julia would have been rendered hysterical by this statement. She'd have been jumping out of the car on the spot, heading off into the distance at top speed.

But now?

Now everything was different. There was no denying it: in her situation, the college did seem to be the right choice. If you could say it was a choice.

Alex switched the high beam on. White light flooded the road like fog that contained some kind of phosphorescent substance. Stardust, maybe, or comet dust? 'This landscape's the business, isn't it?' Alex said. He did sort of have a point. 'Believe me, once you're there, you'll never want to leave. You get addicted to the mountains!' The car slowed down. 'Okay, folks, we're at the pass. Not far to go now.'

Julia had imagined that she'd be able to see down into the valley from the pass. However, the highest point of the road wasn't all that different from the road that lay behind them. Here, too, the pine trees were densely packed, and blocked her view. There was just one weather-beaten wooden sign telling them that they'd reached the summit: *White Escape, 7,916 feet.* Underneath, it said: *2,413 meters.*

Seconds later, she could feel that they were going downhill. Alex put his foot on the accelerator, and he sped rather too fast for Julia's liking down the snaking road. Until now, the asphalt had just been wet, but now the water sprayed up from gigantic puddles, and every now and then the car jolted over the stones. The dog on the dirty floor smelled revolting.

'By the way, Mrs Hill – she's the head of first year – didn't tell me why you weren't arriving until now.' Julia became aware that Alex was speaking again. 'The semester started a week ago.'

'Robert was ill for ages, and couldn't fly before,' Julia murmured.

'What was wrong with him?'

'Pneumonia.' The lie came automatically. In order to turn his attention away from Robert, she asked him: 'Is everyone else already there?'

'Yes, of course they are. Your year is the only one that's not complete yet. You'll be sharing with three other girls, Deborah Wilder, Katie West and Rose Gardner in apartment 213.'

Names that meant nothing to her. People that Julia didn't want to know.

'What about me?' asked Robert.

'Apartment 113. One floor down. You'll be with David Freeman, Benjamin Fox and Christopher Bishop. Boys and girls are kept on separate floors.' Alex laughed. 'There's one senior mentor on every floor. Isabel Hill is in charge of the second floor, and I'm in charge of the first one. If you have any problems, just ask me or Isabel. We share an office and work closely together.'

Mentor? The way he described it, it sounded more like a minder, Julia thought.

She shut her eyes and thought of the song that her iPod battery had so abruptly interrupted.

'I Know It's Over' by Emilie Autumn.

Not exactly what you'd expect of Little Miss Perfect.

For the next ten minutes, silence reigned in the Land Rover.

If you have any problems, just ask me.

It might have been hilarious, if it hadn't all been so horrendous.

Problems?

That word didn't apply to her situation. A 'problem' was what people had if they missed the bus, or if their spots started spreading or, for all she cared, their bank card was rejected. No: Julia didn't have problems. She was the very embodiment of catastrophe. A catastrophe that would never end – just like the road outside, or so it seemed.

Alex was steering the car with one hand, and he still hadn't slowed down. But Julia was too exhausted to say anything.

Her gaze followed the lurid glow of the headlights, which seemed to illuminate the same bit of the forest track: black trees, lit up for a matter of seconds, as if they were going to catch fire when the headlights hit them. Every one a copy of the others.

The road.

The future.

A rattlesnake that gives you the creeps as it slithers along with its strange, unexpected movements. And nobody can guess which direction it's going to choose next.

Suddenly, Julia felt that Robert's prattling about parallel universes wasn't quite so absurd after all.

'Look after him!' her mother had exhorted her more than once. 'Look after your brother. He's not made for this world. He's different.'

And me? Julia wanted to ask. What about me?

'What do you reckon, Julia?' whispered Robert. 'How long have we been now?'

'No idea.'

'Time is relative ... we've probably been travelling for forty-eight hours, but it feels to me as if time's standing still.'

'Robert, I'm tired. I really don't want to think about the phenomenon of time.'

'What I mean,' she heard him say, 'it's just that ... there are moments when you can't feel time passing because nothing's changing – or everything is! But how are you supposed to orient yourself if time and space ...'

Julia shut her eyes and tried to tune out his voice. She knew that she would be well and truly left behind if Robert started on one of his scientific discourses. And at that moment, she couldn't even be bothered to try to follow him: all she wanted was to get there, go to bed, and hope that the future would soon pass.

The dog growled at her feet.

'Quiet, Ike,' she heard Robert murmuring. 'Good dog.'

The car slowed down. Julia opened her eyes.

During the few seconds in which she'd tuned out the world, everything had changed. It was as if someone had transported her to a different location, beamed her up to somewhere completely new.

The dense forest lay behind them, and the road ahead

11

suddenly widened. To the left and right were street lamps, their orange light illuminating their way in the night. Julia felt her hands beginning to perspire with anticipation. Alex steered straight towards a huge glistening area.

Despite the darkness, Julia couldn't just sense the lake: she could see it clearly. It was almost as if it were giving off some inner glow. As if countless lights were glittering beneath the surface of the water. And the lake was spreading out endlessly into the valley – as if it knew no boundaries, or so it felt to Julia, at any rate. In the darkness, she couldn't see the mountains opposite or the shore which presumably marked the end of the lake somewhere in the distance.

And then there it was. On the left at the end of the street was the college building, about a quarter of a mile away. It was brightly lit.

Julia had imagined it to be more modern. Instead, they were heading for a massive building that, with its numerous chimneys, balconies, windows and bays, looked as if it had been altered more than once over the years. And instead of looking inviting – as Julia had hoped it would after their long journey – it looked off-putting, if not downright spooky. Like an alien that didn't belong in the valley. Like the gleaming black surface of Mirror Lake was recoiling from the building.

Alex started braking, and the car slowed down.

Julia craned her neck. The headlights had lit up a red and white striped barrier. Like a frontier post, thought Julia, wondering where she'd put her passport. With that frightful mug-shot that should have a prisoner number beneath it – but which instead bore the name Julia Frost.

The car wheels crunched.

'Won't be a moment,' said Alex. He wound down the window, leaned out, and spoke into an invisible intercom. 'Alex Cooper. Can you open the barrier?'

Seconds later, the barrier rose silently and Alex set off again. The raw night air came through the open window; so cold that Julia thought she might as well be sticking her head in a freezer. Why couldn't he shut the bloody window? But before she could complain, the sign appeared. Squiggly green writing on a white background, illuminated by countless little lights, as if Christmas had come in the middle of summer.

Welcome to Grace Valley.

They'd done it. Time wasn't standing still.

'Here we are!' said Alex, turning briefly to look at her.

No, Julia thought, we're not here at all. We've gone forever.

'Watch out!' Robert yelled. 'Someone's there!'

Alex whirled round. The tyres skidded and the car came to a sudden standstill.

The dog jumped up and put its paws on Julia's lap.

Robert's voice was trembling. 'What was that?'

'For God's sake, you scared me!' Alex looked angrily at Robert.

'Sorry – but by the side of the road. There was something there. You almost hit it. I think it was a person!'

Julia stared out of the window. The next street lamp was about a hundred yards away, so the headlights were the only things that lit up the area around them. To the right were trees; to the left a field that sloped away to the college, which was covered in foliage. Boulders and stones, big and small, lay everywhere, but there wasn't a person in sight.

Alex looked around too, then shook his head.

'You're mistaken,' he said, starting the Land Rover. 'It's easy to mistake these stones for animals or people in the dark.'

'I wasn't mistaken,' Robert said firmly. 'Someone was there.' Julia recognised the customary stubbornness in his voice. Once her brother had an idea in his head, nothing was going to shift it. Long experience had taught her that.

Was that why she turned round?

The rear lights left trails of red dots behind them on the dark, narrow road, like tracer shells. Alex slowed down. The brake-lights lit up briefly and ... there it was. Something was standing in the road, watching the car.

A person? No – something else; something smaller, more compact ...

Was it an animal after all?

No. Robert was right.

It was a person! For a second, Julia could make out a hand waving to them. A hand that belonged to someone in a wheelchair.

Alex's and Robert's voices became indistinct. They were drowned out by a loud cawing. Julia could hear the birds, but she couldn't see them. It was only their screeching that told her that they were somewhere above their heads. They grew louder for a moment, then faded away.

The birds had fled from the valley.

Something or someone had frightened them.

Julia wished she could have fled with them.

CHAPTER 2

The room was horribly stuffy. Robert found it hard to breathe. It hadn't been far down from the mountain pass: Grace College was still some two thousand metres up. Although there were presumably still frosty nights in early May, Robert was sweating. But he knew that it was nothing to do with the outside temperature.

His mind was wandering. Fleeing from the loud echoes of memories. He knew what was happening, but couldn't do anything about it. It became worse and worse. His thoughts raced through the twisting, labyrinthine corridors of his brain. It was just biology, he told himself. Chemistry, synapses.

So why couldn't he control them?

What had changed?

He couldn't grasp this question either. Instead, he was overcome again by insights that came to him in a flash and scared him to death. He could see through things, and could perceive another world behind them, a world that might be harmless but might also harbour hidden dangers.

Robert had felt unbearably crushed by the very sight of the college campus.

'Unbearably' because he couldn't tell anyone how he felt,

and because there was nobody who could comfort him or who would believe him.

In his room, he stared out of the little window at the alien landscape. To the south east, the silhouette of the highest peak stood out against the black sky which now looked even blacker in the lurid moonlight.

The mountain was called the Ghost. He'd asked Alex.

A weird name, but somehow right.

The Ghost consisted of three linked peaks, the middle of which was several hundred metres higher than the ones to the left and right. As if shrouded in grey cloth, the mountain range rose up above the valley and the aptly named Mirror Lake.

Robert screwed up his eyes behind his glasses. The middle peak did look like a ghost's face. The dark lines on its left and right looked like two eye-slits in a pale ghostly sheet. And the peaks to either side of it looked like two arms embracing the lake.

Stop it, Robert said to himself, and tried in vain to breathe more slowly. He listened to the water lapping softly against the reinforced shoreline. The lake was so near that it could be heard even through shut windows, and the longer Robert listened, the more it seemed to him as if the water were murmuring words.

Which, of course, was nonsense.

Completely ridiculous.

But the spooky feeling increased. A feeling of foreboding started to build up within him, quietly and barely perceptibly. As fleeting as the gentle breeze that wafted through the rickety window-frame and made him shiver despite the stuffy air.

As always, this spooky feeling was based on something that was annoying Robert.

In this case, it was the architecture of Grace.

At first sight, the historic main college building appeared to be a gigantic, castle-like edifice consisting of a vast central complex and two side wings. Behind the main building were the modern additions: the sports centre, the supermarket and the bungalows for the teaching staff and older students – though they were so skilfully integrated into the hilly landscape that Robert paid them no attention.

What really interested him was the facade of the main building. At first sight it looked capricious in its complexity, and Robert was initially confused by the countless balconies, dormers, arcade arches and cross-bar windows.

But first impressions were deceptive.

And this deception was to do with numbers. Robert normally found numbers reassuring, but the reverse was true here.

2, 4, 8, 12, 16.

These numbers frightened him.

2, 4, 8, 12, 16.

Two side wings, each with four floors and eight balconies. Each of the side wings was framed by two stairways, making four in total. The main building, in turn, consisted of a gigantic glazed central area which housed the foyer and refectory. To the left and right were sixteen windows apiece, and up in the roof were twelve dormers.

Every apartment in the side wings housed four students. There were eight apartments on each floor, four facing the front and four facing the back. That made thirty-two students per floor. That in turn made one hundred and twenty-eight students per side wing, or two hundred and fifty-six in total. Then there were the further hundred and twenty-two senior students who were, apart from the mentors, all accommodated in the more spacious and modern buildings at the back of the campus. In total, that made precisely three hundred and seventy-eight students. Exactly the number that Robert had read in the college prospectus.

Yes, Robert thought, the numbering system was simple, even verging on the primitive. Yet whoever built the college had put an awful lot of thought into the architecture.

Or was he just imagining it? After all, architecture – and indeed the whole world – was based on numbers and mathematical principles.

So was it just coincidence?

But it wasn't this that was making him feel irritated and uneasy. No, it was the system that he'd detected. Every apartment, every room had the same square layout. And the squares were lined up together like prison cells. Clearly arranged, orderly, and easy to keep an eye on at all times.

And then there was something else: the Grace College building and the Ghost faced one another like mirror images. Grace rose up above the western bank and the mountain dominated the eastern bank. And if Robert weren't mistaken, then ... no. Not that. The numerical ratio between the side peaks and the main peak of the Ghost surely couldn't be identical to that of the main building and its side wings.

Robert shivered again. He turned abruptly away from the window. He could feel the panic rising. It felt as if he were falling into a dark abyss.

CHAPTER 3

When Isabel Hill, the senior student in charge of the second floor of North Wing, opened the door to the tiny room, Julia was plunged into a state of shock. During the journey, she had been merely tired and irritable – but now she could clearly feel herself sinking into total despondency.

It was already late, almost half past ten, and although Alex had offered them something to eat, Julia and Robert had both declined.

Alex had parked the Land Rover by the side entrance of North Wing. The landings and corridors of North Wing had been relatively empty when they arrived; on the way to Alex's office on the first floor, they had encountered just a few students, who'd given them curious looks. Julia could see the questions whizzing through their minds. Who were these new students? Why had they only just arrived? In the middle of the night – and a week after the beginning of term, too? Why all the luggage?

At the same time, Julia had been too tired to take in her surroundings. All she saw was endlessly long corridors, only dimly lit, with seriously worn carpets whose pattern had long been rendered unrecognisable. It covered the parquet, made slippery by the feet of countless students.

It smelled kind of weird. As if decades of dirt had eaten their way into the timber in the walls and floors, and someone were now scrubbing away at it with super-strength cleaning products – to no avail. The eternal battle of humans against relentless dirt and filth. Their mum had almost always won it. No wonder. She was obsessed with cleaning and always lugged disinfectant hand-spray and wet-wipes around in her handbag.

'So, what do you reckon? Cosy, isn't it?' Isabel was a tall, slim blonde girl with the kind of short, just-got-out-of-bed hair that actually involves a vastly expensive cut and a thirty-minute daily styling ritual. Julia could tell by the way that she walked that she was one of the sporty crew; the type who went to bed wearing her trainers, went jogging before breakfast and stuck to a precise training timetable instead of having a life. In the old days, Julia and Kristian used to slag off people like that: people who go jogging are running away from life.

In the old days.

It was time to ditch this phrase from her vocabulary for once and for all. Along with the name Kristian.

'The shared bathroom's over there. The toilet's separate,' explained Isabel, 'and the glass door diagonally opposite leads to the kitchen, though you can have all your meals in the refectory.' She looked at Julia. 'What's up? Do you want to meet the girls you're sharing with?'

Julia shook her head. 'I'd rather do it tomorrow,' she managed. 'I'm pretty done in. We've had a long journey.'

Isabel nodded and heaved one of Julia's suitcases onto the

chair by the desk. 'Okay, I get you. By the way, you're lucky. Your apartment's right on the corner of the main wing, so you get a view of the lake. And you've got your own access to the balcony. It faces north, though, so the shutters rattle more loudly when it's really stormy, and you get frost on the windows in winter.'

Julia dutifully went over to the glass door. In the dim glow of the outside lights, she could see the grey silhouette of the lake and the mighty mountain scenery.

'Fantastic.' Julia nodded and forced her mouth into a smile. She smiled as Isabel gave her a pile of bed linen and towels; she smiled as Isabel showed her the wardrobe and put a campus map on the desk. She carried on smiling as the older student gave her a copy of the house rules, saying as she did so: 'Rules at Grace are there to be kept.'

Julia quite honestly thought that the corners of her mouth were going to get stuck halfway up her face. She'd have to go through the rest of her life sporting this rictus grin.

However, she pulled herself together and thanked Isabel. But as soon as Isabel had left the room, she threw herself on the bed, the mattress of which sagged down almost to the floor, and stared into space.

This room was tiny. And tawdry. It was vile. So far as she knew, the building dated back to the century before last. It had been turned into a college in the seventies. It seemed that little had been done to it since then, or not in the side wings and apartments, at any rate.

The fake carvings on the ceiling gave Julia the creeps. She was convinced that the rattling shutters would give her chronic tinnitus, the wormy wooden panelling would make her wheeze, and the carpet would make her come out in a rash. And then there was the furniture. Straight out of the seventies, but without the slightest hint of retro cool. The only thing she liked was the brown armchair right beside the balcony door.

But otherwise, there was a wooden chair, and a desk that could never take a pile of books. And if the refectory food was as bad as the bedroom, she would presumably die of malnutrition.

Only God and the architect knew which toxic materials had been used to build this place and keep it standing for all eternity. And Mum – Mum would have taken her home on the spot and booked her in for a full-scale session with the homeopath.

Mum.

Julia felt as if she'd been dropped into an agonising nightmare in which time was running backwards. It was crazy: with her inner eye, she could see the big hand racing round the clock.

Just in the wrong direction.

Julia couldn't forget the terrible row. Dad had yelled; Mum had tried to smooth things over.

'You can't tie her down,' she'd said. Her Bristol accent was more pronounced than normal, as it always was when she was upset.

'I don't have to tie her down, because I hope I've given her enough sense not to hang around with people who aren't worth the dust under her feet. Look at her. Our daughter. Look at the state of her. Is that really still my daughter?'

And Julia had turned and slammed the door behind her in true Hollywood style. She'd run off to her room and, later, had crept out to see Kristian. In short, she'd done what everyone her age has to do: she'd done her own thing. She'd told her parents where her boundaries were, and that was that.

Now, in retrospect, she knew that it had been a mistake. God, life would be so much easier if you knew in advance that something bad was going to happen.

Headache.

Goddamn headache.

Julia sat up, fumbled around in the dark for her new mobile, and pressed a random key. The display read 01:23.

She hadn't managed to get undressed, and was lying on the uncomfortable bed, unable to sleep. But what else had she expected? She hadn't slept for weeks; at best, she fell into a kind of short-term unconsciousness, then started up, drenched in sweat. Why on earth had she thought that would change as soon as she was at the college?

For a while, she stared up at the ceiling. The outside lights, which bathed the college buildings in a hazy glow, cast odd shapes on it.

Maybe she should unpack her suitcase.

Or get up, and deliver the promised sign of life?

Sign of life.

A phrase that had recently taken on a particular meaning

for Robert and her. How was her brother doing, she wondered.

Could he sleep?

Julia pictured again his look of despair when Alex had handed them the keys. Robert would rather have gone with her into her room, where he would have rolled himself up in her bedside rug. Just so that he didn't have to sleep alone. But he hadn't said anything, as Alex – exhausted after the long drive – had barely even looked at them. Or was he still pissed off with Robert for almost causing an accident in the car? Though Robert was right: there really had been someone in the road. But neither of them had mentioned the figure in the wheelchair to Alex. Julia couldn't explain why not, even to herself.

She raised her head and stared outside through the glazed balcony door into the night. Everything was silent – but in a tense kind of way. She felt as if someone had spread a black blanket over her which enveloped her but offered no warmth, and suffocated every sound bar one: a grinding noise outside in the corridor that awoke memories within her.

She shivered.

There was a draught somewhere.

And there was that grinding noise again. It penetrated her consciousness, lodged itself in her ears, bored its way firmly and inexorably into her brain.

She listened. Could she hear footsteps?

She concentrated. A scraping sound, then footsteps again.

Was someone in her bedroom?

26

Yes.

Now she could clearly feel it. Someone was coming towards her bed. Someone was staring at her. Someone was breathing loudly.

Suddenly, Julia found the light-switch and the bedside lamp came on. She couldn't see anything, but she heard a soft giggle.

'Oh, you're awake.' Then there was another giggle, and then: 'Welcome to the valley!'

Pale blue eyes stared at Julia for twenty seconds solid without blinking once.

Julia didn't feel so much shock as utter irritation. She took in every detail, as if her brain were trying to put together all the separate elements of what she saw before her.

Pale, rather watery eyes. Freckles, a slender neck. Orangey strands in brown hair. A lurid orange that reminded Julia of life-jackets. If the campus hairdresser were responsible for this crime against colour, she'd grow her hair so long that she could warm her permanently cold feet with it. The girl was wearing baggy grey jogging bottoms and a shirt.

'You're staring at me as if I were a ghost,' she said, holding out her hand.

Was that really surprising, when she came creeping into Julia's room after midnight without knocking?

But rather than saying that, Julia took a deep breath, sat up, and forced a smile for the hundredth time in recent hours.

The hand that was held out was dotted with freckles and felt as cold as the skin of a newly plucked dead chicken.

The girl licked her lips and sniffed noisily. 'Sorry, but I did knock. I thought you were bound to be awake, and might fancy a bit of company.'

Julia didn't believe a word of it. All the same, she said: 'Well, you're right that I couldn't sleep.'

'Course you can't, when it's all so new.'

Julia couldn't disagree with that. But she had no chance to reply anyway, as the other girl carried on babbling. She made the Niagara Falls seem like a little stream.

'I can tell you everything you want to know about Grace. It's pretty confusing to start with, but you'll find your way round after a couple of days. And to be honest, the college is the best thing that could have happened to me. I've finally got rid of my parents. No more lectures, no telling me how to live my life. I've only been in the valley for a week, but I feel as if I've been here forever.'

You kind of look that way too, thought Julia.

'Shove up.' The strange girl clambered over Julia and made herself at home in the narrow bed, her back against the wall. 'Why've you come a week late?'

Julia took a deep breath. The true master of lies, the professional hide-and-seeker, answered questions with counter-questions.

'What's your name?'

'Deborah. Deborah Wilder, but everyone calls me Debbie.'

Debbie leaned forward and reached for the jewellery on Julia's bedside table. 'Why've you got two gold rings on that chain?' She was looking to see if they were engraved when Julia wrenched them away.

'Oh, sorry, I didn't mean to be nosy. Are you engaged?'

In love, engaged, married. That was definitely not going to be part of Julia's future. All the same, memories suddenly flooded her head as if they had been queuing up, waiting to get in.

Had Kristian already forgotten her? Or was he still looking for her? And what had he thought when she'd suddenly disappeared without saying anything, without even a goodbye?

One day, in years to come, someone might ask him: Do you still remember the first girl you slept with? Do you remember that Saturday evening, the evening of the disaster?

How long would it be before Julia turned to mist in his memory?

How long would it be before he forgot who she was?

Which girl? Kristian would say.

'My room's right next to yours, by the way.' Debbie was looking around, full of curiosity. 'Why've you got so much luggage? D'you want to stay here forever? There are teachers who were here in the seventies and came back when the valley was reopened.'

'Reopened? So was it shut once?'

Debbie made a dismissive gesture. 'Long story. Ancient history. Let's think about the present. I'm sure you want to know all about the other two who live here. We share the kitchen and bathroom, but Isabel's presumably told you that.' She tugged at Julia's bedcover. 'To be honest, we haven't exactly won the lottery with them.' Debbie didn't wait for Julia to reply, but carried on talking. 'So, there's Rose. Dear, beautiful, wonderful Rose. Apart from the baldness.'

'Baldness?'

Debbie giggled.

'Bald as a coot!'

'Is she ill?'

'No idea. Haven't asked her. Or, rather, I have asked her, but she didn't give me a proper answer.' Debbie grimaced. 'I know her type. She acts all gentle and innocent, but she's untouchable in real life. Untouchable – know what I mean?'

No, Julia didn't know what she meant. She wasn't interested either, but so long as Debbie was talking about other people, she was at least not plaguing Julia with questions. Maybe that was what bitching was all about. If you were slagging off someone else, you didn't have to give away anything about yourself.

'Are you actually listening to me?' Debbie stared at Julia. The way she was grumpily pursing her lips made her look as if she had a narrow slit in her face instead of a mouth. Kind of creepy.

'Of course I'm listening to you. What's the other girl like?'

Julia had hoped that her question would get rid of the peevish look on Debbie's face, but now her pale blue eyes were blinking nervously.

'Katie?'

'Is that her name?'

'Yes, Katie West. From some Asian country. Stay away from her,' whispered Debbie. 'She's weird. Hardly ever talks to anyone. Keeps herself to herself. But the boys in our year are fine. Especially the gang on the floor beneath ours. You'll like them.' She sighed. 'I'm so jealous that they've got Alex.

We have to contend with that stuck-up cow Isabel on our floor. She really thinks she's it, just because her parents are teachers at the college. "Rules at Grace are there to be kept",' she imitated the older student. Julia had to admit that it was a pretty good impression. 'As if she were our mother. But whatever. Have you heard, on Thursday evening . . . '

A loud crackling sound interrupted Debbie's torrent of words, followed by a buzzing that seemed to come from the bowels of the old building. Then the light suddenly went out. Instantly, the room was plunged into total darkness, along with everything outside.

'What's going on now?'

Julia felt a hand clutching her shoulder.

'Oh my God,' Debbie whispered. She could barely speak. 'Dark! I've been terrified of the dark ever since I was a child. I totally believe in monsters!'

Debbie sounded as if she did genuinely believe what she was saying. Julia felt like laughing out loud – but a second later, she heard a new sound, and was so horrified that she bit her lip.

It was a scream that rang out along the college corridors. A scream that came from the very depths of utter despair.

CHAPTER 4

When the lights came back on, Debbie had already flung open Julia's door and was racing into the hallway of the apartment, where a passage led to the main corridor. Julia followed her, her sense of foreboding increasing. Right next to her room a tall, slim girl was standing in a doorway. Her head was shaven, though Julia thought nothing of it. She also paid no attention to a second girl, who was emerging sleepily from the furthermost room. She was pushing back her long black hair, an impatient look on her face. This must be the Katie girl Debbie had been complaining about.

The light flickered once more, went off briefly and then came back on again, this time oddly dim. Julia ran through the hallway into the main corridor and looked around wildly.

Four apartments lay opposite the four on her side. The pale, sleepy faces of unknown girls were now appearing. They were hugging themselves, shivering with cold.

'Do any of you know what that was all about?' Debbie cried, raising her hands theatrically.

'No idea. But something must have happened! It freaked me out so bad that it woke me up!' exclaimed a girl in a blue nightgown.

The fear that Debbie had been talking about only a few seconds ago had suddenly vanished, and she was quite evidently in her element. Indeed, she actually seemed to be enjoying the whole thing. 'What do you think, guys? Did that scream come from outside?' she asked excitedly. 'Or from downstairs? Oh my God, I was crapping myself, I was so scared!'

Isabel appeared, saying: 'Hey, calm down girls. The best thing is for you just to go back to your own rooms.'

But Debbie simply ignored her. 'I bet it's on the floor below us!' she exclaimed.

She ran past Isabel, down the corridor and to the staircase. Julia was hot on her heels.

That scream – she could still hear it ringing in her ears. It was floating above her, as if it had implanted itself in the wood panelling, as if it were ingrained in the beams on the ceiling, clinging to the very fibres of the carpets.

And then all the commotion around her. The hysterical giggling, someone even murmuring a prayer – or was she going completely mad? She shut her eyes for a second. All the noise was like a background beat to that high, shrill voice that just wouldn't stop screaming. Couldn't someone switch off that screaming?

Couldn't someone finally press stop?

Then Julia understood.

She could read it in the faces of the other girls, who were gradually relaxing and generally returning to their rooms. She, Julia, was the only one who could still hear the scream.

33

And it wasn't the piercing noise as such that had scared her to death just minutes ago. It was the scream from her past that was resounding in her ears. It had followed her to the valley.

And now she knew what had happened.

'Come on, Julia,' Debbie was calling. 'The stairs will be faster than the lift.'

Debbie was in front of her, lumbering down the stairs, clutching the banisters, babbling away non-stop. It all sounded pretty crazy. 'D'you reckon it was one of the boys? Maybe they were torturing someone. As, like, a dare. Boys do that kind of thing, don't they? And that scream was really grue—'

She stopped abruptly. They had arrived on the first floor. Behind the big glass door that separated the corridor from the stairwell, Debbie had almost bumped straight into Alex. He was wearing bright checked boxer shorts and a white t-shirt with a black fire-breathing dragon on it. A grinning skull was on fire and ... Julia shut her eyes ... a cold, revolting vampire red was dripping from its bony jaw.

'Debbie, there's nothing to gawp at here. Back you go upstairs. But you, Julia ... would you mind ... ' Alex broke off, but Julia could tell from the way he was looking at her that her sense of foreboding had turned into a terrible certainty.

'Where?' she just asked.

'First apartment at the start of the corridor, same as on your floor,' Alex replied briefly.

Julia pushed past Debbie and ran off, past a group of boys

who stared after her. Some of them called out, and she heard a lewd whistle. But she was immune to that. Nothing mattered. She only caught her breath again once she was standing outside apartment 113.

'Hey, you've got a lady visitor,' said one of the boys who was standing in the corridor.

Another one was whispering. 'Cool or what? That's our alien's sister. God, I love filming on location.'

The only thing that Julia could see of this guy was his naked, hairless upper body and his pink pyjama trousers. His face was hidden by a camera.

And – for Christ's sake! thought Julia – he carried on filming as the light went out once more.

Julia was glad that the power didn't go back on this time. This gave her the chance to catch her breath and focus. Power cuts were evidently not unusual in the college, to judge by the students' supply of emergency lighting. Some had lit candles, and others were waving their torches around so wildly that it felt to Julia as if the earth were moving. She started to feel sick.

'So you're Julia?' A tall, slender boy was standing in the doorway of the room that must be directly beneath her own. His short, light-brown hair made him look oddly earnest in the semi-darkness. He was the only one who had got fully dressed. Black trousers, black trainers, and a black jumper. He was even wearing a belt.

'I'm David. Something's wrong with your brother. I've tried to wake him, but the more I talk to him, the more he panics. He doesn't wake up, but he won't let anyone touch him.'

'Okay.' That was the only answer she could give.

'Is that normal?' she heard someone asking behind her, but she didn't turn round.

Her mind was whirling. She had to calm Robert down – and stop him talking. Had he said anything in his sleep? Something that nobody should, could know?

She pulled herself together and pushed past David. 'It's fine, I'll take care of him. And ... ' She pointed behind her. 'I don't need an audience.'

'Does he often have that kind of nightmare?' David ignored her request.

For a moment, Julia forgot that she was Little Miss Perfect. 'It's a nightmare, so what?' she snapped. 'Can't you just get rid of the audience?'

'Hey, I'm only trying to help!' David raised his hands.

'He doesn't need your help! He'll laugh about it when he wakes up.' She tried to keep her voice light as she entered Robert's room – but she was thinking: no, he won't.

Her brother's room was identical to hers. Like her, Robert hadn't unpacked his suitcase. An empty picture frame stood on his bedside table. Julia felt a stab of pain.

Then she finally ventured to look at her brother. In the checked bedding, his thin body looked as if he were on hunger strike. He was lying on his back, staring up at the hideous wooden ceiling. No, of course he wasn't staring, because he had his eyes shut; but what if his eyes were open beneath his lids?

The very thought made an icy shiver run down her spine. Something heavy detached itself and landed on her chest, where it would remain forever. She took some deep breaths. She'd been taught relaxation techniques in an attempt to quell the panic. Relaxation techniques. Concentration games.

Ha, bloody ha. How exactly were breathing exercises going to drive out Debbie's monsters?

'Robert,' she whispered. 'Wake up. It's me.' She stretched out her fingers, touched her brother's hand in the darkness and at the very moment that Robert opened his eyes, there was a buzzing sound as the light came back on.

Robert blinked.

Beads of sweat were trickling down his high forehead. A thinker's forehead, Mum had always called it.

His dark brown hair was stuck to his head and his mouth was contorted as he started to speak.

'What's happened?'

'Nothing,' she reassured him. But then she heard a voice behind her.

'What do you mean, "nothing"?'

Julia suppressed a groan. Hadn't she asked that David person to leave her alone?

Robert reached for his glasses on the bedside table, as if wearing them would remind him of what had been going on. 'Everything was all over the place,' he murmured. 'Nothing was where it belonged. The books had all been pulled off the shelves ... and behind the table ... '

Julia was on the point of clamping her hand over his mouth just to shut him up. But she managed to pull herself together, and said brightly: 'You're fine, it was just a dream. Must be because you're in a strange place. Or have you been reading one of your weird books again, Rob?'

Keep smiling, Julia.

My God, keeping up this bloody grinning didn't half hurt.

And why Rob?

She'd never called him Rob before.

But he'd cottoned on, and was trying to play it down. Embarrassed, he pulled up his covers and turned to David. 'I'm sorry if I woke you.'

David came over to Julia and gave her brother a friendly thump on the shoulder. 'It must have been a really horrible dream to make you scream like that.'

'I screamed?' Robert's eyes widened.

'Yeah, like a stuck pig,' Julia said quickly. 'They ought to put you in a soundproof room here, before you're arrested for breach of the nocturnal peace.'

She didn't care what nonsense she was spouting. All that mattered was that he came round.

A low buzzing was coming from behind them. At first, she thought it was coming from the flickering bulb in the ceiling light, but then she spied the lens of a video camera. The boy in the hideous pink pyjama trousers was pointing the camera straight at Robert's face, and was calling: 'Brilliant, brilliant, brilliant. Look right at me. Yeah, like that. Wow, look at the size of your pupils! Like someone had burnt holes in your eyes. Or did you put something in them?' He was now coming closer to Robert and bending down to him. 'Can you pretend to be asleep again? I didn't get the scream properly, y'know?'

Something exploded inside Julia. A gigantic ball of fire in her head that scorched out all trace of reason.

Her hand met the cheek of the video guy. 'What kind of perv are you? One of those weirdos who goes following people around, getting off on their misery, and posting it all on YouTube? You switch that camera off right now, or I'll stick it up your arse!'

God, it felt so good to yell.

'Benjamin, she's right – turn the camera off,' she heard David saying before he put a reassuring hand on her shoulder. 'Benjamin doesn't mean any harm.'

Was David some kind of pastoral helper at the college? Not impossible, to judge by the way he dressed. At some deep level, Julia couldn't bear that kind of do-gooder. They were just aliens sent to earth to proselytise the poor, black-souled earthlings.

She was very glad to see Alex appear at the end of the bed. Although he was only four years older, he looked as if he was the only one with the necessary authority to put a stop to all this madness. And that's what he did. He looked at the clock and declared firmly: 'I think we can all go back to bed now. As you can see, Robert's fine.'

David and Benjamin exchanged looks, but then they left the room without further comment. Alex followed them, having called a reassuring 'Good night, you two' to Julia and

Robert. 'I think you'd better have a really good lie-in tomorrow morning.'

As the door snapped shut behind him, Julia walked round the bed to the window, where she stared out at the lake, the dark blot in the night.

'We can't stay here, Julia,' she heard Robert whispering behind her. 'This place is evil – evil!'

CHAPTER 5

Whatever it was that Robert had to say, Julia didn't want to know. She didn't want to hear his grim premonitions and prophecies. But at the same time she knew that he was normally right. He had this weird gift of sensing things that she hadn't remotely suspected.

She was acting entirely on impulse when she simply turned and left Robert's room without a word. She didn't even properly see the boy leaning by the door in the hallway who hadn't been there a minute ago. His voice came to her as if through cotton wool:

'Your brother's clever if it's only taken him three hours to work it out. It's taken the others up here years to do that.'

Julia pushed past him without replying – but as she made for the stairwell, struggling to maintain her facade of composure, she could feel that he wasn't the only one watching her. Students were standing around in little groups, giggling in a mocking way, murmuring. That's Julia Frost. She's new. It was her brother who was screaming just now, like someone was trying to kill him.

Julia started to run. She fled. And the funny thing was: it felt right. She had no choice but to flee from Robert or, rather, from the fact that everyone here was going to regard him as a freak from now on.

What she needed now was fresh air and time to think. She couldn't get that in these endless stuffy corridors where the walls were closing in more and more and the wood-panelled ceiling was pressing down on her. She passed one glass door, then another. Then to her left and right, she saw stairs leading down to the ground floor.

On the spur of the moment she chose the right-hand one – only to find herself in yet another long, windowless corridor on the ground floor.

For God's sake, wasn't there any way to get outside? Evidently not. Instead, there was one glass door after another, with endless further corridors and staircases branching off them. Where on earth was the side door that they'd used that evening?

The light suddenly flickered again and went out, plunging her back into an alarming darkness. She stopped. Her heart was pounding. She desperately wanted to scream, and she knew that her scream would sound like Robert's desperate terror that had shocked them all out of their sleep.

The ceiling light flickered once more. The light came on briefly, then it went dark again, and then the corridor was suddenly bathed in a ghostly green light. The emergency lighting had come on. At intervals of a few yards, dim lighting picked out the escape route.

She had no idea whereabouts in the building she was. Still in the north wing? So why couldn't she hear any noise anywhere? No footsteps, no voices. Nothing.

Puzzled, she looked around. This part of the building had evidently been recently renovated. It smelled of fresh paint. The dark wood-panelling on the walls and ceiling had gone, and instead the atmosphere was one of cold greyness. The same colour that had been used on all the doors. It took a while for Julia to work out what it said on the signs.

Lecture Theater
Laboratory
Learning Center
Seminar Rooms 1–5

Julia knew that Grace had some of the best facilities of all the colleges in the entire continent. Computer suites, libraries, dining rooms, modern lecture theatres, a cinema, a little theatre, swimming pools, several playing fields, two huge sports halls and all sorts of other things were available for the students on campus. But Julia had had no idea how big the main building alone would be, how full of nooks and crannies. It was so easy to get lost. You could presumably spend days wandering round corridors, climbing stairs to infinity, taking elevators into the inside of the earth – and you'd still never get there. Damn. There simply had to be a door to the outside.

This place is evil.

For God's sake, Robert, can't you just think for once that everything's going to be fine?

Oh God, I can't breathe. I have to get out of here.

Just as panic was threatening to overwhelm her, it became

lighter. The corridor turned sharply and Julia suddenly found herself standing in a gigantic atrium that was more like the foyer of a five-star hotel than a college.

A huge chandelier was hanging from the ceiling. The bright gleam of its countless little lights merged with the dimmer external lights that shone through the glass frontage to the inside, making an orangey glow. The ceiling, supported by columns of grey, unworked stone, had to be more than twenty feet high. Two wide, dark wooden staircases to the left and right led to the upper floor, ending in a wooden galleried landing. From there, people could look down into the foyer with its numerous cosy little seating nooks. In the massive open fireplace on the opposite wall, a few logs were still glowing. It all had nothing – nothing! – in common with the dated, Spartan student rooms, or with the shimmering greenish coldness of the corridor that she had just been in.

It all felt completely unreal. After a moment, Julia worked out why. This brightly lit entrance foyer was made for large numbers of people; for hustle and bustle, for noise, for life. But everything around her was deathly silent and empty.

Julia's attention was drawn to a row of blue flickering flat screens near to the entrance. She didn't stop to find out what they were for.

She ran across the hall. Her trainers barely made a sound on the stone floor; it felt as if the whole building were holding its breath with her.

And then she was at the revolving door. As it started

moving with a gentle whirring sound, Julia could have wept for sheer relief.

It was cold outside: an icy cold May night in the mountains. Once again, Julia was struck by how high up the college was. She immediately started shivering in her thin shirt, a clear reminder of how overheated and stuffy it had been in the building. No wonder she hadn't been able to get any fresh air.

She hugged her arms to her chest and looked around. Behind her rose the college building. It lay on a mighty plateau above Mirror Lake. Outside the glass-fronted entrance foyer the light fell on a broad, well tended lawn with gravel paths and neatly laid-out flower beds. The college authorities evidently invested a lot of money in the grounds and the reception area, and neglected the student accommodation. First impressions count.

Julia took a deep breath. The fresh air was doing her good; her heart was no longer pounding. Her behaviour suddenly felt silly and over the top. What would the others make of her running off like that? Was Robert really the freak, or was she the one who was going crazy?

Julia shook her head and set off. At a brisk pace, she took the main path. Moving would help to clear her head. Ball-shaped lights to the left and right of the path suddenly came on; they were evidently sensitive to movement. The plateau ended after some three hundred yards and Julia found herself at a set of wide steps which led straight down to the lakeside.

Astonished, Julia stopped. She had never imagined that the lake was so close to the college building. From the rooms, it looked as if it were further away.

For a moment she just stood there staring down at the lake. Its surface glimmered in the darkness as if it were made of glass. She could see now why it was called Mirror Lake. The mountains were reflected in the water even in the middle of the night.

Slowly, she made her way down, taking care not to slip on the wet steps. Now she noticed how quiet it was out here too. Strangely enough, though, it didn't give her goose bumps – unlike the way it had inside the building.

Once she had reached the end of the steps, it was considerably darker. The light in the reception area had evidently gone out, along with the lights on the lawn.

She looked to her right – but from here, she couldn't see the side wing with Robert's room.

Instead, she saw only endless rows of windows to the left and right of the glazed middle section. There was nothing to suggest that anything was wrong. But Julia felt somehow compelled to get out of sight of the building. As if the windows were countless eyes that were watching her.

People were evil – not places.

Julia quickly turned back to the lake. A narrow gravel path led from the steps down to the shore and alongside the water.

She turned right and set off briskly. The further she went, the calmer she felt, and the feeling of unreality abated. Being near water had always given her a sense of well-being, and she listened with relief to the waves as they gently lapped the shore. Suddenly everything became crystal clear.

She was at last in a position to reconsider the facts. Robert had lost the plot barely five hours after they'd arrived. Which meant they couldn't stay there. They would have to leave. Robert wouldn't be able to stick it out. Tonight had shown that all too clearly. It was her responsibility, and she had to do something as quickly as possible.

Resolutely, Julia pulled out her mobile. Robert was right. It was in any case time to get in touch. She'd promised to do so, but hadn't been in any kind of contact since the start of their journey. What was the time difference again? She looked at the display. Okay, it might work.

Julia keyed in the number. She knew it by heart. Every key made its electronic bleep. Then it rang twice, three times, four times . . .

. . . eleven times, twelve times.

Damn it! It was no use.

Julia was about to give up when her mobile vibrated.

She pressed the 'end call' button and stared at the phone. New Message.

Her fingers trembled with cold and anticipation as she read the text.

Dear Julia, Welcome to Grace. Thurs May 13 8pm Party at the Boathouse. Loa.loa!

What?

She hadn't given anyone this number. No, she hadn't used her mobile even once since buying it at the airport in Seattle.

So where had the sender got her number from? Who on earth was Loa.loa?

Without a second's thought, Julia flung the mobile away from her. As it landed on the mirrored surface of the lake, she was surprised not to hear shattering glass. The lake simply swallowed the phone. It sank noiselessly to the bottom.

Then she turned on her heel and ran back to the steps. She was still almost a hundred yards away when she suddenly heard a voice behind her.

'You're in a hurry, aren't you?'

Terrified, she whirled round.

A dark figure was emerging from the shadows. 'What are you doing outside?'

Her heart began to pound.

'Me? Nothing! I . . . '

'Did you just throw something into the water?'

'No, I just . . . '

'Whatever. Makes no difference anyway.'

The figure came closer. Julia tried in vain to make out the face in the darkness. A hand touched her shoulder. She shrank back and bit her lip so as not to scream with fear.

Then she heard a low laugh. 'Hey, don't worry. I'm Chris. Christopher Bishop. I'm sharing apartment 113 with your brother. You raced past me a few minutes ago as if you'd seen a ghost.'

Julia couldn't utter a word. Her throat was dry, and she swallowed convulsively.

'I worked out that you'd left the building, and I followed

you just to be on the safe side,' Chris continued. 'It's easy to get lost out here.'

'Thanks, there was no need,' Julia choked. 'I don't get lost that easily.'

'Are you sure?' Chris asked, his voice taking on a strangely hoarse undertone. 'That's just what the others thought too.'

CHAPTER 6

Waiting. That's how Julia spent the first couple of days in the valley. Or that's how it felt, at any rate. And that was why she was watching everything going on around her as an outsider. Everything about the college seemed blurred, out of focus and somehow magnified, as if she were looking at it through a maladjusted microscope.

As Julia and Robert were late arrivals, they had missed not only the Dean's welcome speech to the freshers but also all the important Induction Week events. Was that why it all felt so unreal?

A long time ago – well, six months ago, to be precise – she'd arrived late at the cinema. She couldn't remember now what the film had been; at any rate, she and Kristian had missed the first ten minutes. As a result, Julia had spent the rest of the film completely uninvolved in the plot. Just because she'd missed the start.

That's exactly how it felt at the college. She was an add-on at best, despite all the efforts of Mrs Hill, her head of year; Alex and Isabel, her mentors; and all the others in her class. They were making too much of an effort, Julia sometimes thought peevishly as she yet again bumped into Debbie or David, who would ask her anxiously if they could help her.

I'm beyond help, she wanted to reply; but instead, she merely produced a tortured smile which just made her look totally helpless.

Generally, it seemed that you were seldom alone at Grace College. The eerie silence of the first night had given way to the busy goings-on of daily life. Students bustled around the endless passageways and corridors. The basement library and computer department were permanently full. The various college teams were training in the campus sports halls. From wrestling to baseball to swimming, every sport was on offer. And the entrance foyer and refectory above the entrance seemed to be both meeting place and gossip factory.

Julia tried to go with the flow. She smiled non-stop; she thanked people left, right and centre; and was so exceptionally polite that she could have won a prize for it. She dutifully attended her seminars and ploughed her way through the Freshmen's Handbook that Alex had imposed on her. She attempted to remember all the rules and regulations; met up with the other students in the refectory; and forced down the Canadian food that she disliked. And she feigned interest when Debbie blathered on and on about her core subjects and options and how many credits each thing was worth.

And she even tried out the athletics club and went on a five-mile jog alongside the lake with them. Her of all people – jogging. What would Kristian have said? To add insult to injury, she was so fast that she was selected for the team.

But while all this was happening, Julia felt like she were

on hold in some kind of slow, tortuous way. Never before had time seemed to grind like this. Never before had she felt so alien to herself.

Ultimately, the only thing that enabled her to stand these first few days at the college was the hope that at long last she would get the news she wanted, and that she and Robert could leave the valley. She didn't care what happened after that.

That was the thought that kept her going; the thought that she had been clinging to since that first dreadful night.

Time and again she told herself that it wouldn't be long now and that the waiting would soon come to an end. They must have seen that she'd tried to call them on that first night. They'd surely find some way to get in touch. Soon.

But nobody got in touch. And with every minute that passed, Julia felt more and more cut off from the outside world.

No. She didn't just feel cut off. She had been cut off.

On the evening of the second day, Julia was sitting at a table in the refectory with her flatmates, Robert, and the boys from Robert's apartment. She dipped her spoon into the bowl of gooey potato soup that they called clam chowder and which, as she only noticed too late, had countless prawns floating around in it. She hated prawns. They looked like mini tampons. But Julia wasn't hungry anyway. All her senses seemed to have given up. She wasn't even really taking in the bustle and noise in the refectory.

'Don't you like the soup?' she heard Debbie's voice to her

left as the pale, freckled hands reached for Julia's dish. 'God, the extra calories can't harm after a day like today. A couple of the courses are absolute killers. Especially the ones that are anything to do with math. I didn't understand a word.'

'Math is numbers. The subject with "words" is English,' replied Benjamin. He was sitting on Julia's right. He put his camera down on the table to add an extra layer of maple syrup to a pancake that was already dripping with the stuff. 'And if I were you, I wouldn't go around in these hallowed halls bellowing about how you don't understand something.' Benjamin looked around theatrically before leaning over and whispering to Debbie: 'Don't forget, we Graceians are the elite of the future. The pillars of mankind, chosen by the sacred rite of the entrance exam. Or, that is, if you choose to believe Brandon, our god of philosophy.' He took a bite and said through a mouthful of pancake: 'Ladies and gentlemen, until now I had no idea that I held such an important post. Compared to me, the American president is a mere couch potato!'

The others laughed.

Julia alone had to force herself not to roll her eyes. She too had been in the philosophy class and had heard what Professor Brandon had said. And it had shot through her mind that most of the students and even the freshers in her year had evidently already internalised this notion. During lectures, they all acted in an extremely elitist, ambitious way – not surprising, given the standards that Grace set. However, outside was different. As soon as the students left the classrooms to hang out in the entrance foyer, to chill out on campus or just to chat in their apartments, most conversations revolved around parties, alcohol and, of course, Debbie's favourite topic, sex.

'I think a lot of the lecturers are okay,' came Rose's pleasantly soft voice. 'And Brandon's cool. Have you heard about the lecturer who takes his dog into lectures with him?'

She smiled at Julia, and Julia had no choice but to return the smile. Rose Gardner had the room next to her and was beautiful, incredibly beautiful. Not the sort of beauty that soon fades, but the classical kind of beauty like Katherine Heigl, Scarlett Johansson and Julia's great idol, Kate Winslet. Evenly tanned skin – and her teeth! Compared to them, ivory looked cheap and nasty. Then those legs – which Julia would have bought from her in a flash.

And Rose's baldness didn't in any way detract from her beauty. Quite the reverse. All the same, Julia kept wondering why she'd shaved her hair off.

One thing was for sure: it made her stand out from the crowd. But did it make her unapproachable, as Debbie claimed? That wasn't the impression that Julia had got. Debbie was probably just jealous of Rose, because Debbie wanted to stand out too, especially where boys were concerned. But none of them stood a chance when Rose was around.

'Ro-Ro, you surely don't think that the lecturers here are real?' Benjamin frowned. 'No, no, they're all operated by remote control.'

They all laughed again.

'I'm serious! In the Introduction to Math course today, Mr

Lennon beamed the formulae directly from his head on to the whiteboard. I couldn't copy it all down fast enough.'

'I'm not surprised.' This was one of Katie's rare comments. She was slowly peeling the skin off a grapefruit. 'You didn't put your camera down for a second.'

Julia had meanwhile gathered that the third girl in her apartment was from Korea and had lived in the USA since she was ten. But that's all the girl had revealed, apart from the pretty obvious fact that she seemed to eat nothing but fruit and raw vegetables.

'Because I was filming everything while he was busy with his formula-infested PowerPoint presentation.' Benjamin grinned and mimicked the lecturer's high falsetto. 'Let us prove the following result. If we assume that blah-di-blah, then it follows that blah-di-blah. And in two weeks, you will submit a paper in which you use a counter example to show that the inverse is wrong, in other words, nightmare, night-mare, nightmare.'

At this point, they all started howling.

'Math,' Katie now declared with an earnestness that in her case merely sounded like arrogance, 'is something for people who are trying to escape from the complexity of the world. They construct a system that leads them to believe that everything is calculable and rational, and is merely a ques-tion of understanding and logical thinking.'

Julia looked at her, baffled. This was the longest sentence she'd ever heard Katie utter.

'Did you know that the head of math here at Grace is supposed to be a great luminary?' Debbie joined in again.

'Someone said he was even on the nominations list for a Nobel Prize. God, I admire anyone who has math as their main subject.'

David groaned softly. He and Robert were the only two who weren't doing Mr Lennon's core maths course but had instead chosen to major in maths with Professor Vernon. 'You can say that again. I was writing like mad today, and I still didn't understand half of what was going on,' he said as he pushed his plate aside. 'That all started when I did the Grace entrance exam.' His expression darkened briefly. 'It would have been a mega disaster if I hadn't passed the exam.' He turned to Robert. 'What did you make of the lecture today?' he asked anxiously. 'I couldn't believe the way you were just sitting there. You didn't even write down the formulae.'

Julia exchanged glances with her brother. He was sitting with them, but hadn't joined in the conversation at all up to that point.

'Making notes distracts me,' Robert replied, frowning. 'I can't understand stuff if I'm busy writing it down.'

'Too right,' David agreed. 'It'd be better if they photo-copied the lecture notes then explained them to us. That'd be much simpler.'

'If you listened carefully, you'd understand it, David,' Robert replied patiently.

'So you say you can remember the whole line of argu-ment? All the formulae from the whole lecture? And in Advanced Math with a nearly-Nobel Prize winner?' Debbie looked at Robert as if he were an alien. At the very least.

'Yes,' Robert replied simply, straightening his glasses.

'Anyway, if you've got problems with our course, Debbie, I can help you.' Julia quickly tried to draw attention away from her brother. 'I'm quite good at maths.'

It was true that the standards at Grace were very high and that everyone who had passed the stiff college entrance exam was well above average intelligence. But Robert – Robert was on a level of his own. Under no circumstances did Julia want people to realise that too soon.

'Oh, that's so kind of you, Julia.' Debbie looked like a smiley emoticon. She was beaming from ear to ear as she pulled out her orange Filofax. 'When are you free? We could study together in my room, then watch a film afterwards.'

'Sounds like a hot date,' Rose commented, giving Julia a conspiratorial wink. Julia grinned back, thinking in spite of herself that she could come to like Rose.

'On the subject of dates.' Benjamin was leaning over again. 'While we're at it, did you know that that our oh-so-virtuous second-floor senior mentor Isabel is secretly in love with Mr Forster? I bet you ten dollars that she's sending him hot emails.' He bent across Julia and whispered to the giggling Debbie: 'At the serving counter, I saw her putting her hand on his butt when he went past her with half a trout on his plate. He couldn't stop her.'

So far as Julia was aware, Mr Forster was head of French. He and his wife lived in one of the staff bungalows.

'Maybe Isabel's in with a chance. Forster's wife isn't remotely his type,' Rose said with surprising venom as she cast her spoon aside. 'That's the only thing I've thought is really crap up to now. How Female Forster manages to cope as an art lecturer at an elite college is a complete mystery to me.'

Rose had an art scholarship to Grace. According to Debbie, she'd won all kinds of prizes – although Rose herself preferred not to talk about it.

'French Impressionism's supposed to be her specialism.' Rose snorted. 'So much for the "progressive orientation of the college with special focus on students' independent creative activity". Instead, they lumber us with a lecturer who rambles on about Degas and Monet. I mean, really! The only creative thing about her is that she changes her clothes three times a day.'

'Better than the stupid environmental studies that I've got to put up with,' said Debbie. Geography was her main subject. 'I mean, we're in the Rocky Mountains. Why do I need to know what causes a monsoon? I think I'll be spending most of my time in the library and computer department before our final exams.'

'Yeah, this doesn't look much like relaxation,' Rose agreed. 'This isn't like a luxury hotel in the middle of the mountains, but ... '

'A boot camp,' interrupted a hoarse voice from the other end of the table. Despite herself, Julia looked up – into disconcerting slate grey eyes. They belonged to someone who had evidently not shaved for a couple of days.

She quickly looked down. The palms of her hands were drenched in sweat. For two days now, Julia had done her utmost to avoid Christopher Bishop or at the very least to ignore him – which wasn't so easy, as he was always hanging around with David and Robert.

But every time Julia encountered him, she recalled that moment at the lake on her first night – the noise of the mobile sinking into the lake, and his expression, at once curious and knowing.

He couldn't have seen what she'd thrown into the water. Or could he?

While David was proving to be the good guy of her year and Benjamin the clown, Chris didn't fit into any role. Yesterday Julia had caught him leaning against a door staring at her, evidently quite convinced that she wasn't going to notice. And that morning he'd suddenly appeared at the lakeside at the crack of dawn, just as she was coming back from jogging with the athletics club.

If only she could figure him out.

'Believe me, Grace is nothing but a boot camp,' he continued, leaning back in his chair. 'But there's one thing I still don't get. Do they really want to recruit the geniuses of the future? Or do they want to lock us away because we're too clever for the outside world?' He folded his arms. 'What do you think, Julia? Should we run away together? Escape across the pass? The White Escape? Or how about blowing up the whole place? I'll help you. You look as if you could do with a bit of help.' He gave her a challenging look. Julia felt her throat tightening. She gasped for air.

There was a sudden loud bang. David was banging his fist on the table for the second time. 'Shut up, Chris! Or I'll ... '

Chris laughed scornfully. 'Or you'll what, David?'

Silence suddenly fell at the table.

It was Benjamin who relieved the tension. He reached for the white tablecloth, used it to wipe the sticky maple syrup off his fingers, and removed the lens cap from his camera. 'Would you mind repeating that scene? I've only had really boring stuff up to now. Well, there was Robert losing it – but that aside, it's all just too harmonious for words. Come on, then, David Freeman, what were you going to threaten Chris Bishop with?'

'Hey! Shut up.' Debbie half got up from her chair and looked across the tables at the serving counter. The refectory had meanwhile emptied; it was getting late. 'We're being watched. By Angela. Angela Finder. She's a celebrity at Grace.'

'By who?' Chris asked, irritated.

'The girl in the wheelchair. Angela Finder. Haven't you heard of her yet?' Debbie must have a volume switch hidden in her brain. One minute she was shouting; the next she was whispering. Julia had never met anyone who could modulate their voice to that extent.

'And – oh my God! She's coming over to us.'

Julia turned her head to the left. The first thing she saw was long, slender hands with red varnished fingernails. Then one of those bracelets dripping with countless little charms that enabled the wearer to cart around their star sign, their hobbies and – even worse – their holiday souvenirs.

The hands were resting on the broad wheels of a wheelchair. The girl was wearing jeans and a hoody that bore the logo Grace College. She was probably four or five years older than Julia and the others. She was wearing so much make-up that it was hard to tell her age. Her hair was dyed almost as red as her fingernails.

'Why the whispering all of a sudden, Debbie?' Chris asked spitefully, whipping the lid off his yoghurt pot in one go.

'I don't think she likes people talking about her.'

'And that bothers you of all people?'

He was interrupted by a loud, energetic voice from behind. 'You, stop that. Now!'

The girl had stopped right behind Benjamin, who had climbed onto the chair and was pointing his video camera directly at her.

'Didn't you hear me? You switch that camera off! Otherwise I'll report you for discrimination and offensive behaviour towards disabled people. And you'll get done for breaching human rights and data protection.'

Now it wasn't just their table that was silent. The few students who remained in the refectory craned their necks inquisitively.

'Oh, chill out,' said Benjamin, hopping off the chair. 'Being in a wheelchair isn't such a big deal that you have to get all worked up. You imagine it – I've filmed it. Midgets, transvestites, and one woman whose nose was literally eaten away by cancer.'

'Benjamin Fox,' retorted the girl. She raised her pale, slender hand, and her elegant middle finger made an unmistakably insulting gesture. 'You can kiss my ass.'

'And you can kiss mine, Angela.' Before they knew it,

Benjamin had turned his back to her and had pulled his baggy jeans down so quickly that Julia thought she was imagining the whole thing.

Whispering, then loud laughter.

Julia took in Robert's disgusted face. By nature polite and reserved, he couldn't understand why other people had to cross the line. He always had problems with people like Benjamin who got a laugh at the expense of other people.

Everyone else, though, was looking at Angela, enthralled. They were all intrigued to see how she would react. But the girl remained surprisingly calm. 'That will be my pleasure, Benjamin. You can count on it.'

She narrowed her eyes, and an odd smile appeared on her face. Her long, slender hands lay quietly on the wheels – and then the wheelchair turned and Angela made her way through the refectory door without looking back.

Flabbergasted, Julia watched her go. She was fascinated by the girl's self-possession. Angela had just been insulted and embarrassed. And instead of freaking out, she'd just smiled. But it was precisely that smile that had so clearly shown who was really in control of the situation. It had been more effective than any amount of bluster and threats.

All of a sudden, Julia realised whom she'd just met. Angela was the girl Alex had almost run over when they'd arrived. Angela Finder had been in her wheelchair in the middle of the road, watching them from behind.

'So are you lot going to this mysterious party at the boat-house the day after tomorrow?' Benjamin's voice jerked her back to reality. He was evidently trying to wipe out the embarrassing scene. 'Or was the email to my college account just a joke?'

David was also keen to change the subject. He shook his head. 'No, I got an invitation too.'

'Me too,' said Debbie excitedly. 'What about you, Julia?'

Julia started. What should she say? Her mobile was at the bottom of Mirror Lake. Nobody but Robert knew that she'd ever had one. No, wait, the sender of the mysterious text – Loa.loa – knew too.

'Hey, Julia, are you still with us? Or is it just your body sitting at the table?' Chris asked.

Julia didn't reply. And for once, she was grateful to Debbie, who prattled on regardless.

'Oh, it's so exciting. D'you really think there's going to be a party at the boathouse? I think there's more to this invitation than meets the eye. Don't all colleges have, like, induction rites for freshmen?' She ran her fingers through her orange hair, which stood up from her head even more wildly than normal. 'Whatever. For now, I'm just going to believe that it's a party. The very word "party" gets me going – quite apart from all the upperclassmen guys who might be there.'

'Are you thinking of anyone in particular?' Benjamin said mockingly.

Debbie's hot face glowed red above her white shirt with its puffed sleeves. 'Who'd be interested in me?'

She looked to her left at Julia, in the hope that Julia would contradict her. Julia did her duty. 'Don't be silly – you look great. Really natural.'

'As natural as a mouldy fish.'

'More like a windbag,' Chris muttered at the end of the table.

Julia had a sudden stab of pity for Debbie. It must be the worst thing, to be seventeen and scurrying through life like a little grey mouse, only able to attract male attention by your speed.

And yet, through the walls, she'd heard moaning coming from Debbie's room last night, and had assumed that Debbie was sleeping with someone. But who? Once she and her friends would have chatted about it until they were blue in the face. Now, though, it all left her strangely cold.

'My invitation came by email.' She heard Robert's voice. She looked across at him. He hadn't mentioned it to her. 'But I'm not going. No way.'

He sounded decided. There wasn't a trace of doubt in his voice. Julia immediately realised what was wrong with him. His gaze was firmly fixed on some point that was outside this room and outside her perception. His blue eyes mirrored the same blue of the lake which she could see from where she was sitting, through the long glass panes.

'Hey, don't let Debbie scare you. Even if it's a couple of the older students who are having us on, it's all bound to be completely harmless,' David reassured him. 'And there's supposed to be a really good fishing place at the boathouse. I used to go with my ... with my father ... um, we often used to go fishing together. If you like, I'll teach you fly-fishing.' David glanced at Julia. As if she'd asked him to get involved.

'There aren't any fish in the lake.'

'How do you know that?'

Robert shrugged, took off his round glasses, and rubbed his eyes as he always did when he was worrying about something.

'I can see where Robert's coming from.' Katie reached for her black bag, pulled the strap over her head, and stood up. 'Party. The very word makes me feel like hitting someone.'

Everyone ignored her. Instead, Debbie reached for Julia's hand. 'What about you, Julia?'

'I don't know anything about any party.'

'But why would you be the only one who isn't invited?' Debbie frowned. 'Probably just an oversight.'

Julia stood up hastily. 'Are you going up to our apartment, Katie? Or have you got other plans?'

The other girl looked at her, surprised. Her eyes changed from dark grey to black, and then a mistrustful expression spread across her face. She was evidently afraid that Julia might try to befriend her.

The next moment, Chris was standing beside Julia, giving her that same intensive look that she couldn't quite fathom. He pointed through the glazed frontage. 'I was thinking about going to down to the lake. D'you want to come with me?' He didn't take his eyes off her. 'I love still evenings like this, when the lake looks as if it really were made of glass. Sometimes, just sometimes, I'm tempted to throw something in just to see if it's true.'

Julia's throat tightened with fear.

He knew. He knew very well what she'd thrown into the lake. The only question was: what else did he know?

She shook her head. 'No, I'm sorry, I . . . I'm tired.'

God, her voice sounded as if one of her vocal cords had snapped. But that was just a tiny defect compared to all the others.

CHAPTER 7

Julia was standing in the gallery, looking down irresolutely into the vast entrance foyer. Now that supper had finished, this was the student meeting place. They were standing around in groups, making plans for the evening. The really lucky ones had managed to squeeze into the cosy seating nooks.

Julia spotted Alex and Isabel. They were standing close to one another by the fireplace, chatting and laughing. From up in the gallery, the two mentors looked incredibly alike: tall and slim with short fair hair and tanned skin, they were the types who spent all summer surfing and all winter tearing down the mountains on a snowboard. Even that particular haircut was a giveaway: it suggested outdoorsy types, that breed of human that thrives on fresh air and constant movement. But where Alex was concerned, at any rate, Julia knew that this exaggeratedly casual appearance was deceptive. She'd heard that he was one of the best in his year, and was pretty ambitious. According to Debbie, he was even on the recommended list for a full scholarship to study medicine at Yale. That figured. He could have walked straight into one of those American hospital dramas. He'd start by saving someone's life, then he'd run a marathon, then he'd top it off by spending the evening seducing stunning female doctors.

Julia's gaze wandered elsewhere, and she spotted Rose running across the hall and outside. To her surprise, Robert was with her. What on earth were the two of them up to?

Nobody else from their group had followed Julia as she'd left the refectory, much to her relief. After Chris's strange remark, she urgently needed time to think, and she could only do that without Debbie's incessant wall-to-wall prattle or Benjamin's irritating jokes.

The question was: what should she do now?

The way things looked, her strategy of simply waiting was the wrong one. It had been a seriously stupid mistake, throwing her mobile into the lake like that. Without her phone, she was completely cut off from the outside world, and had no safe way to make contact with it.

She could, of course, send an email.

She immediately rejected the idea.

Absolutely not via Grace's server. Even if she'd had her old laptop with her, which she hadn't, all communications went via the college's central server, and she didn't want to take that risk. That also excluded the computers in the computer department.

The familiar feeling of fear started to rise in her. Six months ago, she wouldn't have believed it possible to live in such a constant state of panic. And maybe you couldn't live in it. Maybe all you could do was survive.

She ran down the stairs, two at a time.

It was just an impulse. One of those reactions that are

neither planned nor considered. Sometimes they were good, sometimes not. You never knew, which was what made them truly tricky.

Once in the hall, she cast aside all the politeness that Little Miss Perfect specialised in and simply burst into the conversation between Alex and Isabel without warning. 'Alex, can I ask you something?'

Her student mentor looked at her, annoyed. 'Not now. Isabel and I are in the middle of something.'

'Sorry, but ... how can I get to Fields tomorrow after classes?'

Isabel and Alex looked at her in horror. 'You want to go to Fields tomorrow?'

'Yes, why? Is it a problem?'

'I'd say it is.' Isabel frowned and shook her head.

'But it's important!'

'There's nothing in Fields that you can't do up here,' Alex replied calmly. 'What's this all about?'

Be careful, Julia.

'I ... erm ... I just have to get out.' She ignored Isabel's aghast expression.

'Yes, so do we all,' replied Alex, shrugging. 'But we can't.'

'Why not?'

'Who do you think is going to drive you down there?'

'You could ...'

Now Isabel started to laugh. 'So what have you got in mind? Alex is your mentor, not your personal chauffeur. Do you realise that it takes almost two hours to get to Fields?'

'But ...'

Isabel rolled her eyes. 'God, honestly, you freshmen get some crazy ideas ... '

Alex evidently realised that Julia was on the verge of tears. 'Okay, Julia, sit down and spit it out. What's the problem?'

Julia slumped down on to a leather armchair. She clenched her teeth. *Just hold your nerve.* 'I need to go to Fields to ... ' She stopped.

'To?' asked Alex, looking at her expectantly. 'Come on, out with it. Or is it a secret? Don't worry, we'll keep it to ourselves, won't we Isabel?'

'Too right. We're experts in keeping secrets.' The girl grinned conspiratorially. 'Okay, fire away.'

'I have to send an important email.' Even before Julia had finished her sentence, she already knew the answer.

'Well, if that's all it is.' Alex raised his eyebrows. 'We have the fastest internet connection you can get, here at Grace.'

'Yes, of course, but ... ' Oh God, the more she talked, the more absurd it sounded.

Alex raised both hands. 'Where's the problem?'

'I have to get out of here. I can't stand it any more. I'll ... '

'Hey, it's totally normal to feel a bit panicky in your first few days up here.' Isabel looked closely at Julia, but this time her gaze was almost pitying rather than mocking. 'We've all been there. But at some point, you'll come to love the valley – okay, "love" might be a bit of an exaggeration, given the crazy things that happen here sometimes.'

This place is evil.

'What do you mean?'

Isabel looked long and hard at Alex.

He leant down to Julia. 'Listen. You can't just go to Fields. If you want to use one of the college cars, you have to have college approval, come up with some important reason, or wait until one of the tutors or another student wants to leave the valley. You can put your name down on the list in the office. Or you can go on the bus next weekend.'

Julia thought about Robert, and could feel herself slowly becoming hysterical. Somehow her vocal cords seemed to be working again. At any rate, she had an urgent need to start screaming.

'Isabel, what did you mean when you said that crazy things happen here?'

'Don't worry. They're just stories that the students make up. Sorry if I upset you.'

'Stories?'

'Well, you know, that things aren't entirely normal around here.'

'What things? What's not normal?'

The older students exchanged glances once more.

'Well, things up here just aren't quite the same as you're used to. Take the weather, for example. It's sometimes a bit crazy. You're from London, aren't you?' Alex looked at her expectantly.

How did he know that? How did he know where she came from?

He continued. 'What I mean is, London's climate is pretty temperate. But you're in the Rockies now. That means you'll see more storms than normal, and they'll be more violent. The weather changes from one minute to the next. Heavy rainfall. In winter, the snow can be as deep as fifty feet. And then the next day, you get the Chinook, the warm, dry westerly wind, and the temperature's suddenly seventy degrees. You can't rely on anything up here.'

'So why was the college built here in the middle of the wilderness?' Julia shook her head, baffled.

'Well,' Isabel replied. 'Grace isn't just any old college. It's an elite university. Take Dartmouth in New Hampshire. That's in the middle of nowhere too.'

'Or Yale – one of the best universities in the US,' added Alex. 'And where is it? In some god-forsaken hole called New Haven, more than a hundred miles from New York.'

'No distractions, that's what it's all about, y'know,' Isabel continued. 'The students can devote their full attention to their studies. That's why Grace has everything from bookshops to supermarkets. Did you know you can even buy golf balls here? And golf is – I think – the only sport that we don't offer.'

Julia wasn't in the slightest bit reassured. 'It doesn't have to be New York City,' she said. 'Maybe I just want to go out sometimes. Meet other people. But it feels like we're locked in here. I've never heard of Yale doing that.'

'Nobody's locking you in, Julia,' Alex assured her, smiling. 'Believe me, up here you can do everything that every normal college student in the whole wide world does.'

'Precisely.' Isabel nodded. 'Sex and drugs and all kinds of fun. Okay, the drugs bit is tricky. The security checks are pretty tough. But where's that any different? You just have to not get caught.'

'That's great, but I'm not allowed to leave the valley.'

'Of course you're allowed to! You can go to Fields, but just not at the drop of a hat.'

'But ... what if something were to happen to one of us? What if one of us got sick?'

Alex looked at her in surprise. 'Then there's the medical centre. They're damn good in there. Some of them studied at Grace and chose to come back. So it can't be that bad, can it?'

'But I mean if someone's really seriously ill. If it's an emergency? Then they wouldn't spend two hours being transported over the pass, would they?'

Alex raised his eyebrows. 'Have you ever heard of helicopters?' He was sounding distinctly tetchy now. 'It's a perfectly normal mode of transport in the Rocky Mountains.'

'But you can't seriously expect one to land here specially for you to send an email.' Isabel was evidently convinced that Julia was completely crazy. 'Oh well, maybe your parents have enough cash to pay for it. That's a different matter.'

'But this just isn't normal!' Julia shook her head. Okay, she sounded hysterical – but she had every reason to. Alex stood up, went over to her, and put his hand on Julia's shoulder. Once more in his role of older, more experienced student and mentor. 'Hey, chill out. There's an outing to civilisation next weekend, and if it matters to you that much, I'll personally make sure tomorrow that you get a seat on the bus.' He smiled at her. 'In any case, you've chosen to be here, haven't you? You can leave whenever you like. Nobody's forcing you to stay in the valley.'

With every fibre of her being, Julia was screaming to contradict him. Of course she was forced to stay here – or, at least, so long as nobody got in touch. That was what this was all about.

And even if she managed to come to terms with what was making her so miserable, if she somehow managed to pull herself together – then what about Robert?

Her gaze fell on Isabel, who was now eyeing her suspiciously from the side. Thus far, the older student hadn't taken the matter very seriously – but now it looked like the cogs were starting to whirr in her brain. She was evidently wondering what was wrong with Julia. Any minute now, she'd start asking questions.

'Okay,' Julia said hastily, summoning up a kind of grin. 'You're right, of course. I think I'm just really stressed out by everything being new. Everything's so strange and, well, the classes here aren't exactly a walk in the park. No, it's fine. I'll take the bus to Fields at the weekend, it's not a problem.'

Isabel and Alex exchanged understanding looks. Or was there a bit of relief mixed in there too?

'So, everything's fine, yeah?' said Alex.

Julia smiled at them once more, then quickly turned away. No way was she going to let the older students see the tears that were welling up.

Mum had always told them a bedtime story, and throughout her entire life Julia had gone to sleep safe in the knowledge that everything was fine. However many poisoned apples, enchanted spindles, evil queens and wicked witches might be out there: everything was fine. But now she knew: happy endings were just the inventions of storytellers. It was the nightmares that came true.

Blindly she forged a path through the crowd. The babble of voices around her grew louder, enveloped her. Indecipherable words, laughter, whispered remarks.

'She's weird, isn't she?' One voice cut across all the others, although Julia couldn't make out whose. 'There's something the matter with her. And whatever her secret is, I promise you, I'll find it out.'

Julia whirled round. But Alex and Isabel had turned their attention elsewhere. And in that packed foyer, she couldn't even begin to tell whether it was one of them who'd spoken.

CHAPTER 8

The weather was unusually fine on the day of the boathouse party. The sky was a deep, even blue of a type that Julia had never witnessed in her home city.

It was her fourth day in the valley, and she'd slept through the night for the first time. Was that the reason why the nightmarish feeling had diminished over the course of the day? Or had she just let herself be intimidated by the place's atmosphere and her bad start?

Now, bathed in beaming sunlight, the college seemed to have been transformed. The old apartments were flooded with light, the seminar rooms seemed thrillingly modern, and Julia had suddenly found the panoramic mountain views breathtaking, while the lake had in some incomprehensible way become mysterious and incredibly beautiful.

Even Robert had thawed out today, and had spent the lunch break telling Julia how brilliant and cool he thought Professor Vernon was.

'Guess what?' he said. 'Vernon says maths is entirely a matter of logic – only it unfortunately doesn't correspond to the way that the human brain works. That's the whole problem, he says.'

'Well,' Julia had replied with a wink. 'That's about as stupid as it gets.'

It had, meanwhile, grown late, and Julia had retreated to her room after supper. She stared, undecided, into her wardrobe. What on earth should she wear for the party? She couldn't decide. A dress? No – it absolutely wouldn't do to be over-dressed. Or maybe just jeans? Boring, and she really wasn't in the mood for yet another deliberate under-statement. Oh, just chill out, she thought, as she pulled half of her stuff out of the wardrobe and deposited it on the floor.

That morning, she'd been jogging by the lake again. With Katie this time, though Katie had barely said a word. But that was fine by Julia.

Then the day had been crammed full of classes. Christ, she already had the stuff coming out of her ears. Perhaps this was why she was no longer in a dreamlike state. Daily life, distraction and exertion did have their advantages.

First it was philosophy with Professor Brandon, then Elementary Physics Part One, which was compulsory for all freshers unless, like Robert or David, they'd chosen to specialise in maths.

Then Julia had her first literature seminar, where the tutor, Mrs Hill, Isabel's mother, went through an endless list of literature from Shakespeare to the present day that the students had to read for next term. Then, after a lunch break which she spent lazing around outside in the sunshine, she was almost late for sociology. In the afternoon, there was another introductory session held by Alex for freshers about major fields of study and optional lectures; then, shortly before supper, Julia took the lift down to the *Grace Chronicle* offices in the basement, as advised by Mrs Hill, to apply to work for the college newspaper. In the editorial office, she was surprised to bump not only into Benjamin, who had had the same idea, but also into Angela Finder, the girl in the wheelchair. It turned out that she was editor of the *Grace Chronicle*.

Angela had subjected Julia to a cross-examination, scrutinising her journalistic abilities and previous experience – but she had instantly sent Benjamin packing.

It was the first time her brother's room-mate hadn't made stupid jokes. On the contrary, he looked furious as he stormed out of the editorial office empty-handed.

Julia's conversation with Angela, however, lasted for more than half an hour, making her almost too late to eat in the refectory.

It was then that she realised that she'd not thought once that day about how she could leave. Quite the reverse. She'd felt as if she really could stay longer at Grace – without feeling the old familiar panic. Maybe the vast plethora of course material wasn't just a burden and a duty but, rather, something along the lines of her salvation. Couldn't this perhaps be a way to overcome her fear after all? To start the new life that she so desperately wanted?

Julia looked at the clock and picked up the pale blue, one hundred per cent organic cotton shirt that she'd bought at the Seattle airport. She held it up to herself and looked in the mirror.

She'd changed somehow. Her light brown eyes which, according to Kristian, looked like snakeskin, looked enormous in her pale face, and even her legs – right at the top of her list of bodily defects – no longer looked too short, but long and slender. Baffled, she turned round in front of the mirror. Hey, she thought, I've lost weight. At least half a stone.

She suddenly grinned. So a new life could have its advantages.

Just yesterday evening, she'd promised herself that she would go to the party for one reason alone: to find out who this mysterious Loa.loa was. But, hey, maybe this party could be the start of all these brilliant college escapades that Debbie was always on about? And anyway, hadn't all the freshers had the same invitation? Whoever Loa.loa might be, there was presumably an innocent explanation.

She looked at her shirt again. No, that wouldn't do. Enough was enough. Light blue? Organic cotton? How on earth could she have bought such a thing? There was a time when she wouldn't have touched it with a bargepole. She screwed the shirt up in a ball and threw it back into the wardrobe. She needed to get a move on. Debbie had arranged with the boys in the apartment below them that they'd go to the boathouse together. Julia hadn't a clue where it was. It wasn't mentioned on the screens in the foyer which gave the students all the information they needed about Grace, and she hadn't seen it while out jogging either. But this didn't seem to bother any of the others, so she assumed that someone must know the way.

Resolutely, Julia reached for her new jeans and pulled on a red top with sequins. Then she stuffed a black jumper in her shoulder bag for later, slipped on her Converse trainers, shook out her ponytail and ran a brush through her hair. Done.

At that moment, she heard an indignant voice behind her. 'You've not got your make-up on yet!'

Debbie was standing in the doorway. A second later, Rose's shaven head appeared behind her.

'I can't be bothered worrying about whether my eye liner's gone smeary or I've got lipstick on my teeth or I've got mascara running down my face.'

'Don't you at least want some lip gloss?' Debbie pulled a tube out of the little white handbag that she wore round her neck and shoulders like a dog harness. She stared at Julia. 'Go on – what about a bit of mascara? God, if I had your eyes ...'

Julia looked at Debbie sceptically. Her peculiar hair had evidently been twisted up in rollers, and seemed twice as big, framing her round face. She was wearing a tight, almost flesh-coloured dress that only served to emphasise her lumps and bumps. Julia couldn't bear to look.

'I don't have any make-up,' she replied.

'Oh my God! You don't have any lip gloss?'

'Why should I? Is it compulsory?'

'It's not a laughing matter.' Debbie shook her head firmly. 'We're going to a party. The first party here at Grace. Our welcome party. We're going to become real students tonight. It's a big event. As big as your first period!'

'Well, I can't say it was a particularly uplifting experience to discover in the school toilets that I'd started,' Katie said drily from the door.

Debbie's eyes filled with tears.

'I can make you up if you like, Julia,' Rose quickly changed the subject. 'I've got it all with me. It won't take me a minute.'

'But the others are waiting for us,' Julia argued – but only half-heartedly. Maybe it wasn't so bad to join in with the whole girly thing just for a change.

'They should wait for us – not the other way round.' Rose laughed and pulled out a make-up bag. Her experienced fingers were warm and gentle as she magicked eye shadow, mascara and lipstick onto Julia's face.

'Benjamin's watching the tutors' office downstairs.' Debbie had calmed down again. 'He's calling David's mobile when the coast's clear.'

'When the coast's clear . . . ?'

'Shh!' Rose interrupted, applying lipstick to Julia.

'The whole thing's a secret,' Debbie cried. 'And this is absolutely not the time to run into Isabel. It's going to be tricky enough, getting past her door and back to our rooms tonight. Don't you all think it's stupid, having to be in our apartments at, like, eleven? I mean, what kind of time's eleven o'clock? We're adults after all. I'm wondering when I'm actually going to be able to do whatever I want. First parents, then teachers – then the lecturers put other students in charge of us. Only a couple of years older, and they're keeping an eye on us. What about our human rights?'

'Absolutely,' murmured Rose. 'We should tell the International Court of Justice, and Amnesty International to boot.'

'Though didn't you think that Alex was, like, really cute again at that introductory session today?' Debbie was not going to be put off her stride. 'He's so serious, isn't he? By the way, d'you know that only two people every year get a full scholarship to Yale?' She ploughed on without waiting for a reply. 'I reckon he noticed me today when I asked about which preliminary courses would be good for studying medicine.' She looked dreamily out of the window.

Julia shook her head involuntarily. 'I think she's been watching too much *Grey's Anatomy*,' she murmured through clenched teeth.

Rose laughed. 'Keep still!' she admonished.

'One thing's for sure, and that's that Mr Big has known for ages about what's going on this evening,' said Katie.

'It's not about that,' Debbie retorted. 'This party is a ...'

'Secret!' Debbie, Julia and Rose shouted all at once. Even Katie couldn't help grinning.

'Look at yourself.' Rose held a mirror up to Julia's face. Julia couldn't recognise herself. She didn't look like herself at all.

'Perfect,' she murmured – and meant it. It was the perfect disguise. And the ultimate look for what she had planned.

'Won't you come after all, Katie?' she asked, turning to look at her.

'I'd rather jump in the lake.'

'Suit yourself,' said Debbie.

The three of them left the apartment and went downstairs,

where David was waiting for them in the stairwell, opposite the lift. As always, he was dressed completely in black. His light brown hair was still wet from the shower, and looked almost gold-tinted.

'So, how do we look?' Debbie did a twirl.

He didn't reply, but Julia could feel him looking at her as if he were seeing her for the first time.

Embarrassed, she asked: 'Do you know where Robert is?'

'He's already down at the lake,' he replied, without taking his eyes off her. 'He took Ike. Or Ike took him, which is probably more accurate.'

Julia shook her head. 'My brother went to this party of his own volition? And without waiting for us?'

'He's not going to the party. He's going fishing,' David grinned.

Julia couldn't help but laugh too. 'Fishing? Is he hoping to find nocturnal fish or something?'

'Where's Chris?' complained Debbie. 'We're going to be late.'

'Here,' a voice came from behind her.

She turned round. Chris was standing on the stairs, his hands in the pockets of his worn jeans. His gaze moved from Debbie to Rose to Julia, where it rested. She raised her hand uncertainly and touched her face.

So much for my disguise, she thought.

At that moment, David's mobile rang. He answered and murmured: 'Okay.'

Then he turned to them. 'The mentors' office is empty. No sign of Isabel or Alex. Let's go.'

Debbie took the lead, followed by the others. She sped down the stairs, turned right on the ground floor and headed for the side entrance. Julia was relieved to find that she already knew her way around very well. Presumably because she'd spent a good half hour looking for the physics seminar room that day. She'd started to think that she'd spend the rest of eternity wandering through corridors, climbing stairs, opening doors.

Together they left the building. Only once they were outside did Julia realise that the beautiful day had, meanwhile, turned into a rather muggy evening. But she was determined that nothing – not even rain – was going to spoil her good mood.

'Hey, so how far is it, Chris?' Benjamin shouted from behind.

'Dunno.' Chris had gone into the lead and had chosen the left path at the lakeside. As Julia knew, this path led to another, narrower, path at the northern high-up river bank another third of a mile or so further along. Until now, Julia had always turned right when jogging with the athletics group or with Katie. This path extended for several miles along the flat southern bank of the river, and was as if made for running.

Chris turned and winked at her. Julia felt herself reddening. She hadn't realised that she'd been staring at him.

God, she just couldn't figure him out. There was something about him that was deeply unsettling. Was it his self-confidence? The ambiguous remarks? Maybe it was his clothes. The combination of refined and relaxed. His low-slung jeans were battered but evidently expensive, and he was the only one wearing leather shoes rather than trainers. And whereas David always wore his beloved black, Chris went for bright, strong colours like the bluey-green checked shirt that he was wearing now.

'Chris, what if we're, like, late?' cried Debbie.

Chris didn't reply, but merely started walking again. The others followed him.

Like lemmings, thought Julia, wiping the sweat from her forehead. It was the hottest day they'd had since she'd arrived in the valley: it had been seventy degrees that lunchtime, and even now that evening had come it was closer but not much cooler.

In silence, they covered the first third of a mile until the paved path ended and became a well-trodden track which led between the dense fir trees and along the water's edge.

By now the sun was lying low over the mirrored surface of the lake, bathing it in a strange orange light. One solitary grey cloud slowly made its way across the glowing red ball, as if it had lost its way.

After around a hundred yards, the path led steeply upwards between the trees and then continued some twenty yards above the shore. Up there, it became distinctly narrower: instead of trees, there were now cliffs looming up right at the side of them. A sign said: *Danger: falling rocks.*

'Hey, there's something hanging up here!' Debbie exclaimed. 'Maybe it's a sign that we're on the right path? What d'you reckon?'

A sleek black ribbon had been tied to a bush that grew

from one of the cliffs, and was dangling down. Benjamin pushed his way to the front and pointed his camera at it.

'You could be right. It hasn't been here long. It's not torn or faded,' David said thoughtfully.

'So there must be signs of human life somewhere around here. Either that, or whoever put the sign there was killed by this rock.' Benjamin pointed dramatically at a tiny stone on the ground.

'Then there must be a body down there,' Chris replied, pointing to the water below them.

'A pretty fresh one,' added Benjamin.

'You're disgusting! Come on, let's go. I get vertigo.' Debbie pressed herself against the cliffs and continued along the path that was by now just a couple of feet wide. The others followed suit. Julia stared at her feet in order not to stray too far to the right. She'd never suffered from vertigo, but even she felt a bit uncomfortable up here. One false move and she'd go plunging down the steep bank and break both legs. At the very least.

At the next bend, she glanced behind her. Through the trees, she could still clearly make out the huge silhouette of the college, although it was well over a mile away. The rays of the low-lying sun were reflected in the windows.

Then she heard water. It was coming from the cliffs, falling almost vertically.

'A waterfall! Oh my God, how on earth are we going to cross it?' Even Debbie could barely drown out the noise of the water.

'There's a bridge over there,' called Chris. He had taken

over as leader again. 'But watch out – some of the wooden planks are loose.'

Julia clung to David. The bridge was swaying gently and one of the hand rails was askew. She didn't dare touch it. Through the wooden slats, she could see the huge drop beneath them.

'Chris,' wailed Debbie. 'I'm dizzy. I can't look down!'

'Then don't,' said Rose sharply. She was behind Julia.

'The path forks again here.' That was Chris.

Julia looked up. Directly beyond the bridge, the path divided into two. The right-hand path led steeply down-wards and carried on beside the lake. The cliffs ended at the left-hand one, where someone had painted a black arrow on them.

'D'you think that's another sign, Chris?' asked Debbie.

'Why do you keep on asking me everything?' retorted Chris.

'Because you know the way.'

'Me? I've not got a clue.'

'You don't know which way to go?' Debbie asked nerv-ously, inserting a piece of chewing gum into her mouth. Dark patches of sweat were already visible under her arms. 'So why are we following you?'

For a moment, Chris turned round. His gaze rested briefly on Julia. 'Because you trust me.'

'But maybe we should have turned right at the college – that's the main path, after all.'

'There aren't that many possibilities, and the lake's round – so we're bound to get there in the end. I mean, we're looking for a boathouse. It has to be at the edge of the water.'

'It could take several hours to walk all the way round the lake,' David added slowly.

'I've got plenty of time,' said Chris, and set off again.

Once more they all followed him down the left-hand path which led into the forest and now seemed not to follow any particular course.

This wasn't even a beaten track. It snaked its way through the trees, using any gap between the dense firs. After only a few yards, they could no longer see Mirror Lake, which had to mean that they were moving further away from the college.

The tall trees stood in dense rows as if they had been cloned. And there was still not even a breath of wind. Instead, the air was intensely filled with fir, pine resin and the mouldy smell that came up from the ground. The soil couldn't be seen beneath the thick layer of pine needles. At least the trees blocked out the muggy heat a bit, Julia was happy to find.

However, it was considerably darker here than by the shore. They ran the risk of getting lost at any moment. Maybe this path was just meant to lead them astray too? What if Debbie was right, and there wasn't really any party and it was really just a test for the freshers?

Julia had always loathed children's parties where beaming mothers had merrily declared: 'Time for a treasure hunt!'

As if to underline her thoughts, she heard Benjamin utter a triumphant yell ahead of her. He had found the next black mark, pointing straight into the undergrowth.

How did I get here, Julia wondered, as she battled her way through the increasingly wild undergrowth.

She kept having to duck, in order to creep through the dense scrub. It was a long time since these trees and undergrowth had seen an axe. Branches tugged at her red top. Her bare knuckles were scratched by thorns. She bent and cautiously pushed a branch aside, then stumbled on through the forest.

'You don't think, do you, that they've led us this way just to drive us crazy? I mean, that would just be stupid, wouldn't it?' Debbie's face was white as Julia turned to look at her.

'No idea.' Julia shrugged. 'Maybe it's their way of welcoming us.'

'But there's nothing here but trees. What kind of party's this going to be? I want to get there now!' Debbie put her head back and looked up into the sky.

No, not to the sky. The sky had disappeared, Julia realised. All she could see was the tops of the trees. How long had they been walking for?

Julia thought about the other night that had changed her life, and about Robert sobbing in the darkness — and now the prickling sensation on her skin wasn't caused solely by the pine needles brushing against her arms. All the same, though, there was no real comparison. Her body felt normal. Not as if it had died. On the contrary, she felt anxious and excited.

'There might be monsters here,' Debbie whispered. 'Maybe they're going to wrest our secrets from us.' She gave Julia a peculiar smile, suddenly more amused than afraid. And all of a sudden, Julia couldn't help feeling that Debbie's hysterical tendencies were all a bit of an act.

89

Julia opened her mouth to ask which secrets Debbie might be harbouring. But then she pulled herself together. 'Yeah,' she said in a studiously relaxed way, and walked on. 'The monsters are in the second year at college and are called ...' She almost said: 'Loa.loa.'

'Where are the monsters?' Benjamin joined in. 'Cool! I love horror films.'

'Oh, God, he's a pain with that camera,' Debbie snapped, following Julia. 'I reckon he's gay.'

'Benjamin? What on earth gives you that idea?'

'Dunno!' Debbie ran her fingers through her hair. 'I like making up stories, y'know. About people. About anything. If I imagine being in some enchanted place, I never think of home. Which reminds me – where do you come from?'

From the past, Julia wanted to say, but Chris saved her from having to reply. He had stopped.

'What's up?' asked Julia.

'Look.'

He pointed to a fence ahead of them.

'Can't we go any further?' Debbie adopted the whingy tone that she'd perfected. She seemed to be able to turn it on by flicking a switch.

'But there's another one of those signs over there.' David pointed to a tree beyond the fence. A black ribbon was clearly visible hanging down from one of the branches.

'Oh great,' said Rose, rubbing her bald head. 'I've heard loads about stupid college initiations, but I had no idea they could be so childish.'

Julia secretly agreed. The fence was more than six feet

high, made of thick green wire mesh, and had no doors. She could see no end to it. A sign at chest height said: *Restricted Area. No Unauthorized Entry.*

'I've read about the restricted areas around the lake,' said Rose. It was clear from her voice that she felt uncomfortable. 'It says in the college rules that students are strictly forbidden to enter them.'

'There's all sorts of stuff in the college rules,' Benjamin said scornfully. 'It also says that freshmen have to be back in their apartments at eleven.'

'I really don't get it,' said Julia, looking irresolutely along the fence.

'I do. Pure trickery. And a test, too.' That was David.

'Or they just want to keep us away,' murmured Chris.

'Away from what?' Debbie asked anxiously.

'From the truth,' Benjamin whispered. The next minute, Julia heard a scream and then Debbie's hysterical voice. 'Benjamin, stop it!'

'I didn't do anything.'

'You put your hand on my shoulder.'

'Me? I didn't. I'm holding my camera and, to be honest, I don't find your shoulder in the slightest bit appealing.'

'Someone touched me!'

'Maybe it was the monster of the forest?' Benjamin laughed.

'Let's just climb over,' Chris said firmly. 'It can't be far now.'

'I thought you didn't know the way,' David said irritably.

'Shh.' Debbie raised her hand. 'Can you hear that?'

Julia listened.

Muffled laughter penetrated the silence of the forest. Fragments of music.

'Look. So there *is* a party!' Debbie's voice had a triumphant note. 'We were right. It must be there, a bit ahead of us!'

Chris looked around. 'Look, if we climb on to that old tree stump we can get over the fence, no problem.'

He ran over, climbed nimbly on to the mossy tree stump, pulled himself up on the green wire mesh and swung himself easily over the fence.

'Dead easy,' he called to the others. 'Come on!'

Julia didn't have to think for long. Restricted area or not, they'd got this far – and now she wanted to know what was behind all this.

She and Rose took the lead. Neither of them had any problem with the fence; however, Debbie, in her tight dress, made a fuss about it, and even helpful David seemed to have lost patience by the time he'd finally managed to hoist her over the fence.

Benjamin was last to go. He carefully passed his camera over to Chris. 'Jesus Christ!' he yelled as he reached for the mesh. 'I reckon this fence is electric. I got a shock.'

'It must have been the monsters in the forest,' Rose and Julia said at the same time, then doubled up with laughter.

CHAPTER 9

The boathouse lay in a little cove, and had a distinctly ramshackle appearance. It was clear that nobody had bothered to maintain it for years. The timber roof and walls had large holes in them. Green paint was peeling off the walls, which were partly covered with graffiti. Above the entrance door, which had a cracked glass pane, it said in big red letters: *We Are The Champions*. On the ground all around lay crisp packets and empty bottles, bottles with candle wax stuck to them, and old jam jars. In short: the whole place had an air of dilapidation which made it the ideal retreat for students who wanted to escape from college control and the stresses of everyday life.

Although everything stank of decay, someone had made quite an effort with the party. Chinese lanterns hung from string that ran diagonally above the veranda. A dance floor had been set up there too. When Julia and the others arrived, students were already dancing, packed tightly together.

'Wow! My favourite song!' Debbie immediately started bawling along.

'Come on, let's dance!' She dragged Benjamin off with her. He gave Rose a pleading look as he went.

'Are you dancing?' asked Rose, looking around.

'Not just yet,' Julia replied uncertainly.

'Hey, look, that's Robert sitting over there,' said David, pointing to the lakeside, where Julia could see a wooden jetty leading far out into Mirror Lake.

Julia looked at her brother in disbelief. Never in a million years could she have imagined her brother actually turning up at a party. And, what's more, he'd gone into the restricted area without hesitation. God knows how he and Ike had got over the fence. But maybe the dog knew his way around better than all the rest of them put together.

Unusually for him, Robert didn't have his nose buried in a book, and wasn't madly scribbling away. No: he was just sitting there, his right hand on Ike's coat, as the dog lay quietly by his side, pressing its body against him.

Julia wondered whether she should go and have a quick word with him. But then again, they weren't joined at the hip. And anyway, it looked as if Robert was doing fine on his own. Julia turned to look at the people dancing madly on the veranda. After their weird walk through the forest, she was glad to be among people again. And there were lots of people at this party. At least seventy or eighty students. Most of the freshers were there, along with some from the other years. Julia noticed that the freshers had formed little cliques during the first few days, which more or less corresponded to the arrangement of the apartments. And Julia could see why; it had worked that way with her. She knew the girls from her apartment and the boys from Robert's best; she'd exchanged no more than a brief hello with the other students in her year.

Strange that they hadn't bumped into any of them on their way there.

Someone raised his hand by way of welcome. Alex was grinning broadly at Julia. He was behind the music system. Julia wandered over to him, stopped beneath the veranda and looked up at him. He held up a Shakira CD enquiringly. *She Wolf.* Julia nodded, although that kind of music wasn't exactly in her Top Ten.

'How are you doing?' he called.

'Okay.'

He grinned. His white teeth gleamed like the basin that Debbie scoured every morning because, by her own admission, she was terrified of bacteria. 'Every speck of dirt,' she would say, scrubbing away almost until her fingers bled, 'is in actual fact a nest harbouring bacteria and germs that are just waiting to make us ill.'

'Okay as in "okay", or okay as in "totally crap, but not going to show it"?' asked Alex.

'I'd say okay as in "okay".' Julia shrugged. 'Hey, was this party your idea?' She looked at the older students. She was seeing a new side to her student mentor. Until now, she'd only known him in his role as responsible older student, someone who held introductory sessions or was on hand to help them during induction week. Someone who made sure that everyone stuck to the rules. But now it looked as if she might have been grossly underestimating him.

Alex grinned and brushed the hair off his face. 'Well, we just wanted to make sure that you didn't just see us as old fossils whose only function in life is to patrol up and down outside your rooms. After all, we were once freshmen too.'

Julia had to laugh. 'You certainly managed to fool us. Though Debbie was in a constant panic that the whole thing was going to turn out to be some kind of weird initiation rite.'

Alex grinned even more broadly. 'The crazy ideas you freshmen come up with ... ' He raised his hands in mock innocence.

Julia was keen to change the subject, but then she suddenly remembered something. 'Hey, if you're behind this, then you sent us the invitations, didn't you?' she asked in a studiedly casual way, hoping that Alex wouldn't notice her heart pounding.

He was busy choosing the next track, and glanced up only fleetingly.

'Course I did. So?'

'Um, I just wondered because of the text.' She held her breath. What was the answer going to be? Some completely harmless explanation? Or something else? She looked Alex straight in the eye.

'The text?' He looked genuinely puzzled. 'We emailed the invitations. A kind of christening for your Grace accounts.'

Julia was still trying to digest what she'd just heard when Isabel came along and shouted across the dance floor: 'Hey, Alex, you seen Ariel?'

'No,' replied Alex. 'Why?'

'She was looking a bit miserable before. I think she'd been crying.' Isabel gave a silly laugh.

'You'd better take care of her – maybe she's not feeling well.' They grinned at one another.

'Okay, I'll go and look for her.'

'You hungry?' Suddenly Rose had appeared next to Julia and was handing her a plate. Rose was one of those people who could eat non-stop without putting on a single ounce.

'Oh, how thoughtful, my dear. Thank you!' David joined the girls and grabbed a chocolate muffin.

'Hey, that wasn't for you.' Rose slapped his hand.

'How on earth did they get all the food and drinks here?' Julia wondered, looking around.

'No idea, but it must all have taken some planning, given that the whole thing was supposed to be a secret. They've even got a proper sound system. D'you want a taste?'

David smiled at Julia as he passed her a mug. Why did someone who smiled like that always go around wearing black? She was tempted to ask David this, then thought better of it. 'Has that got alcohol in it?'

'I'd say that it might have a bit of Coke in it. If you want the same combination, I'll fetch you some of this magical potion. Or you're very welcome to keep mine.'

'No, thanks.'

'Oh, Julia, don't be such a party pooper!' Debbie had left the dance floor and was totally out of breath. 'Let's have fun. We're finally at college, finally adults, let off the parental leash!'

Yes, yes, yes. Debbie was right. New rules applied in this world. Julia remembered her resolution to enjoy herself. And regardless of whatever was behind the invitation business, she decided to forget about it for now. Tomorrow was another day. Time enough to worry about Loa.loa.

'Go on, then,' she said, laughing.

A couple of minutes later David returned with a plastic cup filled to the brim. 'Here's to our new life!' He raised his cup.

'To our new life!' Julia repeated, taking her first sip. The alcohol went straight to her head. Somewhat loosened up, she looked around and saw the same feeling in the others' faces: a sense, or hope, that they'd arrived. She took another sip, and wow! – suddenly there were happy faces everywhere.

Involuntarily, she looked across at the jetty where Robert's red sweatshirt stood out against the grey surface of the water. 'I think I'll go and have a quick word with Robert,' said Julia, leaving David and Debbie standing where they were.

The wooden walkway swayed beneath her feet as she stood on it. Or was the alcohol already having an effect? She stopped suddenly, held tightly to the hand rail, then immediately let it go again. It was at such an angle that she feared it might pull her down into the water. Mirror Lake was completely surrounded by mountains, beyond which loomed the snow-capped peaks of the 10,000-footers. The college couldn't be seen from here, as a group of pine trees was blocking the view. However, Julia could see the bridge that they had used to cross the waterfall.

In the opposite direction, the shore was evidently wilder and more rugged. High cliffs led straight down to the water, and a couple of hundred yards or so further a rock jutted out steeply into the lake. Then the mountains seemed to become even higher, until they turned into the summit of the Ghost somewhere on the horizon.

What if there were nothing behind these mountains?

What if the world ended precisely here?

What if this valley existed only in itself?

What if every day felt like this moment?

Maybe, the thought shot through her head, maybe I could bear to live here.

She walked on until she reached Robert, then sat down beside him. Ike glanced at her briefly out of his brown eyes, then carried on sleeping. Now Julia could see what had stopped Robert reading. A giant fishing rod stretched right out into the lake.

'Where on earth did you get that?'

'From David. Do you reckon I could buy one?'

'I'm sure you could. You can get everything on the internet these days, can't you?'

'What time is it?'

Julia looked at her watch. 'Quarter past eight.'

'David says the fish bite best in the evening.' He laughed. 'If I catch anything, I'll have to defrost the poor thing first. That water's freezing. But I don't think I'll catch anything.' He looked at her earnestly through his round glasses. 'The lake is dead.'

'Oh, nonsense,' she said briskly. 'There are living things in all kinds of water. And the ones in here are probably really into the cold.'

She knelt down and put her hand gingerly into the water.

Shocked, she withdrew it. Robert was right. The air was warm and muggy, but putting her hand in the lake was like putting it into a bucket of ice-cubes.

It wasn't quite dusk yet, but the sun had already disappeared behind the hills near the college. A big, yellowish shimmering cloud hung above Mirror Lake.

Julia remembered another lake from her past. How often had she and Kristian swum in the bathing lake. Mostly in the evenings, at this sort of time. Once the families had packed away their barbecues and had finally set off for home with their brats, the teenagers had reclaimed the lake for themselves. There were camp fires and music and skinny dipping out on the lake. Julia's spine tingled pleasantly. The water had felt soft, so soft, as it enveloped her naked skin.

And although this all seemed pretty much the same – the lake, the party, the alcohol – it was quite different. And she knew why. It was the silence of the valley. She couldn't properly explain it. But despite the music, the laughter and the loud voices, something crucial was missing. Birds singing, insects buzzing, branches rustling. Even the big cloud seemed not to move in the sky. All as if nature had switched itself into standby mode.

Robert's voice wrenched her from her reverie. 'Well, I've been sitting here for more than an hour, and I've not seen a single fish.'

'Maybe you're right and it really is too cold.' She stared at the water.

Beneath the jetty, long grasses and plant tendrils had woven themselves into a thick green carpet from which arose the bare, dead branch of a pine tree. It looked like a skeleton that had been gnawed clean as it tapped the right-hand wooden upright in a regular rhythm. Something must be down there that kept it moving, although Mirror Lake lay motionless before them. There wasn't a single wave; no breath of wind rippled the water – and yet the branch in the green swamp beneath the landing stage kept up its rhythmic movements. Julia shut her eyes and for a fraction of a second she understood how Robert must feel when he had his – what had Mum called them? – visions.

And then the moment had passed.

'You're right, Mirror Lake is dead. There aren't any fish here.'

Julia jumped at the sound of Chris's voice. She was starting to feel that he was following her. She didn't turn round.

'Can you prove it?' asked Robert, suddenly mistrustful.

'No. I just know.'

'But David said ...'

'David hasn't got a clue.'

'I'm going back,' Julia said quickly. Without looking at Chris, she returned to the boathouse. Chris followed her. She speeded up out of sheer nervousness. But at the end of the jetty, she stopped abruptly, whirled round and said: 'Are you following me or what?'

'Is that what you'd like?' He raised his eyebrows enquiringly.

Who was he, and what did he want from her?

'I just want you to leave me alone, okay?'

'What have I done to you?' He raised his hands.

The answer was on the tip of her tongue. She wanted to say that he unsettled her, made her nervous, but ... maybe that's what he was trying to do.

'Nothing,' she murmured.

'I could never do anything to you, Julia,' he replied. God, those pale grey eyes of his. They were like those wintry scenes that you get in a snow globe. Where you see an entire world behind glass, a kaleidoscope of possibilities. And Julia didn't know what else to do other than flee from a world that moved when you rocked it.

It was David who saved her. She couldn't begin to understand now how she could have been irritated by his good-guy act. Julia found him on one of the ancient, dilapidated sofas near to the boathouse.

'Where's Rose?' she asked in an attempt to calm herself.

He pointed.

Rose and Benjamin were wrapped around one another on the dance floor. They made crazy dancing partners. Not just because smooth-shaven Rose was two heads taller than Benjamin, but also because her graceful movements were such a stark contrast to Benjamin's hip-hop leaps. He suddenly leaned forward and whispered something to Rose, and they both burst out laughing.

'Come on, sit down.'

Julia flopped down on the sofa next to David. It almost touched the floor. The mottled red and black cover had already come apart in several places, and the stuffing was bursting out. It smelled of must and mildew.

David leaned back, shut his eyes and asked hesitantly: 'Why are you here?'

'I ... why am I here?'

'Yes.'

'We were all invited ...'

'That's not what I mean.'

'So what do you mean?'

'Why are you at the college?'

Don't ask, Julia thought, then I won't have to lie.

'The college ... it's got a good reputation, hasn't it? An elite place for the gifted and talented and stuff.'

David opened his eyes, put his head on one side and looked at her thoughtfully.

'Did your parents send you?' he asked.

'My parents?'

'Yes, your folks, your progenitors, call them what you like. Did they stand by your bed and cheerfully announce one morning: Oh, by the way, we've put you in for the Grace entrance exam. It's in the back of beyond, but it has an excellent reputation.'

She couldn't help laughing. And that was the first time she'd heard David laugh too. It sounded as free as she felt. She took a long sip from her cup, which was by now half empty.

'No,' she murmured. Oh God, she had such an urge to giggle. Christ, that drink was strong. Like someone were injecting alcohol straight into her veins.

'What, no?'

'They ... they didn't say it was in the back of beyond.'

'Then they were lying to you.'

Now she did giggle. It sounded as silly as it did intimate. She looked up at the sky. The yellowy-grey cloud seemed to be hanging oddly up there. As if it had lost its balance. Hey, she silently yelled at it, nobody invited you to this party. It's our party, you hear? And you're not going to spoil it.

'Look at Mr Big, as Katie calls him.' David pointed to Alex who was on his phone, walking up and down the jetty.

'Dr Big, if you don't mind,' Julia corrected him, again imagining Alex in a white coat with blow-dried hair. 'He's bound to be a surgeon.'

'Cardiologist,' David fired back at her. 'He'll have a consulting room in some hip clinic in Los Angeles. It'll have wood panelling, and his Yale graduation certificate will be on the wall. In a gold frame.'

Julia burst out laughing and elbowed him playfully. Her gaze fell once more on Rose, who was now dancing the tango with Benjamin. The rhythm didn't exactly fit with Lady Gaga. They were stumbling rather than dancing.

They grinned at one another.

'You didn't answer my question,' David said. He didn't take his eyes off her.

'What do you mean?'

'Did your parents want to get rid of you?'

That wasn't hard for Julia to answer. 'Of course all parents would really like to deep freeze their teenagers and thaw them out again once they've grown up. And since they can't, they send us here instead.'

'What are you laughing about?' asked Debbie. She flopped down on the sofa, her face bright red.

'About Benjamin,' replied David.

'He's mean. He should dance with me too, not just with Rose.' She scowled.

'Ask Alex. He hasn't got a partner.'

'Ooh, great idea.' Debbie jumped up, and they watched her heading straight for Alex, who was looking uncertainly at the dance floor. She said something to him and, sure enough, he nodded.

'She'll spend the whole night dreaming about that,' said David. 'She's on the verge of falling in love with him.'

'I think she's got someone else.'

'I don't imagine that'll stop her.'

'True.'

'Tell me something about yourself, Julia.'

'What kind of thing?'

'Like where you're from.'

Oh God, David was really nice. Too nice for her taste – but why all the questions?

'From everywhere and nowhere. My parents, um, we moved around a lot. I don't think my brother or I spent more than a year at any one school.'

'Sounds exhausting.'

'What about you?'

'I've lived in Montana ever since I can remember. Until I decided to go in for the Grace entrance exam.'

'Montana? You grew up in the Rockies?'

'In Great Falls. It's the third biggest town there. More than 56,000 inhabitants.'

'So why on earth are you here in this god-forsaken valley?

Why didn't you go to college in Vancouver or one of the big American cities?'

His expression darkened briefly, then he said: 'I need to think about that.'

'Think?'

'Yes.'

He laughed. But she knew that he hadn't made a joke. She knew how it felt, not to be able to say what was going on in your head.

The next moment, he was resolutely raising his mug to her. 'Cheers, Julia. Let's drink to leaving the valley in four years' time as adults.'

She wouldn't be here in four years' time.

'Cheers.'

She emptied the mug, and handed it to David.

'More?' he asked.

'Please.'

'Sure?'

'No.'

David took her mug, got up, and looked up at the cloud that was pushing its way menacingly across the mountain range. 'I think we might be in for a storm.'

Twilight had now fallen on the lake, and the air was filled with laughter. Julia leaned her head back. Some students were lighting candles. Old jars were being used as lanterns. Someone was asking again about this Ariel who was evidently still missing. Julia could feel the effect of the alcohol but it wasn't making her melancholic, as she'd expected.

106

Instead it was making her feel strikingly relaxed. She looked in the direction of the lake again. Robert was still sitting in the same place on the jetty, but he wasn't alone. Two girls were chatting some distance from him. Benjamin was standing beside them, filming them. Julia watched as he panned the camera across the lake, as if he wanted to capture the entire panorama. She'd never imagined that he'd be into nature photography.

She suddenly had an uncomfortable sensation. Someone was watching her. She could feel eyes on her. She turned her head to the left.

Chris was leaning against a tree beneath the veranda and was staring across at her. She felt her skin begin to tingle. To hell with him! She really wanted to jump up and run. She needed all her strength to pull herself together.

She saw with relief that David was coming back. His smile was the best antidote to Chris's staring. He flopped down beside her. For a moment, they leaned against one another.

Julia, though, was uneasy. She turned her head once more in Chris's direction, hoping that he'd vanished. But, no, he was still staring at her. Julia shivered.

'Are you cold?' David pulled his jumper off his shoulders and handed it to her.

'Thanks.' She took it and put it on, but she knew that it wasn't the cold that was making her shiver.

On the contrary, it was perhaps even more oppressively warm than before. David was right: a storm was brewing. Julia stared at the sky, which was darkening by the minute. Black clouds from the east came scudding across the mountain peaks. The glacier region behind the Ghost was already invisible.

'I think they're planning something,' she heard David saying next to her.

'Who?'

'The seniors.'

And, sure enough, the music stopped and a ripple of anticipation ran through the crowd. The dancers looked at one another in surprise. A black-haired boy left his place behind the sound system, jumped over the balustrade of the veranda, and landed just a few yards away from Julia and David. He was no taller than Julia, incredibly pale and skinny, and wore a white scarf theatrically around his neck. The crowd gathered excitedly around him.

'Who's that?' She looked enquiringly at David.

'Tom. He's in the same year as Alex and Isabel.'

'What's he doing?'

'No idea.'

Tom reached for an old metal drum bearing the inscription *Oil*, and climbed on to it. 'So, guys, are you getting bored?'

'Yeah!'

'Then how about a little show?'

Whooping.

'Here we go, then!'

'Go on, Tom! Show the freshmen what's in store! Let the show begin!' someone yelled from the crowd.

Tom stretched out his arms and bowed. 'Who would my worthy audience like to see?'

'Yoda!'

Tom stopped to think for a moment. He put his hands into his trouser pockets and bent his head. Then he nodded several times, grimaced and said – no, declaimed: 'Do or do not. There is no try.' Then came one *Star Wars* quotation after another. 'Luke, Luke, when gone am I . . . the last of the Jedi you will be.'

Tom raised his arms to quell the applause. 'We should suggest a course in Yoda's philosophy to our esteemed Professor Brandon.'

More whooping.

'Brandon seems pretty popular,' said Julia.

'I don't know. I can't really figure out that guy,' David replied. 'I've heard that he likes playing games.' Something in his voice made Julia prick up her ears.

But then Tom cried: 'You must unlearn what you have learned.' A shiver ran down Julia's spine.

'What's the matter?' asked David. 'Are you cold?'

She shook her head and applauded with the rest of the students as Tom bowed on his oil drum and slipped into his next role. His voice changed from Yoda's mysterious tone to a hoarse, almost creepy voice.

'Most serial killers keep some sort of trophies from their victims – I didn't.'

Pause.

The crowd made mock-disgusted noises.

'No. No, you ate yours.'

Someone yelled: '*The Silence of the Lambs*!' Rose was enjoying herself enormously. 'Hannibal Lecter.'

'Ten dollars for the young lady with the flamboyant hair!' Tom cried, carrying on. 'What does he do, this man you're looking for?'

'Kills women!'

It was Chris who called out the answer.

Before the applause broke out, there came a scream.

Loud and desperate, it resounded across the lake.

Julia's blood froze in her veins.

Please no, she thought. Not again!

CHAPTER 10

For a second at most, there was silence. A confused silence as everyone listened to the scream that went on and on, echoing around the mountains. Not even the dog's hoarse barking could drown it out. Then came the sound of excited voices, some girls started screaming hysterically, and Julia could sense the excitement turning to panic. She saw Tom jumping off the oil drum and running to the jetty. Most of the students followed him.

The wooden planks creaked loudly beneath the weight of countless feet; the hand rail wobbled dangerously and Julia feared that the jetty was about to collapse with them on it. Miraculously, though, it withstood the horde of people who had reached the end and were staring out into the lake which now looked turquoise in the twilight. A powerful wind had started up.

'Something's happened!' David also jumped up and followed the crowd.

Julia stayed where she was. She simply shut her eyes and didn't move. She sat listening to the fear circling around her head like the crows on that first evening that Alex had brought her here to this remote valley.

Where, Julia wondered, did the birds come from? She

hadn't seen any since. Not a single one. She'd never seen them again.

Then she thought about the fish.

She imagined their dead eyes. She imagined the lake over-flowing with the bodies of dead fish.

She heard Robert's voice in her head. *The lake is dead.*

Had there been an element of longing in there?

A yell, a scream rang in her ears. No, it was nothing to do with her. Otherwise the voices would have called her name, wouldn't they?

Julia burrowed deeper into the sofa. She could feel the broken springs pressing into her back as she looked into her own darkness.

Ever since they were children, Robert had trodden the fine line between fantasy and reality – always in danger of falling off. Mum was continually afraid that he would end up living in his own world. To be honest, Julia had never believed in the fine-line idea. It was just a story, an excuse that Mum had made up for when her precious child yet again drifted off into the unknown realms of his mind, where he was beyond control.

She hadn't believed her mother. And that had been a mistake more than once.

'Julia!' Someone was suddenly kneeling in front of her. She looked up. It was Chris.

'Julia, can you hear me? Why are you just sitting there? Robert's jumped in the water! Julia, you have to help us! Can Robert swim? Is he strong enough?'

Slowly, very slowly, the words seeped into her consciousness. She struggled to return to the present. Robert wasn't a bad swimmer, but he had detested the swimming races that Dad had always challenged him to in the past. But why did Chris want to know?

'He's ... he hates ... water!' Now she could feel her whole body starting to tremble.

'I think he's swimming towards Green Eye,' she heard a girl's voice calling from somewhere.

'Green Eye?' someone asked.

'It's the bit below Solomon Cliff,' came the quick reply. 'There, on the left. Sometimes on clear days, you can see a green circle in the water.'

Solomon. What an odd name, Julia thought.

'Julia!' Chris's voice was once again reaching her consciousness, penetrating the blackness into which she yearned to return. 'What's wrong with you for Christ's sake? It's your brother we're talking about! If you don't help us, he's going to drown!'

She felt hands grabbing her, trying to pull her up. She sprang into action, no longer paralysed.

Julia pushed Chris aside, jumped up, ran towards the lake, and crossed the jetty, which suddenly seemed endlessly long. She had to battle her way through the crowd that stared at her.

Their expressions conveyed every reaction from sheer terror to hysterical curiosity. The air was filled with murmuring, and every face betrayed shock and horror. No, some were grinning. Julia couldn't begin to grasp that one. What's there to grin at, for God's sake? she wanted to yell.

A flash of lightning lit up the sky. White light in a zig-zag.

Like an arrow, it was heading straight for the tiny red dot in the lake. Heading for Robert, a small figure in a red jumper, whose thin arms were ploughing through the water as he struggled along parallel to the shore towards the cliffs that Julia had noticed before.

Behind Julia, Chris pushed his way through the crowd. 'For Christ's sake!' she heard him exclaiming. He was staring to his left. 'What on earth's he up to? There isn't a proper shore at Solomon cliff, just a little rocky plateau. It's only a few feet wide. Then the cliff begins, and it's so steep that you can barely cling on. He'll never get up there!'

'Don't worry, Julia.' Rose was suddenly at Julia's other side, squeezing her hand. 'The college is bound to have a speedboat. Alex is already trying to call Security.'

The storm was still a long way off, but the sky above the glacier was as black as night. The wind was gathering force, and the lake was now anything other than mirror-like. The gusts whipped up the water and sent it crashing in waves on to the shore. It was alarming to see how quickly and violently the weather could turn.

Julia realised that silence was falling around her. Debbie alone was sobbing hysterically, crying: 'Oh my God, he's gone mad! He's gone crazy!'

Julia saw Robert's head emerging from the water. She could actually see him desperately gasping for breath.

She bent down to take her shoes off. Now that her kind of unreal paralysis had worn off, she knew what she had to do.

'Robert!' she yelled. 'Keep going!'

Now her shoes and socks were off. Now she was standing at the edge of the jetty, her arms raised.

'No, Julia! Don't do it!' Rose's face appeared. She grabbed Julia, trying to stop her.

'Let go of me! I have to ... look, you can see he's not strong enough! He can't do it!'

The wooden planks beneath her feet were wet, slippery and icy cold. But Julia paid no heed. She shoved Rose aside and was about to jump – when someone pulled her back.

David's expression was unflinching.

'You don't know the lake,' he said. And before Julia knew what was happening, he had disappeared into the water and was following Robert with quick, powerful strokes.

'David will catch him up soon.' Rose took Julia's hand again. The girl was trembling. She was as white as a ghost, her expression a mixture of sympathy and fear.

David swam after Robert faster than Julia thought possible. Although the waves kicked up by the storm slowed him down, every stroke brought him closer to her brother. David could evidently sense the rhythm of the wind, for he used the breaks in it to move forward while the storm re-gathered force for the next attack. For several seconds, the world seemed to be broken down into individual scenes like in a cartoon.

By now, David was only about fifty yards behind Robert. The crowd let out a cry as a big wave grasped Robert and pulled him under the water.

Within the last few minutes, Mirror Lake had completely

changed. Almost as if it were raging with all its might against the two people who refused to acknowledge its power.

It seemed to take an eternity for Robert's head to emerge again. He took a deep breath, paddled with his arms, was forced beneath the surface again. But he doggedly headed for the cliff that jutted out into the tempestuous lake.

'Go on, David!' Julia heard a boy yelling behind her. 'You can do it!'

And then there were just a few yards between the two of them – ten, nine, eight, seven . . . and then they were finally abreast of one another.

Julia gasped with relief as David stretched out his arm to grasp Robert's shoulder. Then the next moment, they both disappeared beneath the crashing waves.

And didn't come up again.

'Oh my God, they're drowning!' Debbie's hysterical sobbing was driving Julia insane. 'That's so unfair! I've only been here a week!'

Then came Rose's gentle voice again. 'Look, there they are. Calm down, Debbie. David will save him, I know it.'

But Debbie didn't calm down. 'What are they doing? They need to come back! David! David! We're over here!'

'I think he knows that,' growled Chris.

Instead of returning to the jetty, David increased his speed, pulling Robert along with him. They were heading for the cliffs. The place that someone had just called Green Eye.

Green Eye.

It didn't sound dangerous.

Kitschy, more like.

And before the next wave had swept over them, they had reached the shore – or, rather, the narrow stone ledge that jutted out into the lake.

'Thank God! They're safe.' There was an odd undertone to Debbie's voice. Almost as if she were disappointed.

'No they're not,' murmured Chris.

His right arm still clasping Robert, David was trying with his left arm to reach the cliff. A wave stopped him. When the surface of the water momentarily calmed down, he tried for a second time. In vain.

'Why doesn't he climb up?' Now even Rose was sounding anxious.

'Mirror Lake is treacherous,' Chris hissed through clenched teeth. 'There are weird currents down there that nobody understands.' He sounded as if he were holding his breath. 'Come on,' he whispered.

The last thing Julia saw before covering her face with her hands was David half-lying on the rocky plateau, desperately grasping Robert's hand as Robert clung to the bit of rock that protruded from the water.

'They're going to die!' She heard Debbie's shrill voice. 'Oh my God, everyone at the party's going to be to blame! I'm going straight back to college! I don't want to get into trouble!'

At that moment Julia heard a loud crack. She opened her eyes and saw Debbie clutching her cheek. Chris's hand-print was clearly visible on it.

'Just shut your goddamn mouth for once,' he murmured. 'Otherwise I won't be responsible for my actions.'

CHAPTER 11

The horizon suddenly lit up. Then came a muffled rumbling sound. The wind churned up the water which kept crashing over the two boys, who still hadn't managed to get on to the stone plateau beneath the rocky ridge. It did look from where the others were standing as if the two of them could now manage to cling tightly on to the ledge.

But it was growing darker by the minute. Before long, it would be pitch black.

'Where's the Security boat?' Rose cried in despair. 'It should have been here ages ago.'

Tom appeared. His hair was sticking to his forehead and he was completely out of breath. Close behind him was Isabel. She was as white as a sheet, her face was covered in sweat, and her hands were tugging nervously at her jumper.

'Alex is doing his best.'

Chris shook his head. 'But we need to do something now!'

Rose glanced along the water's edge. 'How would you get to the cliffs from here?' she asked.

Tom thought for a moment. 'Not along the shore – it's too steep. And going through the forest would take at least fifteen minutes.'

'Doesn't matter.' Chris squared his shoulders resolutely.

'Who knows if they could even get a boat started in these waves? From the cliffs we could at least try to get to them and pull them out of the water before the lake goes even more crazy.'

He pointed across at Green Eye and Julia immediately realised that they had no alternative. The wind was even stronger now and was racing madly across the surface of the water, churning up waves that were becoming stronger and stronger. Robert and David wouldn't be able to hold on to the ledge for long. Even if Alex managed to organise that bloody boat, it might be too late.

'What are we waiting for?' she cried.

'Okay!' Tom and Isabel exchanged quick looks. The older girl nodded. 'Isabel will show you the way. And there are ropes in the boathouse; you'd better take them with you. I'll wait here for Alex, and we'll follow you.'

'Benjamin, I need your torch.' Chris held out his hand impatiently and Benjamin passed him the flashlight.

'We'll need lots of coats and jumpers to warm them up,' said Rose. 'I'll see to that with Benjamin and Debbie.'

'We need to get a move on,' said Chris before adding more quietly, so that only Julia could hear: 'I promise you, he'll be fine.' It sounded more imploring than comforting. She sensed that he wanted to say something else, but instead he stopped and followed Isabel, who had already set off at a run.

It was like running through hell. A kind of hell that Julia no longer feared, as she had long since gone beyond it.

She had no idea how long they'd been running through the forest. The sky was now an unreal yellowish grey, which seemed even more menacing than total darkness. A huge cloud was pushing its way from the glacier and over the valley. It was the shape and size of a spaceship. She could hardly see Chris and Isabel. All she could hear was them panting, their footsteps pounding on the ground, branches cracking as they trod on them, stones kicked aside as they ran.

And then a muffled thud. Thunder rumbled around the valley and then the spaceship seemed to explode. Sparks flew and fell from the sky.

Trees and more trees. They appeared as if from nowhere, got in her way, called things to her that she didn't understand. It sounded like: too late. You're too late.

More thunder. As if someone were beating a gigantic drum to drive them onwards. And how weird. She couldn't see the lake, but she could hear it. The waves matched the rhythm of her heartbeat as they pounded against the cliffs that dropped steeply downwards somewhere to their right.

'Stop! I think it's over there!' Chris yelled in front of her.

As she ran, she turned her head and looked sideways at the cliff rising up barely twenty yards ahead of them.

Isabel turned round. Her blonde hair was sticking to her scalp. 'You're right, Chris. That's Solomon Cliff. But we've got to get up there first. There's a climbing trail from the top down to the water.'

Once more, bright light split the pitch-black sky in half. It shattered into two pieces.

Julia stopped.

Beware: Danger of Death!

The red sign was hanging on a tree. A narrow ridge wound its way past the right-hand side of the tree and up the rocks. More zig-zag flashes were coming from the sky.

'Come on,' panted Chris. He got ready to climb the rock-face – and Julia felt the adrenalin releasing renewed energy inside her.

Step by step, they climbed up. Isabel was somewhere behind her. Julia's hands clawed at the stone; she had to keep going upwards. After just a few yards, she was out of breath.

After what felt like an eternity, they were up on the smooth rocky ridge, where there was no stopping them. They ran along the ridge without looking to either side.

Bare stone everywhere.

To their left and right, crashing waves pounding against the shore.

She and Chris finally reached the end of the ridge which tapered off ahead of them like the bow of a ship. They stood still for a moment, staring at the eerie panorama that stretched out before them.

Above them the sky, dark and desolate like a volcanic landscape. Three hundred feet beneath them the lake, which ...

'Oh my God!'

'What?'

Until now, there hadn't been a single drop of rain. But despite the darkness, Julia could tell that the water was rising. What if the ridge they were standing on was flooded?

'The water's rising, isn't it?' she yelled. 'And I can't see them!'

'Me neither!' Chris rested his hands on his knees and gasped for breath. 'Oh shit! The wall goes more or less vertically down. I'll never get down there in a million years.'

Julia stared at him. He was leaving her in the lurch? He'd brought her here, and now wasn't going to help her?

'Then piss off. Just piss off.' she burst out. 'I'll do it on my own. I don't need you! I don't need anyone!'

Chris whirled round. 'It's not just about you and your crazy brother, you know. David's risked his life for Robert!'

'Stop it!' They suddenly heard an energetic voice behind them. Isabel approached the edge. 'I told you, didn't I, that there was a climbing route down?'

Julia bent even further forward and looked into the black abyss. It was a vertical drop of at least thirty feet. The water was raging below. Relentlessly, the waves were flung up high in the air, flooding the rocky ledge that Julia could now just make out.

'They're not there!' she cried against the wind. 'The water's pulled them down!'

'No,' Isabel replied calmly. 'I can see something. There's someone down there. I'm climbing down. I've done it once before.'

'I'm coming too.' Julia said it so firmly that nobody dared say otherwise.

'But I'm going first,' Isabel declared. 'And we'll rope you up. The wall is smooth and slippery. If you lose your grip, Chris will secure you from above. Chris, give me the torch.'

'I'm coming too,' he retorted.

'No you're not,' Isabel said hotly. 'You're the only one who's strong enough to pull us back up on the rope.'

The lightning flashed at ever decreasing intervals, briefly illuminating Chris's face. He looked at Julia, hesitating.

'Isabel's right,' she said. 'We need you up here.' Isabel pulled Julia away. 'Come on, let's get going.'

Then her head vanished into the darkness. Chris knotted the rope around Julia's waist. She was about to turn away when he reached for her hand. 'I'm sorry I yelled at you just now.' She could barely hear his hoarse voice. 'I didn't mean it. I'll hold on to you. Promise.'

He looked at her, and there was something in his eyes that made Julia believe him.

She nodded silently. Then she turned and followed Isabel down into the black depths. Her hands clung to the edge of the cliff. Her right foot dangled in mid-air. She could feel herself beginning to panic, but then felt the first foothold. Trembling from head to toe, she steadied herself and then her feet found their way in the darkness by themselves. Stone by stone, she clambered down. To keep calm, she counted her steps; after every one, she took a deep breath in and out; felt the air circulating in her chest, until she completely forgot that she was hanging in the air above Mirror Lake, suspended only by a rope.

She'd done it. As she tried uncertainly to find her footing on the wet, slippery rocky ledge, she pressed her back firmly against the wall behind her. She was struggling not to lose her balance in the wind. The storm was whipping across the water; the only light came from the torch that Isabel was carrying.

'Can you see them?' she shouted.

'Yes – there's someone here.'

Isabel shone the torch on to a motionless figure on the ground. Its legs were dangling in the water.

Julia gave an involuntary scream. With one bound, she was at the boy's side. It was her brother.

Isabel bent down to him. Her relief was audible as she murmured: 'It's fine. I can feel his pulse.'

'And David? Where's David?'

'David?' Julia heard the panic in Isabel's voice. She bent over Robert. 'Robert, can you hear me? Where's David? Did he let go of you? Didn't he manage to get on to the rock?'

'David ... trying ... wants to find her, swam off again.'

'The idiot!' Isabel sounded shrill with fear.

A glittering flash lit up the lake, immediately followed by the expected thunder. The waves towered up more and more, and suddenly a massive surge crashed against the ledge, knocking Julia backwards. She instinctively clung to Robert. Together they smashed into the cliff.

And just as the water had so unexpectedly washed over them, so too the anger arose in her. 'Are you insane?' she yelled at her brother. 'What were you thinking of, jumping in the lake? If David ... ' She faltered.

'I had to help her,' he whispered.

'What? What are you talking about?'

'There was a girl in the water. I saw her jump in.'

'What the hell are you talking about?'

'About the girl,' panted Robert.

'Girl?' Julia repeated, still yelling. 'Girl?'

He nodded feebly.

'What the hell goes on in your mind? Have you gone completely crazy? For God's sake, what's wrong with you?'

Her voice cracked. She dearly wanted to shake him, as his eyes widened with shock. She could see the fear in them.

But her body was running only on adrenalin. Not even the next wave that hit her would cool her down. She was operating on a level of pure, immeasurable fury.

Isabel grabbed her arm. 'Stop it. He can't help it! Can't you see what's wrong? He's in shock. And he's frozen stiff. If we don't get him up now, he'll catch pneumonia.'

Isabel's words brought Julia back to earth. 'Enough,' the older student cried urgently. 'We'll tie the rope round him, and Chris'll pull him up.'

'No,' Robert murmured. 'Have to ... wait for David ... I ... promised.'

Suddenly they heard shouts from above. 'Isabel – have you found them? Is everything okay?'

Julia tried to see in the darkness, but all she could make out was bare rock. Was that Alex? Had he finally fetched help?

'David's still in the lake,' Isabel shouted back. 'What's happening with the boat?'

An earsplitting clap of thunder almost entirely drowned out the answer. 'Storm ... take too long,' was all Julia could make out.

Then she felt something caving in inside her. It was the

last bit of hope that she'd still had. At that moment, it was as if the atmosphere exploded above them. The clouds gathered together as if they were planning one final attack. The water was as black as oil. Several flashes of lightning raced across the lake, all together. And in their light, she spotted a figure emerging from the water.

It was David.

In the glare of the lightning, he looked as if he were on fire.

CHAPTER 12

Neon light shone from the ceiling. One of the tubes flickered and buzzed. After the violent thunderclaps that had rocked the valley, the buzzing noise seemed almost comforting. But now the storm, too, was beginning to die away. The occasional flash of lightning raced through the sky and lit up the night for a moment, while the rain sounded almost pleasant as it pattered against the window of apartment 113.

Peace had been restored to the college surprisingly quickly. There were still students buzzing around in the corridors, banging doors – but what was missing was the laughter that rang out every evening in the hallways. Instead, a gloomy silence gave the entire north wing of Grace an atmosphere of strange calm.

Wrapped in blankets, David was sitting next to Julia at the little kitchen table in the first-floor apartment. Robert was sitting opposite them. At regular intervals, he was overcome by an attack of the shivers. Rose was standing at the sink, making tea.

'You ought to go to bed, Robert,' she kept saying, but he repeatedly shook his head.

'Don't you dare start filming,' Julia said to Benjamin, who had retreated to the windowsill.

He shook his head. 'I'm waiting for something more exciting than this gloomy scene,' he replied, giving Debbie a meaningful look. She was looking in the boys' fridge for something edible.

'I have to eat when I'm in a state,' she said. 'Is milk all you've got? No chocolate?'

Nobody replied.

'So, Robert, you say you saw a girl jump in the lake,' began Chris.

'It's true. She jumped off the rocks.' Robert was stubbornly sticking to his version of events.

They all stared at Robert as if he were an alien. And in fact that's what he looked like. His face was white, his lips were blue, and his teeth were chattering – with agitation, with cold, or because he rightly feared that nobody believed his story about the girl.

'So what did this unknown girl look like?' Debbie asked. A mocking smile was playing around her lips.

'I don't know ...' Robert faltered.

Julia could tell that he knew exactly what she looked like. Her brother's memory was housed in a five-star brain. He never forgot a thing, even if he did sometimes fail to separate fantasy from reality.

'Like Lorelei,' he finally murmured.

'Lorelei?' Rose drew the name out.

'He means something like a mermaid,' Julia said reluctantly.

'Mermaid? Wow, that really is strange.' Debbie sat herself down on the windowsill next to Benjamin and dug him in the ribs. 'A mermaid in Mirror Lake. Who'd have believed it!' She'd forgotten her earlier panic, and now seemed to be finding it all highly amusing.

'She had blue hair and she was wearing a green swimsuit,' Robert continued with his absurd story.

'Blue hair?' Benjamin rolled his eyes.

'Let Robert finish.' Suddenly Katie was standing in the doorway. Up until then, she'd just put her head round the door, had registered the state that David and Robert were in without comment, and had disappeared again. 'If you're setting up some kind of tribunal here, the accused has the right to give his version of the story without anyone interrupting.'

'Yes, tell us your story again really precisely, Robert.' David was speaking. 'Where did you see the girl?'

Robert frowned impatiently. 'On Solomon Cliff. Where the rocky ridge drops down into the water. She appeared from nowhere.' He looked at the others. 'She ran along to the edge where Chris and Alex pulled us up, then stopped for maybe one or two seconds, maybe longer. Then she jumped into the lake. Just like that. And she went under. Swallowed up ... the water just swallowed her up.' Robert spoke haltingly, panting for air. The trembling in his body was audible in his voice.

Oh God, don't say he's going to start crying, thought Julia. She quickly ran through the possibilities. Okay, the cliff was pretty high; it must be a good thirty feet and extremely steep – she'd found that out for herself when she'd climbed down to the ledge. But on the other hand, that leap wouldn't be completely impossible for someone really bold, particularly as the storm hadn't set in at that point. There were people who actually enjoyed a risk. Bungee jumping and stuff. But did that make it any more likely that Robert was right?

'And when she was standing on Solomon Cliff, this Lorelei – was she, like, brushing her hair?' Debbie looked disbelievingly at Robert. 'Or was she singing? Like the sirens? Did she lure you in with her bewitching song?'

'No,' said Robert, ignoring the irony in Debbie's tone. 'She was just standing there, and the next minute she jumped in.'

'A girl with blue hair?' Chris repeated sarcastically.

'Yes. And a green swimsuit.' Robert nodded.

Debbie started laughing hysterically. 'You really are weird,' she giggled.

Rose's face darkened with irritation. 'What is there to laugh about?' she snapped. 'Robert wanted to help someone. He risked his life, and so did David.'

Chris shook his head. 'What I don't get, David, is why you didn't stay by the cliffs once you'd finally reached the ledge. You only just made it.'

'I went to look for the girl.'

'So you believe me!' Robert looked at him in relief, but David hesitated. Pity was written across his face. 'I don't know, Robert,' he said, shrugging. 'I went down pretty deep. But I didn't find any trace of her. And blue hair ... sorry, but to me that sounds like you had too much of that cocktail at the party.'

'She was there!' Robert jumped up. 'And I didn't touch a drop.'

Benjamin put the camera down. 'If I may put a stop to this little dispute,' he said, grinning. 'I was standing right beside the jetty and I was pointing the camera straight at Solomon Cliff. And believe me, I'd have noticed a girl with blue hair.'

Robert was about to reply, but then he shook his head in despair.

'Do we have to tell the college? I mean, what if Robert's right?' Rose frowned.

Benjamin screwed up his eyes. His face, normally so humorous, looked suddenly pinched. 'So you mean you're going to go running to the college authorities, blabbing about where we were?' he growled. 'Have you forgotten that the boathouse is in the restricted area? If we say that we had a party there, then it isn't just Alex, Isabel and the others who'll get a bollocking, but us too.'

'I just can't believe that I actually climbed over that fence. And that I was at that party!' Debbie's voice was shrill with panic.

And yet she was the one acting like a complete party animal, thought Julia.

Outside, a rumble of thunder could be heard echoing through the valley.

Chris raised his shoulders. 'For once, Benjamin might be right. You know, it could mean that we're booted out of college when we've only just got here. And anyway, you heard Ben – he was shooting the cliff the whole time. And I just don't believe in this imaginary girl!'

Benjamin nodded and patted his camera. 'If you want proof – it's all in here. Digital and in colour. We can watch it whenever we like.' He grinned mockingly at Robert. 'Well, Rob, we don't mind if you go running off and tell your story to the Dean. He'll say you're mad and he'll stick you in the nuthouse where they'll drug you up to the eyeballs. You'll be on an all-day high.'

Enough, Julia thought. Just stop it. They had to stop tormenting Robert. But she couldn't manage to interrupt Benjamin, who was staggering around the room, rolling his eyes as if he were on speed. 'Complete high,' he murmured. 'Priceless.'

'Robert,' she began slowly. 'You know you sometimes ...'

Her brother looked at her imploringly. His eyes were asking for her support. She had to believe him, shore up his self-confidence, make him feel safe. But Julia didn't believe him. And, moreover, she had no desire to put up with questions and stupid comments; and she particularly didn't want to end up talking to the Dean.

Robert could tell this from her eyes. She knew it. Julia had no idea how, but her brother could read thoughts and hidden feelings; he could sense misfortune and death from a long way off.

She had experienced this.

And was scared of it.

'Okay, it's decision time.' Chris had rejoined the conversation. 'Who believes that Robert saw a blue-haired girl jumping into the lake? And who thinks we should tell the college authorities?'

'Nobody believes him. And nobody's going to the Dean.'

They all whirled round. Alex was standing in the doorway. He was as white as a sheet, but this just made his voice sound all the more determined. Julia had no idea how long he had been there listening to them.

He looked at them one after the other, then came in and put his hand on Robert's shoulder. 'Just you watch it, Rob,' he said. 'You've been acting strange ever since you arrived here. I don't care whether you made the whole thing up to make yourself look big, or whether you had a complete blackout. The fact is, you put your life, and David's, at risk all because of some hallucination. And if anyone goes to the college authorities now, we'll all be in it up to our necks, just because you're going crazy.' He took his hand off Robert's shoulder and looked round at them. 'But that's not how it happens – not here in the valley. We stick together at Grace, come what may. That's the first lesson for freshmen.' His face, otherwise so nice, looked deathly serious. 'So, you guys. You have to decide. What are you going to do? Do you really want to go to the Dean, spread stories that Robert is going insane, and end up with half of you getting a black mark, even though everything turned out fine in the end?'

He looked them in the eye, one after the other. And one after the other, they looked at the ground and shook their heads. First Debbie and Benjamin. Then Chris. Then, finally, Rose and David. Katie had slipped away unnoticed at some point.

Julia was the last one.

Alex fixed her with a long, challenging look. Julia had no defence. She stared desperately down at the worn lino floor. Then she slowly shook her head. She knew full well what she was doing was betraying her brother.

CHAPTER 13

Worn out by the events of the previous night, Julia opened her eyes and found herself staring straight at the huge bright yellow sun. The stormy rain in the night had washed away the black clouds in the sky. Now it was a radiant blue, as if it had been freshly painted; the mist that had made the mountaintops merge with the horizon had vanished too. The glacier that extended beyond the summit of the Ghost was clearly visible; the Ghost itself looked much closer than usual.

Idyllic rather than apocalyptic. As if the valley were setting out to show its two faces.

Which is, of course, nonsense, Julia thought. A valley is just a bit of nature, nothing more. It has no independent existence. And storms are always followed by beautiful mornings.

She had had another sleepless night. Whenever she'd finally dozed off, she'd been startled awake again by images from the previous evening. And for eternally long seconds, when she simply stared up at the ceiling, she had been tormented by guilt.

She had betrayed her brother in front of everyone else.

Rose poked her head round the door. 'Are you awake?'

'Not really.'

'Are you coming down for breakfast?'

'In a minute.'

Rose, however, didn't leave the room but sat down on her bed. 'Your brother's pretty sensitive, isn't he?'

'Might be.'

Again, she heard Mum's words in her head.

You'll see.

That was what she always said. You'll see. When you're grown up and have responsibilities. Well, that was presumably where she was at now. Julia briefly shut her eyes. I must do something, she thought. Since last night, Robert's going to be under constant scrutiny. And that's precisely what mustn't happen.

'You need to do something,' Rose continued, as if she'd read Julia's thoughts. 'You should ... I mean, y'know ... don't you think Robert might benefit from some kind of therapy? There's a psychologist here at Grace. Mr Hill, Isabel's father. He's supposed to be really good. You can just refer yourself ...'

Julia heard Rose's words, but she didn't really grasp their meaning.

As a child, she'd always thought that being grown up looked like fantastically good fun. You could decide when it was hamburgers for tea (every day!); when you wanted something new to wear (always!); which films you were allowed to watch (all of them!) and so on.

But once Julia was in her teens – on the home stretch towards adulthood – the delusion was over. No amount of fancy shoes, smoking, boozing and shagging could mask the truth about adulthood. Mum had been cross when Julia refused to grow up, talked about skiving off school, and said that she couldn't be arsed with anything. Oh, all that grown-up crap!

'What do you think – should I have a word with Robert?' Rose's voice penetrated her consciousness once more.

'I'll take care of my brother,' Julia mumbled. And thought with relief about the next day. Yes, she would take care of Robert. That's what she'd always done.

Tomorrow was the big day. Tomorrow, the bus was finally going to Fields.

A large cup of tea and a yoghurt. That was all Julia put on her tray.

The refectory was particularly busy at that time of day. Students were crowding around the buffet. Several of them, who had also been to the party, looked pale and over-tired.

'Will you wait for me?' Rose had just joined a long queue for fried eggs.

Julia nodded, scrutinising Rose as she did so. You couldn't tell by looking that she'd feared for Robert's and David's lives the night before. Or was it nothing to do with Robert, Julia suddenly wondered. Maybe she shouldn't be quite so quick to trust this girl? On the other hand, Rose was the one who'd shown the greatest degree of understanding for her brother. Apart from wanting to send him to a psychologist without having a clue that it would be the end of him.

This time the flashback came without Julia being able to prevent it. Normally, it was just fragments of memories that arose unbidden, and she could push them out of her mind more or less effortlessly; but this, this was something different.

Julia could see it before her again – could feel it, smell it. When she'd come home after her night with Kristian, her father's study door had been open. The study door of all doors. It had been the death strip, littered with landmines. Dad's room. Nobody went in there.

Then she'd felt for the last time as if life was like this long refectory buffet. You had to stand and wait, but at some point you got what you wanted.

She could smell once more the stench that had filled the air. Julia still felt sick when she thought about it. She had pushed the door further open and – the room had looked as if a mini tornado had swept through it. Every drawer and every cupboard seemed to have been sent flying. Countless files were lying scattered on the ground; papers were strewn across the parquet. Drawers to which only Dad held the key had been wrenched out as far as they would go and were hanging limply from their hinges.

Dad's record collection was lying everywhere. Some of the records were smashed to pieces.

Led Zeppelin, Pink Floyd, Santana.

The bands that he worshipped, as if music had been first invented in the seventies.

But the worst thing was the smell.

And the noise!

An insistent scratching sound. It ate into her mind, stuck fast in her ears, bored its way inexorably into her brain.

'They've run out of fried eggs.' Debbie was standing next to her, scraping out the rest of her cornflakes with her spoon.

'Shit!' exclaimed Rose as she came back. Even though she looked tired, her face was radiantly attractive. The shadows under her eyes just added to her beauty. 'I'm always starving when I've got a hangover.'

'Me too.' Debbie stared at Julia's tray. 'Is that all you're having to eat?'

Julia shrugged.

'Well, that's something you've got in common with your brother. He only drinks water for breakfast. How disgusting is that?' She looked around. 'He's over by the window with David, in case you wondered.'

Together they pushed their way through the throng. Julia caught fragments of sentences. Some chit-chat about the party, but mostly about the weather last night.

'Apocalyptic,' said one of the older students. She recognised him. He'd been on the jetty. Thank God he hadn't noticed her. Julia was dreading anyone talking to her about last night.

'The apocalypse,' Julia heard. 'I wouldn't have chosen to spend the night outside.'

'Yeah, some people have really weird ideas.'

But Julia didn't hear anything more as she was just passing the table where Alex was sitting. She wondered if she ought to just ask him about the bus again. But one look at him told her not to: he looked exhausted and grumpy. And after his appearance last night, she really didn't fancy it. She still resented him for forcing her into a decision that she didn't want to make. Though – was it really his fault? She couldn't really blame him for her own actions, could she?

He didn't look at the little group, not even when Debbie shouted, 'Shall we take our breakfast outside?'

Julia turned her attention to the glass frontage that separated the refectory from the lake and led out on to a long balcony. Some students were already at the tables outside, enjoying the rays of the early morning sun.

'Are you mad?' replied Rose. 'We'll freeze our tits off out there.'

The lake had changed hue and the dark turquoise had turned into an intensive blue. The sun lit up the mountains so that the cliffs no longer looked dark grey and threatening but bright and almost unreal.

Just as Julia was thinking that it would make the perfect backdrop to a film, she saw Benjamin. He was sitting astride the balcony railings, pointing his camera at the northern shore where Solomon Cliff seemed to have moved even further out into the lake overnight.

'Benjamin's filming again,' said Debbie. 'He's a sicko, isn't he?'

Neither Rose nor Julia replied. Instead, they put their trays down beside Robert and David, who were sitting next to one another in silence.

'Hi guys,' trilled Debbie. 'So did you dream about girls

with, like, blue hair?' She ran her fingers affectedly through her thin locks. 'Maybe I ought to dye mine?'

Sitting around made Julia nervous and fidgety, as did the silence at the table. She couldn't talk to Robert with everyone else listening. So she quickly drank her tea and ate her yoghurt. Maybe she'd have a chance to talk to Robert before lectures started. She and David got up together. His face bore its usual serious expression. His light brown hair curled down on to his neck, and he could have done with a haircut – though David wasn't the sort who bothered much about his appearance. Not like Chris, Julia found herself thinking.

Where was he, anyway? And how did she feel about him after what had happened last night? It was too much, all just too much. Too many people, too many new things to take in. She had no chance to sit and gather her thoughts in peace and quiet.

David yawned and winked at her. 'Let me take that.' He reached for her tray and put the used crockery on the conveyor belt. She turned to look at Robert, but he was already disappearing through the door.

Damn. Robert was a terrible one for holding a grudge. He never forgot a thing.

'Are you coming across with me?' asked David. 'I need to fetch my books for philosophy.'

She nodded and followed him. Together they walked down the corridors of North Wing.

'How did you sleep?' asked David.

'All right,' she murmured.

'It'll be fine,' he said reassuringly. 'Believe me, Robert can cope with more than you think. He isn't as weak as everyone believes. Otherwise he'd be lying in bed now with pneumonia and a temperature of forty degrees. But he feels fine, apart from a sore throat and strained muscles.'

'What about you?'

'Me? I think the cold water did me good.' He grinned.

'I need to thank you. Robert ... '

'No you don't.' He stopped, looked at her, reached out his hand, hesitated, and finally brushed a strand of hair off her forehead. Julia's heart was pounding.

She was suddenly aware of how essentially alone she felt here despite being in the midst of so many people. How lonely. How bloody lonely. Making real friends with someone meant having to trust them – and them having to trust her. And that was impossible. Quite apart from the fact that she was decidedly not interested in David, however nice he was.

She quickly started walking again.

David followed her. He had a questioning look on his face, but he didn't get chance to say anything as, at that moment, Chris came up to them. He was wearing dark blue Adidas tracksuit bottoms and trainers, and had a towel slung across his shoulders. He'd evidently just been jogging.

Instead of saying hello, though, he didn't so much as deign to look at them. Instead, he walked straight past David and Julia as if they weren't there. Julia stared after him, completely nonplussed.

'What the hell's up with Chris?' she asked.

'What might be up with him?' David sounded husky.

'I dunno. I just don't get it. Last night, when that stuff happened with you and Robert – it was as if he'd been replaced by someone else. Someone not cynical, someone who doesn't despise people. Someone ... well, he cared. He was concerned. And now he's so ... different.'

'Must be because of the weather in the valley, then,' said David, now grinning again. 'One minute, it's the end of the world, and then it's radiant sunshine.' He set off again. 'Come on, we need to get a move on. Otherwise we'll be late for the seminar.'

Julia hesitated. 'Hey, David ... '

'What?'

'What do you really make of Robert's story?'

'You mean the girl?'

She nodded.

'Why do you want to know?'

'Why? Because ... '

'Are you worried about the girl, or about Robert?'

'Robert.' Julia was surprised by how quickly the answer came tumbling out.

David shook his head. His expression darkened. 'If you were really bothered about Robert, you'd have stuck by him. That's what siblings are for. They stick together. And if they don't listen to one another, there might come a time when it's too late.'

Julia was last in the seminar room on the ground floor of the main wing. Professor Brandon, however, hadn't turned up yet. She made her way past the rows of seats to the top and slid into the last row, which offered her a good view. The philosophy seminar was compulsory for all first-year students and, as a result, most of the seats that rose up to the back of the lecture theatre were occupied. She could see Robert in the third row, sitting between David and Rose. He was bending over one of his books, and seemed not to be noticing the outside world – or the curious gazes that he was attracting.

'Hi,' Katie slid in next to her. 'Debbie's going nuts again. News has somehow got out about last night, and she's running around telling everyone that she wasn't at the party for long.'

Julia craned her neck. Debbie was the only one who was sitting in the front row. She evidently wanted to accost anyone who came in, to exchange rumours with them.

'I was basically here the whole time,' her shrill voice floated up to them. 'Nobody . . . '

Despite her worries, Julia had to laugh. 'Debbie's never going to survive college. I think her brain's going to overheat. Any moment now, she'll catch fire, and we'll have to clear the room for health and safety reasons and go and sit outside.'

'Not a bad idea. I can't stand that philosophy guy. I wouldn't have done this course in a million years if it weren't compulsory.'

'What have you got against Brandon?'

'He just seems shifty.' Katie put her head on one side.

Like an exotic bird, Julia thought, before mentally adding: one that lives in captivity.

'Oh my God.' Katie couldn't take her eyes off Debbie. 'Can't she see how embarrassing she is? Isn't there a law to prevent people like her from opening their mouths?'

She broke off then as the door opened and Professor Brandon walked in. The philosophy lecturer was in his forties and looked distinctly nondescript. His hands were buried in his saggy jacket pockets. His tie was askew, and he wasn't carrying anything. No books, no bag, no notes. He didn't even have a biro in his breast pocket.

Ike was trotting behind him with elegant, rangy movements and took his customary place by the lectern, which his owner was now approaching in order to survey the room in silence for several minutes.

Brandon eventually cleared his throat and, with a confident hand movement, turned the lectern microphone aside. He had an unusually deep and impressive voice. When he started speaking, all the students immediately raised their heads to listen. And that wasn't all. Brandon was also such an outstandingly good rhetorician that it seemed as if he were reading from a book rather than speaking off the cuff.

'Philosophy,' he said, and smiled, 'is Greek for love of knowledge. However, maybe we had better start today with love of truth. What do you reckon?' He moved in front of the lectern, leaned casually against it, and folded his arms. He was still smiling. 'There's a rumour going around that an illegal party took place. At the boathouse. In case you have failed to notice, the boathouse' – he began to patrol up and down at the front, his hands now in his trouser pockets – 'is in the restricted area; that is, in the area of the valley that is

145

blocked off. There's even a sign that says: *Restricted Area. No Unauthorized Entry*. And if I remember rightly, there's also a fence.' He cleared his throat. 'Since everyone at this college has an above average IQ, I take this to mean that you are able to read signs. Am I right? And that you understand what fences are for.' He suddenly became serious. 'Does anyone have anything to say about this episode?'

Silence.

Not a single student spoke.

Brandon's ironic smile appeared once more. 'Aha. It's all about the Grace code of honour,' he said. 'I see. The leaders have agreed to keep schtum, have they? Well, this raises a whole host of interesting questions, don't you find? As if made for our course. When does betrayal start? When does responsibility begin? And what do rules mean in a community like this? To put it more precisely, what do rules mean specifically when you live in an isolated valley where everyone is dependent on everyone else? So, what comes to mind?'

'That people need other people?' came Benjamin's voice. 'And that there's a good chance of getting laid?'

Ripples of laughter.

Brandon raised an eyebrow. 'The only one who makes jokes in my seminars, Mr Fox, is me. But if you are desperate to make a valuable contribution to this seminar, then I suggest you set the topic for today.' Brandon gesticulated to the lectern. 'You are welcome to take my place. How about it? Good idea?'

Benjamin leaned back in his seat and folded his arms. 'Why should I stick to rules that I didn't make?'

'Because you don't have the world all to yourself?' someone further forwards retorted. 'It's the only way for people to coexist.'

'But shouldn't you be allowed to choose the types of people you want to coexist with?' Katie chipped in.

Most students clapped their approval.

'Exactly,' cried Benjamin. 'If we're talking about coexistence – then why do only a few people make up the rules? It starts here with the Grace entrance exam. Who decides who's in and who's out?' He turned to the other students. 'People, let's face facts. Age and rank determine what goes on here, nothing else.'

General laughter and agreement.

Julia saw Robert looking up and finally getting to his feet.

'We shouldn't be talking about rules. It's more about cause and effect. If *A* happens, then *B*. In logic, it's called implication. Rules without a description of their consequences are incomplete. People can only decide whether to stick to the rules or not when the consequences are explained to them.'

'Kant!' a girl with a mass of blonde curls cried. 'Immanuel Kant. That weird German who spent all his life in hicksville. Didn't he say something about that?'

'Enlightenment,' Robert quoted, 'is man's emergence from his self-incurred immaturity.'

'Precisely, and by that he means that you're immature if you're an idiot who just does what someone else tells you to do.'

'And we're not that stupid,' added Benjamin.

'So you're bringing Kant into it.' Brandon smiled. A

147

satisfied smile had spread across his face. Evidently the discussion was what he'd had in mind. He was about to address the students again when there was a knock on the door. One of his younger colleagues came in. She went straight across to the microphone and looked at the slip of paper she was holding.

'Robert Frost,' she read aloud. 'Could you please come along with me to the Dean's office?'

CHAPTER 14

A jolt of icy horror ran through Julia. Whispering and muttering filled the lecture hall. What had happened? Why was Robert having to see the Dean? Did it have anything to do with the forbidden party and the events of last night?

Robert stood up, pushed his way past Rose, who was looking at him sympathetically, and left the row of seats. He was as cool as a cucumber as he made his way down the steps and followed the woman out of the lecture room.

Julia didn't move a muscle. Not even when the whispering and muttering started up in all the rows as several students turned to stare at her.

Why had they summoned Robert? They'd all been at the party. The only explanation could be that the whole business about his story had done the rounds, and now the Dean wanted to interrogate him about it.

What if he said the wrong thing? Her brother was a complete weirdo when he was convinced that he was in the right. She had failed to get him to agree that in future he would lie. But in that case – so she had pleaded with him before they left – at least always lie about the past.

In his customary way, Robert had pondered for what seemed like for ever before eventually replying: 'Okay. I won't say a word about the past, but I won't lie about anything in the future either.' Then he'd looked at his watch. 'It's 18.14 and seven seconds on the 13th of April. The future begins this second.'

And if it wasn't about the party at all, but about her? She remembered Loa.loa. You could never be sure. That had been drummed into her.

Without further ado, Julia started bundling her things together.

Katie looked up, astonished. 'What's wrong?'

'Let me past.'

Clutching her bag, Julia stood up. Her seat flipped up with a loud click, and she pushed past Katie, ran down the steps, and raced out of the door without a word of explanation or excuse.

She finally managed to catch up with Robert and the young lecturer just outside the Dean's office. The woman said something to Robert then disappeared into the lecturers' common room.

Julia was already standing next to Robert when he knocked on the door. He was still staring at her in astonishment as the door opened, revealing Mr Walden, the Dean.

'You wanted to see me?' said Robert.

'Are you Robert Frost?'

'Yes.'

'And who are you?' Mr Walden's irritated gaze fell on Julia.

'Julia Frost.'

'I did really want to speak to your brother alone.'

'We don't have any secrets from one another,' Julia replied, remembering her Little Miss Perfect act just in time. Stay friendly. Keep smiling. Act innocent if need be. She stayed put.

'Hmm,' sighed the Dean, holding the door open. 'Well, I do in fact need to speak to all of you.'

'Why?' asked Robert. He seemed calm, almost sanguine, as if he already knew why he was the first to be summoned.

'Well,' the Dean said slowly, brushing his hand across his forehead. 'I need to speak to you because a girl has gone missing.'

The gigantic office window afforded a breathtaking view of Mirror Lake. The sun was reflected in the deep blue water. And then Julia took a step back in horror: a moose's head was floating weightlessly in the room. It belonged to a hideous chandelier that Julia had at first glance taken to be actual antlers.

'Sit down.' Mr Walden gestured to two chairs in front of his desk. His voice sounded more nervous than stern.

Until then, Julia had only ever seen Mr Walden from a distance. The Dean was barely five foot six, and either his pin-striped suit was too big for him, or he was too small for his suit. Mr Walden was clearly the type who only ever wore slippers at home, never left the house without his nasal spray, kept paper-clips in his wallet, and flossed three times a day. His hair wasn't parted – not because his hair had refused to cooperate, but because he had evidently just failed to comb it.

Julia shook herself. Now was not the time to be thinking about the Dean's hair. He had been talking about a girl who'd disappeared. Which meant that Robert had been right. Hadn't he?

Mr Walden gazed at both of them. Julia felt as if she could see a fuzzy reflection of herself in the watery blue of his eyes.

'So, Robert, there is a rumour going around that you saw a girl fall into the water yesterday evening. Not far from the boathouse.' He grimaced. 'I have no desire to know what might have driven you there; I have other concerns at the moment. What I want is for you to talk me through what happened yesterday.'

Who, Julia wondered, hadn't kept their mouth shut? It could have been anyone. Even though Alex had tried to make everyone who'd been at the party stick to the code of honour, there had presumably been just too many of them.

'Mr Walden,' Robert shook his head firmly, 'I'm afraid you've been misinformed.'

'Oh? You're saying that someone's been lying to me?' Mr Walden frowned and Julia, too, looked up in irritation. Now what was going on?

Robert's voice became quieter. 'That girl, she didn't fall into the lake. She jumped.'

'She jumped?' Mr Walden bent forwards. 'You're telling me that she did it on purpose?' His evident bafflement made him look even smaller behind his huge dark-wooden desk.

'Yes, sir, that's what I'm telling you,' Robert replied firmly.

Mr Walden brushed his right hand across his non-existent

hairdo. His wedding ring was embedded firmly in his fourth finger. The thought flitted across Julia's mind that it would stop him from ever getting divorced. It was such an absurd idea that she had to bite her tongue in order not to laugh out loud. Her nerves weren't like taut cables; they were brittle like paper.

The Dean pressed his hands together. 'Tell me exactly what happened, please.'

Robert took a deep breath. 'I was sitting on the jetty by the boathouse, fishing. I spent the whole time staring at the water, waiting for fish to appear. So I could see the cliff the whole time.'

'Which cliff?'

'Solomon Cliff. Is that its real name, sir? I looked in the library and on the net for a map of the area, but I couldn't find one.'

'The cliff doesn't have a name,' Mr Walden replied quickly. 'So, you were sitting on the jetty?'

'Yes. The boathouse isn't that far from the cliff overhang. A hundred and fifty, two hundred metres maybe.'

Mr Walden sighed. 'Then?'

'There was suddenly this girl on the edge of the cliff, I mean on the bare bit that stretches out like the bow of a ship.'

'Suddenly?'

'It was getting dark, and it was pretty cloudy. I knew a storm was coming. The girl appeared out of nowhere.'

'How long was she standing on the cliff?'

'Not long – maybe a couple of seconds?'

'But you saw her all the same?' The Dean sounded disbelieving.

Julia didn't blame him. Robert, though, wasn't going to be put off his stride.

'Just as I saw her, she jumped. And then she moved for a moment in the water before ... something pulled her down.'

Julia stared at him. He hadn't mentioned this until now.

Mr Walden propped himself up on both hands and leaned forward. 'Something pulled her down?'

Robert rubbed his eyes. He suddenly looked completely exhausted. 'Chris Bishop told me this morning that the bit at the bottom of the cliff is the deepest bit of the lake. He called it Green Eye. It does actually look like an eye from our balcony. If you give me a map, I can show you what I mean.'

The Dean shook his head. 'This girl – so she was standing there. And then she jumped,' he repeated. Was his expression one of dissatisfaction or disbelief? Or both?

'Yes, and I thought at first that she meant to do it. She looked like a good swimmer; why else would she have jumped into the water? After all, it must be more than ten metres. I was looking at the spot the whole time. But she didn't come back up.'

'And I'm supposed to believe that?' Mr Walden frowned.

'It's the truth!'

The Dean got up, walked round the desk and put his left hand on Robert's shoulder. He let it rest there for a second before saying: 'I'd prefer it if you had a reason to lie.'

Julia recalled what David had said.

If you were really bothered about Robert, you'd have stuck by him. That's what siblings are for.

She'd left Robert in the lurch yesterday; today she was going to stand by him. Throwing all caution to the wind, she blazed at the Dean. 'What if he's not lying, and he's telling the truth?' she snapped. 'You just said yourself that a girl disappeared yesterday. If that's the case, how can you sit here so calmly?'

Across Mr Walden's face spread the arrogant look that Julia knew all too well. Adults always looked like that when they had a chance to brag about their inside knowledge. When they had a chance to make anyone under the age of twenty feel as if they were totally immature and hadn't got the first clue about life.

'Yes, a girl has indeed disappeared, Miss Frost. Nobody has seen her since yesterday evening, and she was evidently not in her room last night.'

'Then what I'm saying is true.' Julia saw a glimmer of confidence in Robert's eyes.

'Well . . . it's true that the girl apparently disappeared into thin air yesterday evening. But it's quite certain that she didn't jump off that cliff.' The Dean shook his head firmly. 'It's simply impossible.'

'But . . .'

'No buts.' The Dean stood up and went over to the window. He stared at the mountains rising up beyond the lake, as if the lake had forced them out of their place in primeval times. Then he turned on his heel. His eyes were no longer watery and dim as he fixed his gaze on Robert. 'I don't believe you, Mr Frost. Though maybe you are able to give me a plausible explanation for how a paraplegic could get to the top of the cliff in a wheelchair, stand up and jump in.'

Angela Finder? It was Angela Finder who'd disappeared? Julia felt dizzy. Disappointment lay on her tongue like a bitter taste.

There was no denying it. It had been another of Robert's fictions. And if she'd stopped to think for a moment, rather than letting herself be eaten up by her bloody guilty conscience, she'd have realised it too.

'But . . . ' Robert stammered, staring beseechingly at Julia. She didn't stir.

The Dean sat down, propped his hands on his desk once more, and leaned forward again. This time there was nothing gentle about his penetrating gaze. 'I've already informed the police. The access road to the valley is impassable thanks to fallen trees. The valley hasn't seen a storm like that for a long time. But Security have been out since first thing this morning, looking for Miss Finder.' He was silent for a moment, then continued. 'Robert, I now expect you to tell me the truth.'

Julia held her breath. Robert, though, didn't lose an ounce of his composure. 'I'm sorry, but I can't help you. I saw a different girl. The girl I saw wasn't in a wheelchair. She had blue hair and was wearing a green swimsuit.'

Once they were out in the corridor, returning to the lecture theatre, Julia could no longer contain herself. 'Robert, I mean it. You have to stop this right now.'

'Stop what?' Robert looked at her in surprise.

'Stop telling these stories!'

He halted and put his head on one side, as if he were thinking. 'That's not fair. I may not always have the best grip on reality, but I'm sure' – his voice became louder – 'that girl jumped. It wasn't Angela. And no, I'm not lying!'

She grabbed his shoulder and forced him to stop again. 'Your whole life is one big lie. Or have you forgotten?'

The look he gave her before turning and running cut Julia to the quick.

Blind with despair she turned and almost crashed into Debbie, who was standing right behind her. Curiosity was written across her whole face.

CHAPTER 15

Robert's interest in maths was based on its strict exactitude and rigorous rules. But his real enthusiasm for the subject derived quite simply from the fact that maths was based on proof. After all the events of recent months, that gave Robert the security he so desperately craved. However complicated the problem might be, there was ultimately always a straightforward answer. Precisely the opposite of his life at the moment. No assertion without proof! This sentence kept whizzing round his mind that morning.

He had seen the doubt in Julia's eyes; the disappointment and fear. And he knew that he could only alleviate her doubt if he could provide some objective proof.

He sighed involuntarily. It was much easier with David than with Julia. David didn't know anything about him. David didn't question everything.

He raised his head and stared straight in front of him. There was something weird about this corridor. It seemed endless, almost as if the architect had constructed it in such a way that everything hurtled towards one vanishing point that moved further and further away the closer you came to it. What's more, Robert had repeatedly noticed that there was something wrong with the look of the building. Sometimes, when the sun was shining through the windows, the walls looked to him as if they were curving outwards, and the long corridors seemed crooked. That was something else he needed to think about. Something else that needed explaining.

Robert's throat felt scratchy, and he had a headache too. The water had been so cold, almost icy. As if shards of ice were floating around in it. His skin had been burnt by the cold, and he was still frozen.

But he couldn't think about that now. He shut his eyes and concentrated. The distance from one door to the next was around four metres. He turned round. There were already six doors behind him, and the same number ahead. As he walked on, he calculated. So this corridor – including the doors and the bits at the start and the end – measured around sixty-four metres.

Robert continued walking and calculating. The ceiling was 3.2 metres high. He had measured it in his bedroom. Every stairway had twelve steps up to the first landing. Framed photos on the walls. The opening of the college in 1969; class photos from 1969 to 1977; more from the reopening in 2009. The only one missing was their photo.

Move everything into the right dimensions. Express it in numbers. Find rules.

Robert felt his head clearing. It always worked. Proof demands logical links. You had to stick to the facts. It was as simple as that.

He passed through the entrance hall, which seemed exaggeratedly elegant compared to the rest of the building.

As if it were there to deceive people, to act out something didn't really exist.

He quickly crossed it and went outside, only to find that a security officer had been stationed by the entrance. His uniform proudly bore the college emblem. The man was talking into his mobile, saying something that sounded like: 'Okay, I'll be in touch.'

He paid no attention to Robert. In the distance was a rhythmic clatter that cut through the silence of the valley.

The lawn in front of the building was normally empty at that time of day as most students had classes. Today, though, was different, and there were more students around. Robert saw a few of the older ones hanging around two of the lecturers, and he also spotted Rose with Katie.

He quickly buried his hands in his jeans pockets and strode up the steps. Several students recognised him and gave him curious looks. Then they huddled together in a way that suggested that he would be featured as a laughing-stock in the next issue of the *Grace Chronicle*.

He didn't care what they thought of him, though. He was used to people thinking he was a weirdo. Before, and again now. That would presumably never change.

He simply had to go. He had to find somewhere to think. He needed silence, peace, time.

A thought flashed through his mind. A hiding place. I need a hiding place, somewhere away from other students.

'Hey, Rob!'

Robert stopped.

Alex, of all people. 'Wait a sec.'

Robert speeded up. He had no desire to talk to Alex. Particularly not now.

The rhythmic clatter was becoming louder. Alex stopped and looked up into the sky. Robert followed suit. A helicopter had appeared above the trees and was heading for the college building.

State Police.

Men in uniform. Robert knew all about that. What now? Was it never going to stop?

Alex paused for a moment, undecided, then turned and disappeared in the direction of the sports hall, which had the helicopter landing-pad on its roof.

Robert breathed a sigh of relief.

At the same moment, he felt a damp nose on his leg, and then thick, wiry fur brushed against him.

'Ike!' Robert stroked the huge dog. It sat down in front of him, looking at him with faithful eyes. Robert was pleased to see him. Dogs can't lie. That's how easy it was. Humans were far too complicated.

'What's up, Ike?' he asked quietly. 'Are you coming?'

Together they set off, heading leftwards. Robert cut diagonally across the neatly mown grass. Artificial: that's what this lawn was. It might just as well have been made of plastic.

It was about a third of a mile from the college entrance to the lakeside. From the bridge to the eastern shore would take around twenty-five minutes. Just beyond that lay the prohibited area with the boathouse.

Ike trotted on ahead. Robert followed him without hesitation. The helicopter was landing behind him, but Robert paid it no heed. The further away he went from the college, the lighter the air felt around him. He could breathe again.

Down at the lakeside, he stopped briefly and surveyed his surroundings. Nobody would ever guess what the lake was capable of. Robert, though, had experienced it for himself; had felt how quickly it had changed and how very forcefully the water had tried to pull him down into the depths. Could he have survived without David?

It was impossible to calculate the strength of a person. It all depended on the individual's will to survive. That's all that mattered.

Sometimes Robert believed he could have parallel thought processes. If he really concentrated, something happened to him. It was hard to explain. Maybe it had some logical explanation that nobody had yet discovered. Someone would presumably find it out one day. Science was always making new discoveries.

When he was younger, he had always thought that he could see things that weren't really there. But he had come to think that it was similar to seeing a magnified image of everything. The unimportant bits looked fuzzy, whereas you could see the crucial thing clearly and in full detail.

That breakfast time, there hadn't been a single cloud in the sky. Now, though, they were once again pushing their way across the glacier.

By now Robert had left the college behind him along with the paved path. He had clambered up the steep path to the high bank and was walking parallel to the cliff that loomed up to the side of the path.

Below him to his right lay the lake; to his left, the cliffs. Fifteen minutes or so and he'd be at the bridge.

Robert glanced down the embankment as he walked on. Once more, he felt the icy cold that had taken his breath away after he'd jumped from the jetty. He had swum. Not just to find this girl, but also so as not to freeze to death.

It hadn't been Angela. It couldn't have been. Angela couldn't move. She was wheelchair-bound.

He heard again the screeching of the Land Rover's brakes on the day that they had arrived. He remembered Angela's angry voice. Her face during the quarrel with Benjamin in the refectory.

Angela Finder.

Had she been at the party? No, of course not. The path to the boathouse was far too steep and rough. Then there was the fence. She could only have gone as far as the end of the paved path.

Robert heard Ike barking. The noise barely penetrated his consciousness. It was no different from the gentle sound of wind blowing up the dust. The noise of the waterfall that he was approaching. The crunching of stones under his shoes.

Ike's barking became louder.

Be quiet! I can't hear myself think.

Angela wouldn't have got this far. Not under her own steam.

Maybe someone had pushed her. Up the bumpy track, past the cliffs. Robert looked around. Yes, the path was wide enough, if somewhat rough. But it would be possible.

Robert shook his head reluctantly. False start. He needed to think again.

Two girls. Both had disappeared. Angela Finder, who definitely existed, and a girl that only he had seen. Not the same. Not the same.

Two.

Two girls.

The waterfall appeared ahead of him, and Robert crossed the little bridge. Beyond the bridge, they had taken the left-hand turn off into the forest; to his right, a steep path led down the embankment and to the lake. From where he was standing, he couldn't see through the water, although it was a radiant blue. He couldn't see down to the bottom. For, down there, was darkness.

Shut your eyes and it will be light.

Robert's heart pounded. He suddenly felt sick. The darkness would lift, but he didn't want to see.

Ike came bounding down the embankment. He was carrying something in his mouth. It glittered in the sunlight.

The moment had passed. Robert's mind had suppressed the images.

'Hey, come here. Ike!'

Ike hesitated.

'Come on. What have you got there? Show me!'

As cool as anything, the dog trotted closer and Robert gradually realised that something was glittering in his jaws.

He went up to the dog. 'Good boy. Show me what you've found.'

Now he was on a level with the dog.
Ike opened his mouth and something shiny fell out.
A bracelet.
A bracelet with numerous charms.
Robert picked it up.
And the first thing he saw was a silver skull.

CHAPTER 16

Where was Robert?

Julia's brother had vanished more than an hour ago. Where the hell had he got to? Julia had watched in panic as the security officers, together with the policemen who had landed in the helicopter, had taken over the entire college.

She couldn't bear the sight of uniforms and, in a state of semi shock, had fled to the basement, where she could get online in the computer lab.

Most freshers and many of the older students had evidently had the same idea. Some had wanted to join in with the security service's search patrol, but the Dean had refused. He was obviously afraid that too many volunteers would do more harm than good.

The computer department was a popular place to work in. Movable partitions divided the room up so that people could work either on their own or in bigger groups. The students spent a lot of time here writing essays, working on presentations, chatting to friends outside the valley on Facebook, or just looking stuff up on the internet.

After Robert had left her, Julia had had a thought that made a shiver run down her spine. In all the turmoil of last night, she hadn't had time to think much about Loa.loa.

Now, though, she remembered what Alex had said when she'd asked him about the party invitations.

The others had all had email invitations. Julia was the only one whose invitation had come by text.

And something else had lodged itself in her mind, although she knew that it was probably just as absurd a notion as Robert's stories.

What if it wasn't a coincidence that her brother of everyone there was the one who'd started off this commotion? What if it was all part of some bigger plan that was in some way connected with what Julia and Robert had been through? She pulled herself together. Nonsense. That was a crazy idea.

And yet – she couldn't get rid of it. She chewed her bottom lip and looked at the screen. She had just tried for the third time to Google 'Loa.loa' along with every possible search term. But all she'd found was the Latin name for the so-called eye worm. Loa loa – a species of roundworm – were, she'd discovered, parasites that lodge themselves in the human eye. The idea made Julia shiver.

But it had to be someone. After all, someone had found out her mobile number. Julia raised her head and gazed across the work stations. How was she supposed to work out who was behind it?

And where the hell was Robert?

'Why should I care what happened sixty million years ago?' Debbie sighed to Julia's left. She was hammering away at the keyboard, busily writing an essay about the formation of the Rocky Mountains, as she had told everyone regardless of whether or not they wanted to know. 'You only start thinking about the past when you're, like, eighty. I'm only seventeen.'

Nobody replied.

To Julia's right, Chris was staring at the screen of his own personal laptop. He was ignoring her, as he had done that morning. She screwed up her eyes and tried to see what was on his screen.

He suddenly turned to look at her. 'Something the matter?' he asked.

'No.' Julia felt herself going red. 'Erm, I just wondered what you were up to.'

'I'm playing,' he replied curtly.

'Playing what?' Julia got up and leaned over him. The smell of tobacco filled her nostrils. It reminded her of her dad sitting in his study, smoking his pipe.

Chris, though, had already clicked off the image. Instead, the home page of the *Grace Chronicle* appeared on the screen. *Grace Chronicle Editor Vanishes Without Trace*, read the headline.

It was only yesterday that Julia had applied to Angela to work for the college paper.

'Wow, they're fast.' She shook her head.

'Yes, there are people here who always hear stuff a bit before everyone else.'

'What do you mean?'

Chris shrugged. 'Just that.'

'Hey, what are you whispering about?' cried Debbie, peeling the top off an extra-extra-large pot of yoghurt. Several students looked up and glared at her.

'Just imagine we've got secrets that you're not supposed to know,' replied Chris.

'I love secrets!'

'Oh yeah? That's a new one on me,' retorted Katie, who was sitting with her back to Debbie.

Julia would have loved to know what was going on in Katie's mind. What did go on in the mind of someone who was so quiet? Someone who made no attempt at eye contact? Who basically never responded to outside events? A smile on her face was as rare as a total eclipse of the sun.

Benjamin, however, was the exact opposite. At that moment he came storming into the computer room so highly charged that Julia thought he must have some form of high-level hyperactivity. 'Is there a computer free anywhere? I absolutely have to edit one of my films.'

'I think films are all you ever think about,' said Rose. 'Life is one long screenplay so far as you're concerned.'

'Yeah, I firmly reject reality,' grinned Benjamin.

Debbie was still spooning her revolting pink strawberry-flavoured yoghurt out of its pot. 'Yeah, screenplay reminds me. Did you know that the cops are quizzing Angela's room-mates? D'you reckon it's, like, a thriller? Only with real police?' Her eyes flashed with excitement. 'Maybe Angela disappearing has something to do with her always getting post. There were six big envelopes for her today. I mean, who gets post now that we've got email? That's suspicious in itself if you ask me. Maybe I should tell the police.'

Rose groaned. 'God, I've had it with your gossip! Has it never occurred to you that poor Angela might have had an accident out there and is now lying on the ground in need of help – while you're spreading your crazy theories around?'

Julia, who had returned to her own screen, could sense Chris watching her. As she turned her head, she could see that he had a thoughtful expression on his face.

'What?' she was about to ask when he smiled unexpectedly.

'Do you know the feeling that the present is so absurd that it suddenly makes you look at the past with new eyes?' he whispered so quietly that only she could hear him.

Julia caught her breath.

What was it about this guy? What was he on about now? What did he know about her? Could he be Loa.loa?

She remembered how he had snapped her out of her paralysis at the boathouse the day before. She could feel his hand once more, his urgent words and his promise to help Robert. He had sounded so genuine.

But then these allusions, these remarks that she couldn't make head nor tail of, like this one now. Quite apart from the fact that he'd completely ignored her that morning in the corridor.

What if his personality were made up of two different characters? That's almost how it seemed.

'My theories aren't crazy!' Debbie squeaked next to her.

'Could you lot please shut up?' Alex's voice came from somewhere behind one of the partition walls towards the rear of the computer department. Julia hadn't realised that he was in the room.

Debbie duly lowered her voice to a theatrical whisper.

'Don't forget that Angela was editor in chief of the *Grace Chronicle*. Journalists live dangerously. What do you think – if she doesn't appear again, should I apply for her job?'

'If that means you'll go and live in the editorial offices, then that's fine by us,' said Chris. 'I've heard that they're down here too. Then we wouldn't have to look at you quite so often.'

Debbie's eyes filled with tears. They were so large and round that Julia feared they might burst on her cheeks like bubble-gum bubbles.

'How can you be so mean, Chris?' asked Rose. 'What if something bad's happened to Angela?'

'Angela?' Chris asked, irritated. 'Who is Angela anyway? Why are you all so interested in her? Did any of you know her? Ever speak to her?'

Alex interrupted once more. 'Haven't you got anything better to do? Other people are trying to work in here!'

Chris shrugged and turned back to his screen.

But at that moment, the door was pushed open. Before Julia realised what was happening, Robert was in the doorway, throwing up the entire contents of his stomach on to the garish green polyester carpet.

While David set about cleaning the carpet, Julia and Rose took Robert to his room. Benjamin followed them, filming the whole time; it had long since ceased to bother anyone. Debbie, of course, had not discreetly withdrawn. She could probably only exist so long as the gossip nerves and rumour synapses in her brain were being constantly re-energised.

Julia, however, was glad that Chris was there, even though she couldn't quite explain to herself when her mood had changed towards him. 'Are you feeling any better?' Rose asked, feeling Robert's pulse. 'You're still really pale.'

'Pale?' interjected Benjamin. 'He looks like death.' He shook his head. 'I'd love to know why these things always happen to you. You give me the creeps.'

'You'd better fetch a bucket, or he'll be puking all over here too,' said Debbie.

'Leave him alone,' Rose said firmly.

Julia, who'd sat herself down in the armchair, watched as Rose used a flannel to cool down her brother's forehead. Benjamin was right. Robert looked as if he'd seen a ghost – but there was something else bothering him. He always looked like that when some problem was gnawing away at him and he couldn't stop worrying away at it until he found the solution.

'I'm fine,' he was saying now. 'Honest. It was ... it wasn't so bad. After all, Ike found the bracelet, not me. When he didn't stop barking, I just went to see what was up and then ...'

'And then you found it?' The remains of Debbie's pink yoghurt were clinging to the corners of her mouth.

'What?' David and Katie were standing in the doorway. 'What's he found?'

Rose held the bracelet out to them.

'Where?'

'Just after the bridge.'

Robert looked at Julia through his round glasses. His gaze was earnest and introspective. 'It's Angela's. I saw her wearing it when she had that row with Benjamin in the refectory.'

'I didn't have a row with her!' Benjamin looked angry.

Julia, too, had seen Angela wearing the bracelet. There was no doubt whose it was.

David came into the room and sat down at the desk. Katie remained standing in the doorway, as if there were some invisible line she didn't want to cross.

'What were you actually doing at the lakeside?' asked David.

'I was thinking. About a solution.' Robert leaned forward. 'To the equation.'

'What equation?' cried Debbie.

'Two girls go missing on the same evening. There has to be some solution to that.'

There was a tense silence. Julia could almost see the tension. A tissue of threads that were just about to snap. Nobody believed in the second girl, but there was such finality in Robert's voice that nobody contradicted him.

'A girl suddenly appears on the cliff, runs off and jumps into the lake. She has blue hair and is wearing a green swimsuit,' he began. 'I saw her, which means she exists. And then there's the second girl, the one in the wheelchair. She can't walk, she can't run, she can't jump. She can't have been at the party, never mind on Solomon Cliff. But she disappeared. A classic paradox, isn't it?'

Nobody replied.

'My mistake was leaping to the conclusion that the girls were one and the same. Which is nonsense.' There was a note of something like triumph in Robert's voice. 'This has to be about two girls – or, rather, two players in a game.'

They all looked at him with irritation.

'Never heard of game theory in maths?'

'No,' Chris replied impatiently. 'Just tell us where you're going with this.'

'The girl in the wheelchair really does exist. In mathematical terms, you could say she's the constant. A fixed value, you know. Whereas the girl on the cliff ... '

'Lorelei?' Debbie interrupted sarcastically.

'Yes, maybe that's what we should call her. Anyway, Lorelei – she's the variable in this unsolved equation.'

'I don't get it,' murmured Debbie.

She's pretty close to zero, thought Julia, sticking with the maths analogy. She suddenly felt something like pride in her brother, who wouldn't let Debbie put him off his stride.

'Variables are placeholders,' Robert explained patiently. 'You can substitute pretty much anything for them. You're right that Lorelei doesn't really exist. But anyone could have been Lorelei.'

'Anyone?' Rose frowned.

'Anyone apart from Angela. Because she was in a wheelchair.' He looked around at them. 'When I told all of you my story, what bothered you most? Why did you think I was talking nonsense?'

'Um, how about the blue hair, the green swimsuit ... ' Benjamin raised his eyebrows.

Robert smiled. 'Yes, precisely. The blue hair. Do you remember that people kept asking about Ariel at the party?

Ariel, the mermaid. Ariel and Lorelei are one and the same, see? And some of the older students know that too.'

He's right, Julia thought. Of course he's right. The whole party – the rumours before about initiation rites. Someone planned it.

'Hey, man,' said Benjamin sceptically. 'So why didn't I see the girl? I was standing next to you the whole time. With the camera.'

Robert looked at him. 'Then show me the video.'

Benjamin switched the camera on and rewound to the point where they had all been unaware of what was about to happen. They all leaned over the display. The camera showed the jetty and Robert, who was staring out on to the lake – or, rather, at the fishing line in the lake. Two students were sitting to his right. Julia recognised one of them. She was also a fresher, in her maths class. The other girl looked older. They both had their backs to Robert.

Then the camera panned over in the direction of the boathouse. For a second, Julia saw herself sitting next to David on the sofa, holding her mug. She looked extremely relaxed. Then the camera swung round to the dance floor, which was heaving. A completely normal party.

'Where were you standing, Benjamin?' asked David.

'Near the girls, in the middle of the jetty.'

'Look!' Julia's brother interrupted him. 'This is where it happens.'

Tom was climbing on to the oil drum to begin his performance. All eyes were on him. Then the camera panned across the crowd towards Robert and then further out on to the lake. To the left was the Green Eye, then the Ghost with black clouds scudding above it, as if Benjamin were fast-forwarding. Then the camera came to rest on the path that they'd walked down. Julia could clearly see the cliff wall. Beyond the slope was the bridge over the waterfall. And something else which she couldn't quite identify at that speed.

Then she saw her brother again, Solomon Cliff and the Green Eye in the background to his left. So far as Julia could see, there was nobody standing on the cliff, never mind jumping off it. But it was hard to say, as Benjamin's camera work was somewhat unconventional: a mixture of long, drawn-out passages and sequences in which the images danced around all over the place.

Suddenly Robert was no longer sitting down, but was standing on the jetty, staring up to his left at the rocky ridge – and then he disappeared into the water. It all happened within a few seconds.

The camera remained fixed on Robert. They saw him struggling through the water again, and Julia felt the same panic that she had felt that night. Then cut. Now Julia appeared, standing on the jetty with Rose. David was pushing his way through the crowds. He was taking his shoes off as he ran. Julia saw him put his hand on her shoulder and follow Robert into the water.

Benjamin switched the camera off. 'Nothing there,' he said.

'The picture went wobbly at that bit,' said Robert. 'Didn't you notice? Just rewind it again.'

Benjamin obliged.

'When I say stop, you pause the camera, okay?' said Robert.

The image began to flicker again. The clouds. Their path along the shore. Solomon Cliff with the Green Eye in front of it. At that point Robert cried 'Stop!'

Now Julia could see it. There was a slight jump in the footage just there.

'Can you play it in slow motion?' she asked.

'Yeah, sure.'

Benjamin switched to slow motion, and now they could all see it clearly. The image wobbled for a moment and no longer showed Solomon Cliff, although at normal speed it looked as though it did. Instead, it showed a lower down spur of rock between the boathouse and the Green Eye. Then the camera panned round to Robert, who was leaping up.

Benjamin gave a low whistle. 'I remember now,' he said. 'I think one of the girls on the jetty bumped into me. I remember snapping at her, but I didn't think I'd wrecked my picture.'

'So there we have it: conclusive proof,' Robert said triumphantly, closing the camera. 'The whole thing was a game.'

'But why?'

'Speaking in terms of game theory, games are always based on a crisis point with several participants, all of whom make decisions that influence each other's actions.'

From outside, a piercing sound came through the window. It sounded like the pitiful yowling of a cat.

Julia looked over at the window.

A bird of prey was circling over the lake. It was making noises that sounded like cries for help.

A bird of prey. It was the first time she'd seen any form of animal life in the valley, Ike aside. She hadn't been aware of it until now. It was as if the valley had died out and they were the only things keeping it alive. All of them. An icy shiver ran down her spine.

'Robert's right. It was just a game. We were pranking you.'

Alex was standing in the doorway. He held his hands up. 'I'm sorry, guys. I know – it was a dumb idea.'

CHAPTER 17

Julia had retreated to the windowsill in Robert's room. As she listened to the conversation, she was also watching what was happening on the campus. By now it was late afternoon, but a helicopter was still circling around outside. And there were uniforms everywhere, which scared her.

Moreover, the quiet of the valley had been broken, and frenzied activity had taken its place. But although the previous quiet had made Julia anxious, she now longed for it to return.

'It was just a game,' said Alex. He took a deep breath and ran his hand nervously through his blond hair. He looked exhausted beneath his tan, and there was suddenly no trace of Mr Sunshine. 'And I admit it, we never imagined that the whole thing could get so out of hand.'

'But . . . '

Alex pointed to Benjamin's camera. 'Would you mind switching that thing off? Then I'll carry on.'

'Why?'

'Oh, stop all the questions – just do it,' growled Chris. 'I want to know what's been going on.'

Benjamin shrugged, and the humming noise that Julia had become accustomed to instantly stopped.

'Come on then, out with it!' Chris was leaning against the balcony door, his arms folded.

'Let's just wait for Isabel.' As Alex spoke, Isabel came through the door.

'Have you already ...' she asked, turning to Alex.

'Show them.'

Isabel opened her rucksack, pulled something out, and put it on over her hair.

'Do you get it now?' asked Alex.

Isabel was wearing a wig. Long blue hair hung down over her shoulders.

'It was you? You were the girl?' Robert screwed up his eyes behind his glasses. 'You jumped into the water?'

'Got it in one.'

Silence.

'Isabel's a top-class swimmer,' Alex explained. 'She jumped off the cliff, and swam round it underwater. On the other side, maybe a hundred yards on, there's a hidden place where you can get back on to the shore pretty safely.'

'Unbelievable,' Benjamin managed.

'So the whole thing was ... what? ... a joke?' Chris drew the final word out ominously.

Isabel shrugged. 'We didn't mean any harm ...'

'A joke?' Julia had never seen David angry before. 'Maybe you could explain the punchline? Nobody here gets it. What possessed you? For Christ's sake, I risked my life trying to find that girl!'

'It was supposed to be like a murder mystery party,' said Isabel.

'Murder mystery party?' David repeated icily.

'Well, yeah, like, you know the stories that go round about Grace Valley.'

'What stories?' Debbie chewed her lip excitedly.

'About the lake, about it having dangerous shoals, about the water sometimes rising for no reason, about whirlpools forming that nobody can explain, and that ...'

'We're really sorry,' Alex interrupted her abruptly. 'You have to believe us.'

Everyone ignored him.

'Is that why you chose Solomon Cliff?' asked Chris. 'Because the Green Eye's supposed to be the deepest bit of the lake?'

'Yeah, that too,' said Isabel reluctantly. 'But mainly because you get a good view of the ledge from the boathouse. And a jump from there looks pretty spectacular. But it's really not dangerous, jumping from there, if you know what you're doing.'

'A murder mystery party.' Rose looked at them all, completely nonplussed. Julia couldn't blame her. The extent of the whole elaborate prank was starting to dawn on her. Isabel, Alex and Tom: not only had they been worried last night – they'd also known that it was all their doing. She remembered how Isabel had appeared late in the piece – wearing clothes that she'd hastily thrown on. And her hair had been damp.

'We just intended to give you a shock,' Alex struggled to explain. 'D'you see? A bit of action. A girl jumps into the water and doesn't come up again, excitement, chaos, panic.'

'And that's why there was that performance just at that moment? The Yoda quotes and stuff. So the whole thing seemed really dramatic and scary.' That was Benjamin.

Alex shrugged resignedly.

'So, Robert was sitting on the jetty and ...' Isabel faltered, '... we thought he'd be the perfect hero.'

'Hero?' Julia asked, feeling the anger rising inside her. 'Are you crazy? You risked my brother's life and David's. And now you just produce a wig and think that it's all over and done with? Do you have the faintest idea what the last few months ...' Robert's look stopped Julia in her tracks. She bit her lip.

'How were we supposed to know that Robert would go jumping straight into the ice-cold water like a lifeguard?' Isabel retorted defensively.

'So I was your bait, was I? The lure?' Robert no longer seemed angry but, rather, relieved. His expression had turned to one of recognition, as if he had found the solution to a mathematical problem. 'You thought I was a wimp, didn't you? You never guessed in a million years that I'd jump, did you?'

'Honestly, it was a game. We just wanted to keep you all on tenterhooks for a bit and see who worked it out,' Alex explained. 'We were going to own up at the end of the party.'

'So why didn't you?' David was almost yelling.

'Well, the storm started, and it all came to a head. And in the end, Robert and David got out safe.'

Julia glared at the older students. The way they were standing there, tall, good-looking, self-confident, with their designer jeans and unblemished faces – their student mentors. The ones who were supposed to ease them into college life. And what did they do instead? They put them in danger – and only admitted it when they were forced to.

'So what about the next morning?' Rose joined in. 'What do you think Robert went through when nobody believed him?'

'Um, well, Angela had gone missing by then,' murmured Isabel. 'And it all got a bit complicated.'

Chris detached himself from the balcony door. It was hard to read the look in his grey eyes. 'Let's sum this up. You invited us to a party, making out that it was a kind of welcome celebration, all quite harmless. You wanted to create a bit of excitement so you could have your little joke and risked the lives of two people ... '

'... which we couldn't have predicted,' Alex interrupted him.

'Let me finish, will you,' Chris snapped. 'So you risked the lives of two people. And just to top it all, you got us to swear yesterday evening that we wouldn't go to the Dean. Although you knew for a fact that Robert was telling the truth.' He gave Julia a sidelong glance.

'Yeah, well,' Alex rubbed his hands together nervously. 'We only did what generations of seniors have done to fresh-men in the first few weeks. It's a kind of tradition here at Grace too. We got you to swear loyalty to the code of honour. The code of silence.'

Robert rejoined the conversation. He was the only one who had retained his composure. This whole event had given him back the security that he had lacked during the first few days. 'So that's what this party was really about, is it?' he asked. 'About your code of silence? You wanted to see what we'd do – who you could trust and who you couldn't. Or who would go running off to the Dean.'

Isabel nodded.

'And you risked getting thrown out of the college for the sake of some stupid ... initiation rite?' Katie stared at them in disbelief. 'If this all comes out, you'll be lucky to get a Yale scholarship, Alex.'

Julia decided not to wonder whether Alex had actually tried to contact Security. He'd only been worried about himself. No way was he going to get himself into trouble.

Alex rubbed his face. 'As I said – the whole thing got completely out of hand. We didn't plan it that way.'

Julia felt exhaustion overwhelming her once more. She just wanted to lie down on one of the beds and shut her eyes.

Isabel took off the wig. 'We're really sorry. It was a crap idea.'

'What about Angela?' asked David. 'Is she just hiding somewhere in the forest so you can carry on your double-crossing little game? And did you select Robert to be the hero again so that he could find the bracelet?'

'No! Angela had absolutely nothing to do with the party, honest. She wasn't even there. She thinks that kind of stuff is childish.' Isabel paused. 'Hang on – what do you mean?' She looked enquiringly at David. 'What bracelet?'

Rose held up the charm bracelet. 'Robert found it by the lake. Have you ever seen it before?'

Alex turned pale, and Isabel took a deep breath. 'Of course I have,' she said. 'It's Angela's. She never takes it off, or hasn't since last summer, I know that for a fact.'

David was first off the mark. 'Robert – you have to show us exactly where you found that bracelet. Now!'

CHAPTER 18

The temperature had dropped again. The massive thermometer in the main college now read fifty degrees. The morning sun had vanished and the valley was now enveloped in mist, as if someone had wrapped it in an impenetrable shroud.

The group had gone down to the lake and had set off along the path to the bridge.

'If I find Angela,' Debbie was saying, 'I'll get, like, a commendation, and it'll say in my files that I rendered outstanding services in the search for a missing student.'

'Yeah, stumbling over a dead body looks great on any resumé,' Chris replied sarcastically.

'We don't know that she's dead.'

'But you'd get more Brownie points if she is.'

Julia looked across at Robert and motioned to him to hang back slightly. Her brother looked at her quizzically. 'Are you still sure that you want to go through with this?' she whispered to him.

Robert nodded. He looked serious and pale, but composed. 'I'm not going to stand before the Dean again and have him say I'm a liar,' he said quietly. 'I worked out the stuff about the game – now I want to know what's going on with Angela.'

It had been Robert who had convinced the others to go

and look for Angela themselves. Katie, Chris, Benjamin and David had immediately agreed. 'After all Robert's been through, it's the least we can do for him,' Katie had said. The others had nodded.

Debbie alone had hesitated, but had then changed her mind. She was evidently afraid that she might miss something if she didn't go.

At the last minute, just as the group was about to set off, Alex had joined them too. Chris and David had protested, but Alex had insisted – so the others had finally agreed, even if they did make their disdain for him quite clear.

Julia still couldn't get her mind round what the seniors had done the previous night. Evidently none of them could, with the possible exception of Debbie, who was still looking at Alex with hungry eyes.

'Robert, are you coming?' called David. He was in front. 'I think you ought to go ahead from here. Then you can show us more or less where Ike appeared from.' Robert nodded, glanced briefly at Julia, then squeezed his way past the others who were making their way down the rough path high on the bank of the lake.

'Hey, Julia.' Chris came to join her. He looked over at Alex suspiciously. 'What do you make of all this? Do you think Alex and Isabel are feeding us a pile of crap, or do they really not know where Angela is?'

'I don't know,' Julia replied slowly. 'I haven't really thought about it. I'm just too angry. Do you really believe ... ' Then she remembered once more that Chris knew things that she had no idea about.

'So think about it now. Robert said Ike found the bracelet just after the bridge. But Angela couldn't have got very far in her wheelchair, could she? Just look around you.'

Julia could see what he meant. The path was perhaps wide enough for a wheelchair – but Angela could never have got up there on her own. The track that met up with the paved path was just too steep. And then there were all the roots and stones.

'Let's have a bet,' Benjamin called from in front. 'Fifty dollars says that she's dead.'

'What kind of sicko are you? You're betting about someone's life?' Rose's voice floated across the lake.

'Why not?' asked Benjamin. 'Do the normal rules about morality and humanity apply up here in complete isolation? I reckon all that stuff is a lie anyway.'

'Isolation?' Debbie was surprised. 'But there are, like, four hundred students and teachers in the valley. No way are we alone here.'

'That's a real problem, unfortunately enough,' whispered Chris. He looked sideways at Julia and she noticed for the first time that his eyes weren't just grey but were full of changing colours and shades. Maybe that's what made the expression in them so irritating. 'I'd give anything to be alone with you.'

Julia gulped. Had Chris really just said that, or had she imagined it? The words had come out of his mouth. But the words themselves: they belonged to Kristian. He'd said it the day before that Saturday night.

I'd give anything to be alone with you.

Then he had kissed her.

Julia shut her eyes.

'What's wrong, Julia?' Chris's voice was suddenly very near. He sounded worried. 'You've gone really pale.'

She stopped.

Chris briefly put his hand on her shoulder. 'I can't leave you alone.' His voice was even more hoarse than normal. 'I think you need someone to take care of you, Julia Frost.'

Julia wasn't thinking about Angela Finder or about her brother as she turned off into the forest beyond the bridge. She wasn't thinking about the college or her friends. She wasn't even thinking about Chris, whom she'd simply shaken off.

Julia was thinking only about herself.

She had raced off into the forest, to where there was no path through the undergrowth. She ignored the turn-off to the boathouse and carried on running upwards – not twisting and turning to spare herself, but straight upwards, higher, higher, heedless of her jeans and shoes which were filthy and scratched after just a few yards.

But the higher she ran, and the more out of breath she became, the better she felt. It was as if she were leaving the valley behind her – and, with it, all her worries, fears and nightmares.

The fir trees were densely packed together, but this time Julia didn't feel as if they were conspiring against her. On the contrary, she felt protected and somehow elevated among them.

The voices of the others below gradually died away, but she didn't stop. In some corner of her mind, she wondered where on earth she was finding the strength to run up the mountain at that speed. But she enjoyed being on the move, and could feel her mind gradually emptying.

She was almost disappointed to leave the murderous incline behind her when the ground flattened off all of a sudden.

But then she paused, astonished. Ahead of her lay a little clearing which no longer looked like a wilderness. Someone had uprooted a group of trees to clear a space. The bushes and shrubs had been carefully cut back. And there was something else odd, too. So far as Julia could make out, there was no path up to the clearing. It seemed as if it had been somehow beamed down into the middle of the forest.

Julia suddenly felt a warm sensation. She looked up automatically. The cloak of mist had dispersed, and a couple of rays of sunshine penetrated the bit of sky above her head. Laser beams. Unreal and somehow magical.

Stairway to Heaven.

Dad was always listening to that song.

Julia stood directly under the rays of the sun, raised her face to the sky, and shut her eyes.

The silence was overwhelming. There wasn't a single sound – which wasn't normal, was it? There was no such thing as complete silence. Nowhere in the world. And if there were such a thing, it would drive you mad, wouldn't it? Nobody could bear it.

She stood there for several minutes, completely absorbed,

and when she opened her eyes again she was looking straight at a large boulder at the far end of the clearing. It looked as if it had fallen from the sky.

She took a step forwards. Nothing rustled beneath her feet. The thick green moss swallowed up any sound. And suddenly, as if from nowhere, there came a voice – from right behind her.

'What on earth are you doing?'

Julia whirled round. Katie was standing directly behind her. 'God, you scared me!'

'I didn't mean to.'

'What are you doing here?'

'I might ask you the same thing. I followed you.'

Julia stopped breathing for a second.

Katie put her head on one side. 'Come on, Julia, don't act so shocked. I'm curious.'

Julia stared at her. 'You – curious?'

'About you. Just because I don't go shouting stuff from the rooftops like Debbie, doesn't mean I'm not interested in people.'

Julia screwed up her eyes. 'What's that supposed to mean?'

A hint of a smile appeared on Katie's face, giving it a slightly sphinx-like look. 'Oh, nothing,' she replied simply.

Julia could have screamed with frustration. Didn't any of these people have a life of their own? Why were they all so interested in her? First Chris, who threw up one riddle after another, and now Katie.

Katie looked around. 'Where are we?'

'Don't know,' Julia replied grumpily. She was wondering whether she could just leave her room-mate there. The elevated feeling she'd had earlier had completely vanished.

'Weird place, eh?' Katie took a couple of steps forward. 'A kind of fake clearing in the middle of nowhere. And that rock there, it doesn't look as if it landed there just by chance. Almost like a gravestone.' Katie stared at the rock, which was covered with dense ivy. The next moment, she made a lunge for it. Her hands reached for the bright green leaves, and with one tug she pulled them to the ground.

Behind the ivy was a stone slab with a hollow in it. It reminded Julia of a shrine. The kind that was sometimes erected in churches, on graveyards, at crossroads or – as here – in the forest. All that was missing was the Virgin Mary. Instead there was a slate that had something like a name scratched on to it.

'Wow,' Katie murmured. 'It really is a gravestone. In the middle of the forest!'

Julia went closer. Her gaze was fixed on the inscription. Behind it was a date. *September 10 1974.*

Julia went through the list of names, but the inscription had become weathered over the years. All she could make out were fragments and individual letters.

At the end of the list, she stopped. There was a complete name there. The name Mark.

And then?

The stone was dirty and had started to turn hoary, having been exposed to more than thirty years of snow, rain and storms.

'I wonder whose names they are?' she heard herself asking.

'Maybe the students who went missing?'

Julia stared at Katie. 'What students?'

'Don't you know the story?'

Julia shook her head.

'Debbie told us, I can't remember when. Maybe before you and Robert came. It was in the seventies. Eight college students went on a mountain tour on the Ghost, and they disappeared without trace. Horrible, right?'

'What happened?'

'Nobody ever found out. Eventually the search was called off. And the college was shut down shortly afterwards. Did you know that it used to be called Solomon College?'

Julia shook her head. 'I'd never even heard of Grace College until recently.'

'Well, anyway, they didn't manage to keep it all secret, even though they tried to. There were big stories in all the newspapers, then of course the obituaries.'

'But what were the students doing on the Ghost?'

Katie looked at her in surprise. 'They wanted to climb it – what else?' she said. 'The aim of mountain climbing is to find your way up the mountain. I totally admire them for it.'

A shiver ran down Julia's spine. She suddenly felt her head starting to hurt. The ivy was twisting itself around her head like a kind of wreath; it was getting tighter and tighter. Until she felt as if her head was going to burst.

And then it came again. The cawing that she'd heard before. Directly above her. She opened her eyes. It was circling around high up in the sky, in the laser beams of the sun. A bird of prey. She shut her eyes. And when she opened them again, Julia was alone in the clearing.

Katie had vanished.

As if she'd disappeared into thin air – or had never been there at all.

CHAPTER 19

A loud cry echoed through the valley, repeating itself over and over again, endlessly bouncing off the surrounding cliffs.

Julia was still alone, and the forest seemed endless.

She could see red. Everywhere. A hideous vampire red that glowed through the tree trunks. Past and present. Where are you, Julia, what are you doing? A hand with red-painted fingernails that appeared from behind the fir tree ahead of her, waving to her.

Where had she come from?

Where could she go?

Branches holding her back. A mountain. A slope.

She stopped briefly. Ran onwards. Just get away. Was it a voice? Was someone calling her?

Then red mist rising from the ground. A hand appearing among the trees. Bright red nails digging their way into the ground, making a scraping sound that took her breath away.

Get away. Just get away from here.

But the forest was a labyrinth. No: the trees were alive. They were standing in her way. Whenever she thought she'd found her way out, they were suddenly standing there. They seemed to be growing before her very eyes.

Then more voices. Or was it the trees whispering her name?

She tried to concentrate.

Julia. Julia. Julia.

She called for Katie, to drown out the voices. Had Katie even been there? She surely couldn't have vanished into thin air?

No?

Couldn't she?

Why not?

Anything was possible.

She knew that for a fact.

The red thread hanging from her mother's mouth. And beneath it, the necklace with the cross.

It hadn't helped.

The trees seemed to be reading her mind.

Alone, they whispered, alone. You're all alone.

The branches with the pine needles bending down to her. The forest swirling around her.

Her hands went up and clamped themselves to her ears. Her arms sank back down.

She listened.

Had it gone?

No.

There, there it was again. Someone was desperately calling a name.

The sound was coming from everywhere, and only slowly diminished. Not until its final echo had faded away did Julia realise.

Not Julia.

Angela.

Angela.

The blood rushed to her ears and her heart. She could hear it pounding, could hear its powerful rhythm joining together with the name. Contracting, expanding, contracting again.

Angela.

There was desperation in the name.

Her breath rattled; fear was the bird of prey that was pursuing her. His beak was hacking out holes in her mind so that she couldn't think clearly any longer.

And Julia carried on running. Up the mountain. Steep, so steep.

Then she stumbled. Her foot caught in the ivy that covered the ground like a spider's web. She couldn't stop herself falling; tried to break her fall with her hand; but from far away, she could see herself falling and hitting her head on a stone.

Everything went black before her eyes. The last thing she thought was: if she didn't get up quickly, the buzzard who had been chasing her through the forest would pounce on her.

Julia.

Julia.

The echo didn't stop.

Julia was slowly regaining consciousness.

'Julia?'

There was a familiar smell: forest, wood, tobacco. She lifted her head and opened her eyes. It was Chris's hand that was touching her face.

'Julia, are you okay?' he asked.

She lay there for a moment, thinking that it would be easier just to give up.

'Julia, are you hurt?'

She shook her head, still in shock.

She tried to stand up, but everything swam before her eyes. The next moment, she felt an arm around her, steadying her.

'Hey,' Chris murmured, 'you just stay sitting, okay? Don't move. It'll be fine. I promise.'

He stroked her, pulled her to him. His body was so warm. For a moment, Julia just wanted to shut her eyes and let herself fall. A bit of peace, a bit of security. What had he said before?

You need someone to take care of you, Julia Frost.

She abruptly detached herself from him. 'Everything's fine,' she stammered. 'No harm done.'

But instead of letting go, Chris pulled Julia even more closely to him. Her head was lying on his chest. She could hear his breathing, could feel his hand on hers. And she felt something quietening inside her.

'I'm here for you, Julia,' he whispered. 'Do you hear me? You don't need to be afraid any more. I'll protect you.'

She didn't understand. 'Why?'

'Don't you know?'

She shook her head.

He pulled away from her slightly, but only so that he could look into her eyes. There was an expression on his face that Julia couldn't quite place. Was it possible? Yes, cool, self-confident, inscrutable Chris looked hurt. 'Julia – how on earth can you be so blind?' he said. 'I ... I've liked you since the first moment I saw you. I like you more than is good for either of us.'

Julia froze. She'd imagined everything – except this. 'You like me?' she croaked.

He nodded.

She extracted herself from his arms, and this time he let her. Behind her was the bridge; she must have run all the way down the mountain without noticing. The path directly below them was empty; there was no sign of the others.

She turned to look at Chris again. 'If you really like me – then how come I never know where I stand with you?' she asked.

'Probably because I don't know where I stand with you.' His face darkened. 'Julia, I need to know. Is there something going on between you and David?'

She stared at him. 'Between David and me?'

'Well, yesterday evening at the boathouse, and then again this morning in the corridor ... oh, I don't know.' He brushed the hair off his forehead, embarrassed. 'I just know I get so angry when I see you having fun with him, smiling at him and not me. Whenever you're with him, you look almost happy. But I know that something's bothering you. There's something behind your facade ... '

Her breathing immediately became panicky once more.

This was Chris she was talking to. The same Chris who'd seen her throwing her mobile into the lake. The same Chris who kept alluding to things that he couldn't possibly know anything about.

Don't trust anyone. No. No-one.

'No, there isn't.' Julia desperately shook her head and shut her eyes. 'Leave me alone.'

'But I'm right, aren't I? Something happened to you that you don't want to talk about.' His voice was calm and insistent. 'Julia, maybe it would do you good to tell me what's wrong.'

Her body was in knots. Suddenly every fibre of her was screaming to tell him. It felt so right, so damn right. Her secret would be safe with him.

She gritted her teeth. 'No,' she murmured, 'that's just some nonsense that you've made up.'

He let go of her and stood up.

At that moment, the familiar forest sounds started up again. The wind in the trees, the gentle crackling of branches. The babble of voices, quite close by. She could hear Benjamin and Alex, but she couldn't make out what they were saying.

Then Katie was standing in front of her again, as if she'd never vanished.

'Where've you been?'

'Nowhere.'

'But you suddenly disappeared.'

'I didn't disappear.' Katie turned away. 'You disappeared. I've been looking for you.'

'Chris! Julia! Katie? Where are you?' There was a note of panic in Rose's voice. Although they couldn't see her, it sounded as if she were standing right next to them.

'Here.' Chris looked around.

The next moment, Rose came clambering up the embankment. Gasping for breath, she stopped in front of her friends. Her beautiful face was the picture of horror.

'We've found Angela,' she croaked.

'Where?' asked Chris.

'Down there.' She pointed behind her.

'Is she still alive?'

Rose couldn't reply. She simply shook her head.

Julia stared down at Mirror Lake. At first sight, everything looked completely normal. Alex was kneeling by the shore, as was Benjamin, who was filming. David was on his mobile. Robert was sitting on a stone, looking at them. He was as white as a sheet.

Julia stumbled more than ran down the embankment. Chris was hot on her heels.

Suddenly Debbie was blocking their path. 'She's down there in the water!' she cried hysterically. 'It's horrible! I just can't look!'

Benjamin called over to them. 'Look! D'you see? Down there. The wheelchair! I think I can see the wheels. They're turning! Oh my God. Right down under the water!'

Julia was the first to move. Chris tried to pull her back by the shoulder.

'You really want to see? Why?' he asked.

'I don't know,' she whispered.

The water was gleaming in the last bit of sunlight, and there was no wind. The surface of Mirror Lake was still. The shore fell steeply away at that point – almost like the edge of a cliff. And although the lake must have been at least thirty feet deep, they could see right down to the bottom, for the water was as clear as glass.

Benjamin was right. Julia could clearly see a silver wheel slowly turning on the bottom of Mirror Lake. And as if that weren't bizarre and absurd enough, Julia noticed a gentle movement.

Grasses were waving to and fro, almost as if they were dancing.

No, it wasn't grass: it was hair.

Long hair, like threads, like countless nerve fibres, passing through the water.

'Oh my God,' she whispered. 'Can you see that? Angela's hair.' Somewhere at the very back of her mind, she registered that Chris's arms were around her, as Alex turned and vomited on to the grass. A stone came loose and fell into the water. The body of the girl lying beneath them on the bed of the lake became blurred and then could no longer be seen.

'When's help coming?' Debbie looked hysterically at David, who was shutting his mobile.

'Help?' Chris let go of Julia and rammed his hands into his jeans pockets. 'There's no help to be had here.'

Oddly enough, Julia didn't find Chris's words irreverent. In fact, she was comforted by his manner, his combination of objectivity and distance with a hint of sarcasm. As if Chris were trying to tell her that this particular death was nothing to do with her. She'd barely known the girl. Whatever happened next wouldn't affect her life.

'D'you think she's really dead?' Debbie didn't seem to grasp it. Could anyone really be that stupid?

'Do you think she's practising her diving?' Julia couldn't stop herself.

Chris said: 'She's deader than dead. And I wouldn't want to be here when they pull her out. There's nothing worse than the sight of a drowned body.'

CHAPTER 20

The next day was dank and dreary, but that seemed to go with what had happened. There was even more snow on the Ghost than there had been the day before and, through the fog, the trees in the far distance looked like dark pencil marks on white paper.

The girl on the cliff had just been a game, but Angela, Angela Finder, had drowned in the lake – not far from where the party had taken place.

The security men had sealed off the lakeside and had sent the students back to the college while the state police retrieved Angela's body. According to Debbie, they had helicoptered the body to Vancouver. And Debbie was asking everyone in all seriousness if they'd seen the corpse-copter and if it had been black like a hearse.

Speculation was rife at Grace. Anything seemed possible, from accidents to suicide. There hadn't as yet been any statement from the Dean's office, only that they were to stay away from the lakeside in order not to hinder the work of the police who had made their way into the valley along roads that had meanwhile been cleared. Once or twice, the police had been in the building, and that morning the Dean had issued his orders over the loudspeakers. A voice that made a shiver run down Julia's back every time it resounded, loud and metallic, through the old building:

Classes will take place as normal today.
Anyone who has any information about the incident should go and tell their head of year.
Please help the police if you can – but don't obstruct their work.

It was somehow not surprising that the strangest rumours were going around Grace. There were speculations about a wheelchair gone mad, where the electrical contacts had taken control; then there was talk of a crazy serial killer living in the forest.

But all the students were basically just waiting to find out what had really happened. And so, that Saturday morning, the atmosphere was one of tense calm when Professor Brandon entered the room.

Julia found it somewhat ironic that she should have philosophy again, of all subjects. How very fitting, it flashed through her mind.

But instead of talking about Angela Finder's death, the lecturer acted as if nothing had happened. He started the class just as he had done on the previous day.

'So, which existential question are we going to discuss today?' he asked. His hands buried in his trouser pockets, he marched up and down at the front of the room. Ike had raised his massive head and was watching him closely, as if he understood what Brandon was saying.

It was Rose who spoke without hesitation. She was sitting in the front row and had neither opened her note-pad nor got out her pen. She was wearing jeans and a shirt that went with her name. Her stubbly hair, which was slowly growing back, looked like the down on a chicken, and she was uncharacteristically pale.

'Yes, Miss Gardner?'

'Is there such a thing as a right to the truth?'

Professor Brandon looked thoughtfully at Rose for a moment, then turned to address the other students. 'What do you think?'

Someone called out: 'That depends. Isn't that always the answer?'

'What on?' asked Brandon.

'On the circumstances,' said Debbie.

'Let's say it's about life and death!' It was astonishing, how energetic Rose sounded despite her soft voice.

Julia felt hot. Life and death. Truth and lies.

God, she was fed up with those words, this whole business.

Professor Brandon walked over to Rose's desk so that he was standing right in front of her. His deep, melodious voice didn't change one iota as he asked: 'What exactly are you trying to say?'

'Don't we have the right to find out what happened to Angela?'

Brandon raised an eyebrow. 'Do you want to discuss this?'

'We don't want to discuss it – we want answers.' Before the professor could reply, Rose carried on. 'Was it an accident?'

Brandon turned and went back to his lectern. 'The police are assuming so for the moment.'

'And that's it?' Rose persisted. Inside the gentle, beautiful Rose, Julia suddenly saw a hard core that she hadn't previously noticed. 'Haven't you wondered how Angela managed to get to where we found her in her wheelchair?'

'Well, that still has to be explained,' Brandon said calmly. 'There will be an investigation, forensic evidence. Conclusions will be drawn from the facts.'

'Which is why I can't stop thinking that you don't want to tell us the truth.'

'I don't know the truth,' replied Mr Brandon, and Julia could detect a note of impatience in his voice. 'So long as they're still investigating the scene of the accident and, above all, so long as they haven't completed the postmortem, we don't know the truth. None of us does.'

Now it was Robert's turn to put his hand up.

'Mr Frost? Which theory are you going to delight us with today?' Brandon's voice had an unmistakably ironic edge.

Robert stood up. 'You're trying to tell us that truth is based on facts alone. But isn't the truth more than merely the sum of forensically gathered evidence?'

'Do you reckon it was an accident?' Julia heard Chris whispering next to her. His right hand was next to her left one, as if by accident.

Julia didn't know what to believe. It seemed to her that life was just one misfortune after another, and that the chain would never end unless she managed to break it.

'If Robert hadn't got involved in the whole thing, then it would all ...'

'... just pass you by?' Chris laughed softly. 'See – I said you were just as wrapped up in yourself as I am.'

'What is there to laugh about, Mr Bishop?'

Professor Brandon was looking up at them.

'So is laughing against the rules now? Well, I can't say I'm surprised, given all the rules and prohibitions up here.'

'So do you think that Angela's death is, like, the proof that Robert was asking for in the last session?' The questioner was a strikingly skinny student that Julia didn't know. 'That whole "if ... then" thing? That rules ought to function according the laws of logic?'

There was a cawing sound outside. Julia looked across at the window. A large bird was circling over Mirror Lake, its wings outspread. It was the third time that Julia had set eyes on it; she had started to wonder if it was always the same one.

At that moment, there came a shot. The loud crack echoed around the cliffs. The buzzard plunged downwards and, within seconds, had been swallowed up by Mirror Lake.

'I'll kill those Security guys,' Professor Brandon murmured angrily.

CHAPTER 21

In the refectory that lunchtime, Alex announced that the bus to Fields was cancelled that day due to recent events and the ongoing state police investigation.

Julia was initially shocked by the news. After all, she had spent the whole week waiting to be able to leave the valley. She still hadn't made contact, and she was still afraid that somebody knew about Robert and her. Yet this seemed somehow less important in the light of what had happened recently. And then there was Chris, who was constantly on her mind now. When he'd held her in the forest, it had felt so bloody good: she'd felt protected, no longer alone; and, most importantly of all, he wasn't falling for the Little Miss Perfect act. She didn't have to pretend any more with him. In that respect, he was like Kristian.

That whole Sunday was dominated by the noise of the helicopter. The flashing lights of the police cars were mirrored in the lake, orange circles passing through the water. The security men were manning the college entrances and exits. And they kept hearing the same information: 'The western side of the lake has been sealed off. Please do not hinder the police in their investigations.'

Obviously, this all served to increase the tension and

anxiety felt in the college. The students sat about in the entrance foyer or hung around in the corridors, talking about what was going on. A big group of rubberneckers went out on to the balcony outside the refectory to watch what the state police were doing. Benjamin kept on filming, even though Katie warned him that the state police were even worse than the FBI. 'If they find out that you're filming them, they'll confiscate your camera.'

Julia spent most of the day with Rose and David. But as evening fell, she was fed up with rumours and suppositions and decided to forget about supper and go up to her room instead. She put her earphones in and went to the bathroom first. It was too small to be shared by four people. They all spent as little time as possible in there. The dark brown tiles had to be seventies leftovers – which reminded her of the memorial stone in the forest.

Mark.

She couldn't get the name out of her head.

To get rid of it, she turned her iPod up to full volume. As always, music was a comfort – although comfort was perhaps not the right word. It was more that it stopped her from feeling lonely.

Julia reached for her washbag, pulled out her toothbrush and toothpaste, and started to brush her teeth.

Once again, she was aware of what an insane situation she was in. Wasn't it absurd enough to drive anyone completely crazy?

Only when Debbie wrenched open the door did Julia snap out of her reverie. Damn, she'd forgotten to lock it. It didn't seem to bother Debbie, who went over to the second wash basin and started carefully laying out her things.

And it was disturbing, the way that Debbie performed her morning and evening washing ritual, as Katie called it.

As a rubber-gloved Debbie was spreading some mysterious white liquid on to her face, she seemed to be saying something. Or, at any rate, her mouth was moving underneath the gunk, which looked positively grotesque as the white stuff started to crack slightly.

Julia took one of her earphones out. 'What did you say?'

'Apparently the state police are going to question us all about Angela.'

That was all she needed. Julia's heart, which had just started beating normally, began to pound again.

'I haven't got a clue what I'm supposed to say,' Debbie prattled on. 'D'you think I should tell them about the party?'

'Everyone knows about it anyway. After all, someone told the Dean the next morning. I'd love to know who that was.'

Still wearing her face-mask, Debbie started cleaning her teeth and couldn't reply. Her expression didn't change, but Julia thought there was something odd about her. The way she was staring at her twin in the mirror.

'It was you, wasn't it?' It was a wild guess, and something that Julia didn't really intend to say out loud – but it hit the mark.

Debbie manoeuvred the floss between her teeth as if she were hoping to find the right words there.

Only once she'd finished her protracted teeth cleaning did

Debbie turn round. 'After Angela disappeared, I thought it was just more straightforward to tell the Dean about the party before word got out and we all got dropped in it,' she said testily.

Julia raised her eyebrows. She could still picture Debbie looking longingly at Alex that awful night, nodding faithfully when he asked them not to go to the Dean.

But at the same time, it fitted for her to be the traitor – though Julia would never have imagined that there would be such a magnificent actress lurking within her.

'So, did you manage to negotiate yourself a good deal?' she said sarcastically. 'Mr Walden agreed to forget that you were at the party, on the condition that you hand him Robert's head on a plate? And the rest of us too?'

'Don't be ridiculous.' Debbie wound another piece of dental floss around her finger. Julia noticed that she was looking rather nervous now. 'Mr Walden was really grateful that I'd let him know, and that was that. I mean, nothing happened to your brainbox brother. In any case, it was all about Angela.'

Julia could feel the anger rising in her. 'Yeah, right. As if you give a toss about her!' Her voice took on an acid tone. 'You've been here at college for just two weeks. Have you ever exchanged a single word with her?'

Debbie pulled a face. 'I felt sorry for her because she was in a wheelchair,' she said evasively. 'She had an accident, and was paralysed from the fourth neck vertebra down. She told me so herself. No wonder she was so aggressive.'

'Aggressive?'

'Well, I mean, like, stand-offish. Although I always tried to be nice to her.'

Yeah, right, flashed through Julia's mind. Debbie was only nice to one person: herself.

Julia put her hairbrush and washbag in the cupboard. 'Has anyone ever told you how crap it is, the way you always make yourself the centre of attention?' She was well aware that starting an argument with Debbie wasn't a particularly great idea. But Debbie just made her see red. And she shouldn't have made that remark about Robert.

'What do you mean?' Debbie was now riled too.

'You're suddenly making out that you and Angela were best buddies – just to make yourself seem important. And she's dead. Do you actually understand what that means?'

Debbie narrowed her eyes. 'And it's never occurred to you that I might have known her before I came here?' As she spoke, she immediately looked as if she regretted her words.

Julia stared at her.

They'd known one another before? Was Debbie really telling the truth? You never knew with her. Maybe she just felt that Julia had painted her into a corner.

'You two had met before? Go on, then – when and where?'

'Where do you think?' retorted Debbie. 'I met her online.'

'You knew one another from the internet?'

'You haven't got a clue, have you? Angela was a total tech-head; she was well known on all the hacker forums. Did I never mention it?'

'She was a hacker? Angela?' Rose's elfin face appeared behind Julia. 'And well known?' She picked up the second earphone and put it in her ear. Then she dropped it again and ran her hand over her blonde stubbly head. 'Why didn't you mention this before, Debbie? You're normally so obsessed with spreading gossip about other people.'

'I don't know what you all want. I didn't know her that well anyway. Leave me alone!' Debbie flung everything back into her huge make-up bag and left the bathroom.

She was still wearing the white face-mask, and Julia didn't know whether she'd simply forgotten about it or whether she was too upset to take it off in front of everyone.

CHAPTER 22

For an entire week the state police turned everything upside down. There was a constant stream of police cars parked outside; police officers were crawling all over the college; the students were questioned; Angela's belongings were taken away; but whatever conclusions the police had come to, they didn't filter through to the students. The longer the investigations lasted, though, the less the students believed that it had been an accident. It was just too improbable that Angela had managed to wheel herself up to the high path above the shore – even if she had wanted to go to the party in the first place. And anyway, the police would have pushed off long since if it had been an accident.

Julia had dreaded being interrogated by the police. She'd feared having all her personal data scrutinised; she'd feared their insistent questions, their mistrustful looks and the whole good cop/bad cop act. Unnecessarily, as it happened. They had just asked her where she had been that evening. Then they asked whether she had known Angela. Julia told them about her pre-supper interview with the *Chronicle*, and they made a note of the time that Julia mentioned. Then they let her go.

Having that behind her was a great weight off her mind.

Robert, too, said that it had been pretty similar for him – apart from the fact that he had had to put on record the detailed sequence of events that led to him finding Angela's bracelet.

The week had been ultra-exhausting, and Julia was beginning to realise what being at an elite college really meant. Everyone was groaning about the amount of material they had to cover; their packed timetable, and the list of homework and essays to write. Every evening, Julia studied into the night; every morning, she went jogging first thing, sometimes with other people from the athletics team and sometimes with Katie. Partly to distract herself from what was going on around her, but also in order to fall into bed at midnight and go straight into a deep sleep. And in the meantime she once again adopted the role that she'd practised so doggedly. Little Miss Perfect.

After the literature class on Monday evening, she, Chris and Rose were the last to leave the seminar room.

'I don't want to hear another helicopter or see another uniform ever again,' groaned Chris. 'I sometimes feel as if I'm in a Bruce Willis film.'

'Who's Bruce Willis?' asked Rose.

'Never mind.'

They pushed their way past the students who were sitting around on the windowsills and milling around in the corridors outside the seminar rooms, killing time before supper.

'I'm not going back up to the apartment – I'm going straight to the refectory. You coming, Julia?' Chris sounded quite casual. They hadn't seen one another much over the past few days, and Julia didn't know whether to be relieved or disappointed. But at that moment he glanced again at her with that look in his grey eyes that made her feel as if he could see right behind her facade. It suddenly crossed her mind that she hadn't given a second thought to the idea that he might be Loa.loa. And if she was honest, she didn't believe it now either. No: there was something else up with him.

The face Chris Number One presented to the outer world was the Chris she'd initially encountered: nonchalant, cool, sarcastic and sometimes malicious. But every now and then she could see glimmerings of Chris Number Two: sensitive and caring.

'No, sorry, I'm not hungry,' said Julia.

'Maybe not for poutine,' Rose grinned, giving Chris a meaningful look. Then she waved to them. 'See you!'

For several minutes, Julia and Chris walked along in silence.

'I'm shocked – you mean you don't like our national delicacy, poutine?' Chris finally broke the silence.

Julia pulled a face. 'Chips with cheese – and drowned in thick gravy. Bleurgh!'

He smiled – Chris Number Two smiled. And it was that same Chris who said: 'We've barely seen one another all week.'

'How could we, when all that coursework and homework doesn't even give us any time to think?' Julia tried to sound breezy. 'I can barely even remember to go to the loo.'

'That's their strategy, you know. They want us not to

think – or, at least, not to think about what's going on outside.' He looked at her earnestly. 'How do you fancy going to Starbucks afterwards, or going for a walk? I heard the lakeside isn't sealed off any more.'

'This evening? I should really be writing my literature essay.'

Chris grinned boyishly. 'Great. So that's a date, then?' He didn't wait for her reply. 'I'll call for you at eight.'

'A date? Didn't you just say something about Starbucks?'

'I'll make us a reservation.' He grinned from ear to ear, and she could only smile in return.

'Well, of course,' she said. 'But make it the best seats in the house.'

So she had a date. With Chris. And she didn't want to think about whether that was a good thing or not.

No, she corrected herself. She didn't *need* to think about it. It was a good thing. She was happy, and she was bloody well going to enjoy that feeling again.

In the best possible spirits, she went over to the kitchen to make a cup of tea and a sandwich.

There were still more than two hours to go until eight o'clock. If she really got stuck in, she might be able to finish that essay.

Ah well, she thought as she filled the kettle, Starbucks is a five-star restaurant compared to this dump. The kitchen was just as bad as the rest of the apartment: it had the same murky brown walls and dated wood panelling, and all that could be said of the equipment was that it was functional.

There was a hob with two rings and a little fridge in which each student had their own shelf to store their food. They shared the cost of milk, bread and mineral water.

Julia put the kettle on, sat down at the table, and flicked through *Macbeth* without really reading it.

She had a date.

Thinking about Starbucks made her chuckle again. Wasn't that something like a new start after all the turmoil of the past week?

The kettle started to boil loudly and as she stood up to switch it off and make her cup of tea, she heard a noise out in the corridor. A door had banged shut.

She hadn't even noticed that it was windy. It had been sunny before.

She sat back down at the table with her cup of tea and opened her book again.

Tap ... tap ... tap.

Oh for God's sake. A window was banging somewhere. She couldn't concentrate. Annoyed, she went out into the corridor and then into her room. Had she left her balcony door open? No.

She glanced out across the lake. Nothing had changed outside. The sun was behind her; just a few dark clouds were hanging over the water at the same height as the boathouse, as if they were on a long journey. Not a breath of wind.

Tap ... tap ... tap.

The spruce trees were swaying gently. It looked as if they were dancing a round.

Dancing a round? Hang on a moment, Julia thought,

Shakespeare might talk like that, but I certainly don't. And, while she was at it, it was really unreasonable to expect seventeen-year-olds to read any Shakespeare except *Romeo and Juliet*.

Tap ... tap ... tap.

God, that noise was driving her mad. She went to knock on Rose's door — but there was no-one in there. The windows were firmly shut. Everything was fine. A pleasant aroma of vanilla followed her out of the room.

Julia knew that Debbie still had a class, but she knocked all the same just to be on the safe side. When no reply came, she moved the handle downwards.

Locked.

Typical Debbie, Julia thought. Nosy about other people, but didn't trust anyone else.

That just left Katie's room. Julia hesitated. Katie wasn't mistrustful, but she was extremely private. Or was she? Julia wondered. When they were jogging in the mornings, she rarely said a word, though she still kept on coming. But then there was that whole business in the clearing, which she'd never managed to suss out.

Tap ... tap ... tap.

Julia pushed the handle down.

She had never been in Katie's room, and it was the complete opposite of how Julia had imagined it. She had expected her flatmate's room to be tidy, bare, and impersonal — so she was astounded to see that Katie was the only one who'd turned it into a home.

The walls were covered with photos.

A disturbing number of photos. And their subject matter was hardly varied. Towers, bridge piers and pylons on the empty wall next to the cupboard. Images of mountains above the desk. Photos of Katie and a boy above the bed.

How weird. Julia had never seen Katie taking a photo.

Tap ... tap ... tap.

The window was open and the right-hand shutter in front of it was loose, so that it kept banging against the outside wall.

As Julia clicked it back into the latch, she saw a group of students down on the lawn in front of the entrance foyer. They were deep in animated conversation. Among them was Chris, who was just rolling a cigarette. As if he'd felt her gaze, he looked up and waved at her. Then he pointed to his watch, stretched out both hands, and spread all ten fingers.

What was that supposed to mean?

Did he mean ten minutes? They weren't supposed to be meeting until much later. Whatever. She nodded, and shut the window. Then she turned to go.

The wind had scattered some of the pieces of paper from the heap on Katie's desk. Julia bent to pick them up. As she did so, her eye was caught by the print-out of an email. Or, to be more precise, by four words that made her blood run cold.

I know what happened.

Julia hadn't been paranoid. Her fears had been justified. She stared aghast at the piece of paper in her hand. Ever since that business with the text, she had known that someone in the valley was spying on her. But this email changed everything.

Julia was not Loa.loa's only victim.

This email had been sent by the same person who sent the text to Julia's mobile on the first night, despite the fact that nobody could know the number.

So Loa.loa wasn't just after her, but after Katie too. And whatever was behind that brief sentence *I know what happened*, it was evidently intended to be a threat.

Julia pushed a strand of hair behind her ear and re-read the email.

To: k.west@gracecollege.ca

The sender was loa.loa@gracecollege.ca and it was dated the day that the academic year officially began for the freshers. Katie had had a really special welcome, just like Julia.

She was just about to put the piece of paper back on the desk when she noticed a name written in the bottom margin. It was written in pencil, in Katie's handwriting.

Oh my God!

What did that mean?

Julia dropped the piece of paper, ran out of the room, and fled down the corridor, down the stairs, through the side entrance, and outside.

Just behind the door, she clattered into someone. It was Benjamin. His face was the picture of anger, and he was as white as a sheet. She stared at him.

'Someone's got my camera. Do you have any idea who it might be? I swear to you, I'll kill them.'

She shook her head and let him pass. It was just a camera.

222

That was nothing compared to the fact that Katie had found out who Loa.loa was.

The first drops of rain started to fall as Julia took the main path down to the lake. She shivered in her thin jumper, but more with agitation than fear.

Angela Finder was Loa.loa.

Angela, über-hacker. Angela, chief correspondent. Angela, who had presumably been murdered. Angela with whom, Julia had told the police, she had had as good as no contact.

Which was basically true – but, all the same, she would have had a motive to kill Angela. Only she didn't do it.

But what about Katie?

A thought flashed through Julia's mind. Katie was the only one who hadn't been at the party. She had had plenty of opportunity to meet up with Angela – to offer to take her to the party, perhaps.

And up on the steep bank above the lake, the two of them had been alone ... Another thought crossed her mind. The business in the clearing. Why had Katie followed Julia? Wasn't that suspicious too?

Stop it! You're letting your imagination run away with you, she told herself sternly. If Angela was actually murdered – it could have been anyone. After all, the college had more than three hundred students.

But all the same ... a motive was a motive.

Julia's heart was pounding so hard that she could feel it in her entire body. She absolutely had to talk to someone who knew about her past.

'I'd give anything to know what you're thinking about at the moment.'

Julia gave a yelp of shock. It was Chris who had appeared as if from nowhere. 'I was just about to come up to see you,' he said, and laughed. 'But I never imagined I'd find you out here in the pouring rain.'

Instead of replying, Julia shrugged her shoulders.

Chris's face darkened. 'What's the matter?' he asked. 'Is something wrong?'

Julia shook her head. How on earth could she explain what had happened?

'Weird. An hour ago, I'd have put money on you liking me.'

Julia could feel herself turning red. She glanced across the campus to the lakeside promenade where her gaze rested on a canoodling couple, of all things. The rain didn't seem to be bothering them.

'Do you know that feeling,' she said suddenly, 'when there seems to be an invisible burden on your shoulders, when the air feels heavier than you can imagine, and ... '

'You mean when you see yourself standing alone on the gigantic planet Earth, looking into the abyss? I know that feeling.' He took a step closer. The sharp smell of his tobacco filled her nostrils. 'But then you find another person who is just as alone, and all the evil thoughts just vanish.'

Evil?

No, that wasn't what Julia had meant. But she didn't say so, as he was now pulling her towards him. He didn't seem to care that her face and clothes were soaking wet.

224

The first two buttons of his shirt were open. She could see his bare chest and although her body was involuntarily tensing up, something inside was telling her to put her cheek exactly on this spot. Julia was battling inwardly. Should she give in?

She wasn't in love with Chris; not in the way she'd been in love with Kristian. No, it was completely different with Chris. A unique kind of to-ing and fro-ing. Strange. Unfamiliar. Slightly frightening. Like everything in the valley.

And yet she so yearned for peace and security. Maybe that was why she let him take her head in both his hands so that she had to look at him.

Mum had once said that you could see the innermost being of the man you loved through his eyes.

That was what she had said when Julia had asked her, before that night with Kristian, how you could be certain that you loved someone.

You can tell by looking into his eyes.

It sounded quite straightforward.

Julia now looked directly into Chris's eyes.

That shimmering grey that sometimes seemed to change colour, as if his eyes were reflecting what was going on in his head.

And then he kissed her.

Her feelings had until that point been shrivelled up to the bare minimum. She had been cold inside; no, she was a solid block of ice like the glacier above the Ghost. Now she felt that this could be something to make the ice inside her melt faster than the polar ice caps.

And then it was over, and they just stood there for a while, their arms wrapped around one another. It was still raining, but it was no longer unpleasant. It felt warm and gentle to Julia, as if it were enveloping them both.

It was Chris who broke the silence. 'Now you can tell me what's the matter.'

Julia took a deep breath. 'Have you ever heard of Loa.loa?' she asked.

Did he hesitate for a fraction of a second before asking his next question? 'What's that, then?'

'A nickname,' Julia explained.

'And do you know the real name too?'

'Angela Finder.'

'I haven't got a clue,' said Chris.

'So is our Starbucks date still on?' said Julia, reaching for his hand.

She had made her decision. She was going to tell him the whole story. No, not the whole story; just the bit that had begun with the mysterious text.

CHAPTER 23

The next day, it was yet again pancakes with maple syrup for supper. Julia was starting to dread the sight of them. She was sharing a table with Rose, Katie, David and Benjamin, listening to Benjamin moaning and groaning that someone might have demolished his camera.

'I only left it for a minute while I went to the bathroom,' he kept saying.

'Oh yeah?' Katie replied sarcastically. 'I thought you actually slept with it.'

Rose giggled and David grinned.

They all seemed glad to be able to talk about something that didn't really matter.

In the distance, Julia saw Alex climbing up the steps to the podium where the tutors sat, and going over to the microphone. He was carrying the mail. Julia found this ritual rather stupid; she'd thought that the students would have pigeon-holes for their post. But handing out post after supper was one of Grace's sacred institutions – it had always been done that way, and nobody asked now whether it was meaningful or downright silly.

She reluctantly stabbed her fork into her pancake, pulling a face. She could barely force anything down anyway, and this stuff would finally make her stomach close up. She couldn't stop thinking about Chris and about what had happened between them yesterday. Remembering their kiss gave her butterflies in her stomach. But after that kiss, everything had changed – and she simply didn't know how to handle it.

In Starbucks, she had indeed told Chris about Loa.loa.

He was a good listener. He hadn't gone piling in with assumptions, nor had he expressed any opinion about the business with Katie. Yet when he'd said goodbye to Julia at ten o'clock he'd seemed more than deep in thought: he'd seemed almost completely abstracted. He had kissed her briefly on the forehead, and Julia was now constantly wondering whether she'd done the right thing by taking him into her confidence.

Alex was reading out the names one after the other.

'If I've got mail, I'm not collecting it,' Benjamin said grumpily. He still seemed to be in a bad mood because of his camera. 'It's only ever bad news anyway.'

'I like getting letters,' replied Rose. 'It's like opening presents, don't you think?'

Rose was one of the few who regularly received letters.

'Farley, Fredos, Federman. Finder.' Alex halted.

Benjamin raised an eyebrow. 'Alex looks as if he's seen a ghost.'

'Well,' said Rose, 'it isn't every day that dead people get mail.'

Julia looked across at the podium. Alex was still staring wordlessly at the envelope. Several seconds passed before he put it back into the box and called out the next name.

'Frost.'

Julia didn't move.

'Hey,' Benjamin dug her in the ribs. 'That's you.'

'Me?'

'Julia and Robert Frost!' Alex repeated.

Post? She hadn't been expecting that.

'What's up, Julia?' Alex called over to her. 'Do you want me to read the card out loud, or are you going to collect it?'

'Or go one better,' piped up a tall dreadlocked student. 'Stick it up on the notice board!'

Amid the laughter, Julia hurried to the front to collect the card. A quick glance told her that it had been posted in London.

She turned it over and read.

Best wishes from Mum and Dad.

That was all it said.

She made to shove the card carelessly into the back pocket of her jeans. As she turned, she spotted the brown envelope at the top of the post bag.

Angela Finder
Grace College
PO Box 10
Grace Valley
British Columbia

Only then did she notice the sender's name. And when she saw it, she was so shocked that she dropped the postcard.

Der Tagesspiegel
Askanischer Platz 3
10963 Berlin
Germany

In the middle of the night, Julia awoke with a start. The digital clock on her bedside table said 04.22. She immediately remembered about the postcard.

Best wishes from Mum and Dad.

She hadn't shown it to Robert.

Nor had she told him about the brown envelope. The very fact of a dead person receiving post was gruesome enough. But when she thought about the contents, panic started to overwhelm her.

The Berlin *Tagesspiegel*.

What had Angela to do with that newspaper?

And where was the envelope now?

She suddenly had a thought, and sat bolt upright in bed. The police had seized Angela's belongings! Which meant that the envelope would also make its way to them. The admin office would make sure of that.

She sprang out of bed.

Had Alex taken that envelope back to admin? No – the offices would have closed at five. From then onwards, the student mentors were responsible for students' queries and problems. So wasn't it likely that Alex had the envelope in his office? And that he'd hand it in the following morning?

She hesitated before slipping on her jeans and jumper. Was she overreacting? Perhaps the whole thing was just coincidence? Whatever, it was better to be safe than sorry.

The next moment, Julia was creeping out of the apartment – making sure that she had the torch that hung on the right-hand wall in the hallway. At Grace they were always expecting power cuts, although Julia had personally experienced only the one on her first night.

The mentors' offices were on the first floor of the north wing, in the same corridor as the boys' apartments. As Julia hurried down the stairs, the usual nocturnal silence hung all round the college. It made Julia feel as if her footsteps could be heard in the remotest corners of the building, even though she was only wearing her socks.

Eventually she reached the brown wooden door which said in large letters: *Student Counselors. Office Hours 1–2 p.m. and 6–8 p.m.*

Next to the door was a large window enabling visitors to see if anyone was in the office. Everything looked dark, but Julia spotted a monitor flickering away in the furthest reaches of the room. At first she thought that Alex or Isabel must have forgotten to switch off their computer, when she noticed that something was moving in front of it.

Someone was sitting there! At half past four in the morning! What on earth was going on?

For a moment Julia stood uncertainly in the corridor. She absolutely had to get into that office and find the envelope.

Julia was just about to retreat to the stairwell to wait for the coast to clear when she heard footsteps approaching from the floor above.

What now?

She had absolutely no desire to start explaining what she was doing on the boys' staircase in the middle of the night.

Toilet.

That was it. There were toilets directly opposite the office. She hastily felt her way in the darkness to one of the doors, disappearing behind it just as the footsteps reached the landing above.

She took a couple of steps back and bumped into something. She flicked the torch on for a second to see what she was doing.

Outside, the footsteps were coming closer. Someone was right outside the door. Julia's stomach was turning somersaults. The security men had been regularly checking all the corridors ever since the business with Angela.

Her heart was beating so loudly that the whole college must surely be able to hear it.

But nothing happened. Everything was quiet.

Curiosity finally drove her back to the door.

Footsteps again – one, two, three.

Stop.

Voices.

One, muffled but clearly male, asked: 'What are you doing here? It's the middle of the night! You've got no business here.'

Julia couldn't hear the reply.

'Oh yeah?' came the sarcastic answer.

More indistinct murmuring. It sounded somehow pitiful, indeed tearful.

Then the voices became quieter. Chairs moving. Something falling to the ground. Footsteps in the corridor, on the stairs. Only once a door finally closed did silence return to the corridor.

Julia waited another five minutes, then softly opened the door.

Cautiously she edged her way out into the corridor. She could immediately tell that there was nobody else there, and she felt safe enough to switch on the torch.

A minute later she saw to her surprise that the door of Alex's and Isabel's office was open. The room was empty.

Was that luck or fate? Whatever. She had no time to worry about that one. There were some times in your life when it was necessary to switch your thought-processes off entirely.

She glanced towards the stairwell again. All was quiet. No sign of the security men. Okay, this would only take a matter of seconds.

She went into the office. Where would Alex have put that envelope?

On the wall to the right were two desks. Julia went across to them and found a shelf filled with carefully labelled files. Underneath was another shelf unit with boxes. In the first one were brand-new college prospectuses. Next to them were piles of the lecture lists that they'd been given at the start of term.

Then Julia noticed a red plastic box with the red and blue Canadian post logo on it: Post Canada.

She quickly pulled the box off the shelf and rummaged

through the letters and envelopes. Nothing. Nothing. Nothing.

Her torch didn't give off much more light than a glow worm, but she shone it once more around the room anyway. She remembered from before that Isabel's was the desk on the left. On it there was also a photo of her holding a trophy at the college swimming pool. The other desk was Alex's. Whereas Isabel's papers and lists were piled up all higgledy-piggledy, everything here was neat and tidy. Typical Alex. And lucky for Julia, as it made her search much easier.

She opened the drawers one after the other. Pens and pencils, paper, forms, course brochures, a file with information about Yale – and there it was, in the last one. The big brown envelope.

Angela Finder
Grace College
PO Box 10
Grace Valley
British Columbia

With one swift movement, the letter was under her jumper. The paper felt cold and crackled softly when she moved. She tried to push the desk drawer shut. It had jammed. But she had to leave it, Julia had no desire to be caught now.

She flicked the torch off, scurried out of the office, and seconds later was back up on the second floor. Only once she had closed her bedroom door softly behind her did she hear the hoarse barking of a dog in the distance.

CHAPTER 24

Robert was cold, freezing cold. He could feel rough material pressing against his back: carpet or something. And it was narrow, hideously narrow. His hands and arms were tied with thick sticky tape; the more he tried to free himself, the more he could feel his circulation being cut off. He desperately stretched out his hands and banged into something metal. But worst of all was the smell. Deeply unpleasant, overpowering, so that he tried to breathe only through his mouth. He felt an overwhelming urge to gag, and he gasped for air. But it wasn't air that filled his lungs: it was something else. He wheezed, coughed.

Petrol, it whizzed through his mind. I can smell petrol.

Robert understood now. He was in the boot of the old Mercedes that used to belong to Dad.

It was the barking of a dog directly beneath his window that roused Robert from his nightmare.

Bathed in sweat, he woke up and looked around him. He was in his room in the north wing of the college, lying on his bed. It was still night.

Had he screamed in his sleep again? As if he'd asked out loud, Chris stuck his head round the door and grumbled sleepily: 'Christ, it's only just five, and you're squealing like a stuck pig. Can't you just cut it out?'

'Sorry,' Robert murmured, hoping that Chris would go away again. But Chris stayed standing in the doorway, and his voice conveyed a hint of concern as he asked: 'D'you want me to fetch Julia?'

'I said, everything's fine.' Couldn't Chris just piss off? Robert wasn't keen on him, and the more he saw him with Julia, the more he disliked him.

'I was only trying to help.' Chris turned and shut the door.

Chris wasn't the helping type, Robert was certain of that. Well, ninety-nine per cent certain: there was always some degree of risk.

Robert struggled out of bed and went over to sit on the windowsill. By now, he was wide awake.

In the darkness, the lake was only visible as a silhouette, a black disc. When he'd said to Julia on that first night that the place was evil, it had just been a feeling. Now, though, he was seeing more and more proof of it every day. At the moment, he was busily constructing an accurate and detailed map of the valley. Which wasn't easy, especially as he didn't have anything much to go on. He couldn't find any decent maps, either in the library or the geography department, where he'd been to ask. And the map that was up on the screens in the entrance foyer was a complete disaster on all counts. There was nothing right about it, nothing at all. Robert could have made a better job of it when he was a toddler.

Mirror Lake was pretty much circular. In itself, that wasn't unusual. Circular lakes were often the result of meteorite impacts that happened millions of years ago. One example was the Sudbury Crater in Canada, formed 1.8 million years ago, with a diameter of two hundred kilometres. The asteroid that had crashed had had a diameter of ten kilometres. Imagining a ten-kilometre-wide asteroid was beyond the power of most people's imaginations. Compared to this, Mirror Lake was no more than a hole in the ground.

More barking. It had to be Ike who was being bothered by something. He had extremely sensitive hearing.

Robert stared out of the window. In the orange glow of the outside lights, he could see the lakeside promenade. On it were two figures.

In the middle of the night? He jumped off the windowsill, opened the bottom desk drawer, and took out his father's telescope.

It took him a while to focus on the figures once more.

A tall boy.

Close to him, a girl.

Debbie.

But – who was the guy?

To judge by the silhouette, he looked like Chris.

But Robert couldn't imagine that Chris would choose to go for a walk with Debbie at 5 a.m. And anyway, he'd only just been in Robert's room.

Deep in thought, Robert put the telescope back in the drawer. Moments later, he had filed the whole event away in a compartment in his mind and was giving his full attention once more to his original problem.

Which was: while searching for the solution, Robert had encountered something that terrified him. It was the clearest evidence thus far that something was wrong with Grace Valley.

Immediately after being forced to accept that the maps and college information were a dead end, he had tried to find a more precise map of the valley on Google Earth. But whilst Google Earth showed a detailed satellite image of the area around Fields and the forests in the north, the whole valley, the Ghost included, was blank. And every time Robert had tried to zoom in on it, a warning had come up on the screen that he couldn't forget.

Access denied.

CHAPTER 25

Julia decided not to go back to bed. She knew that she wouldn't be able to sleep anyway. She sat in her armchair and as she waited for the sun to rise, thousands of thoughts chased around in her mind. She was desperate to open the envelope, but something was stopping her.

When morning came and she got ready, the others didn't spare her feelings.

'You look like a ghost,' said Rose, when they bumped into one another in the hallway.

Debbie presumably heard her, because she stuck her head out of the bathroom. 'Never mind ghost. You look like something the cat threw up. Truly scary.'

'Shut up, Debbie.' Rose put her arm round Julia's shoulders. 'Are you okay? Maybe you'd better stay in bed?'

Julia shook her head. 'No, I'm fine.'

Debbie butted in again. 'Have you even had a shower? Don't start letting yourself go. I'm not living with anyone with greasy hair.'

'And I'm not living with anyone whose breath smells,' murmured Katie.

Debbie turned bright red, and her eyes filled with tears.

'Hey, that's enough,' Rose interjected.

Julia's nerves couldn't take bitching and flatmate squabbles, and she fled from the apartment. Rose followed her, looking concerned – and didn't take her eyes off Julia for the rest of the day.

Katie, at least, spared her that kind of attention. Thank God, Julia thought. She still had no idea how to approach Katie after finding that email in her room.

She and Chris didn't have any classes together that morning either. She was longing to see him and to hear his voice. But then she remembered how strangely distant he'd seemed after she'd told him about Loa.loa. And she once again had no idea what to make of him.

At lunchtime, she briefly wondered whether to tell Robert, but he was hunched over his laptop in the computer department, so there was no point talking to him. When her brother was preoccupied with some particular problem, then the normal world simply stopped existing for him.

Her last class that day finished at 3 p.m.

Julia ran to her room, grabbed the envelope that she'd hidden in the wardrobe, and left the apartment without encountering any of her flatmates.

Five minutes later, she was leaving the building. The police presence had been gradually scaled back over the last few days, and it was more or less back to business as usual on campus. The temperature had risen in recent days. There wasn't a cloud in the sky. The air was unusually fresh and clear, in the way that's only possible in the mountains.

As Julia turned out of the car park and on to the road that led to Fields, a car came up behind her and stopped. It was the Land Rover that Alex had driven her up in two weeks earlier; Alex was driving now, too. Next to him was Chris, and on the back seat was Benjamin, who was grinning at her broadly.

Alex stopped and Chris opened the car door.

'Julia. At last! I've been looking for you all day. We're going to Fields. Benjamin wants to get his camera repaired, and Alex has got something important to do. Are you coming?'

Julia shook her head.

Chris got out and took a step towards her. His smile had suddenly vanished. 'We've barely seen each other yesterday or today.' He had lowered his voice.

She swallowed. 'I know.'

He frowned. He scrutinised her with his grey eyes. 'I think it'd really do you good to get out of here for a bit.' He paused briefly. 'It'd do us both good,' he added.

Julia hesitated. Yes, it would. And it would be her chance to get to Fields. She could finally make contact and tell them what had happened to Angela Finder. She'd spent her entire time at Grace waiting for this opportunity, but now the envelope was holding her back. Under her jumper, she could feel the rough paper against her skin, and could feel how scared she was of what might be in there.

'No, I'll go another time,' she said, trying to sound as nonchalant as possible. 'I don't want to spend four hours in the car with Alex.' She still couldn't get over the mean trick that he had played on the freshers, however hard Alex tried to make them forget it. 'And anyway, I was going to go jogging.'

'In that get-up?' Chris stared at her pumps and jeans.

Julia managed a real smile. 'Why not?'

'Just be careful you don't break your ankle in those shoes.' He suddenly sounded bitter. Without saying goodbye, he turned, climbed back into the car, and a few moments later the Land Rover disappeared behind the next corner.

Julia bit her lip. She'd screwed up yet again. That was the last thing she'd wanted. But if he liked her, as he'd said; if he might even be in love with her, then he'd respect that, wouldn't he?

She looked around hesitantly. The broad jogging track led down from the road where she was standing to the lakeside. The sign with all the lights on it that she'd seen on her first evening was here too.

Welcome to Grace Valley.

This was where she'd seen Angela Finder for the first time.

So far as Julia was aware, there hadn't been any further developments in the Angela Finder case. The Dean, Mr Walden, had still not issued an official statement, and the lecturers also remained stubbornly silent. As for the newspaper reports: they only told the students what they already knew.

Julia turned off down the usual jogging track between the forest and the lake. The lakeside was bordered here by trees, and a broad, flat shingle beach led down to the water. This was the only official bathing spot, although Julia had never seen any students swimming there. Isabel, who trained in the pool beneath the sports centre, which was in the rear building of the old college block, had said that the lake was still too cold.

Without thinking, Julia took her shoes off and took several steps into the water.

She had inwardly prepared herself for it to be icy cold – so she was surprised to discover that the lake was almost warm. The water must be at least sixty-five degrees. Could the lake have warmed up that much in the last few weeks? It had been sunny, but Julia wouldn't have thought the sun would be powerful enough.

She stood there for a while undecided, looking out at the lake.

The longer she stared at the horizon, the more the sky and water drifted apart – almost as if Mirror Lake were dividing in the middle into two separate halves.

She was, of course, just imagining it.

But as she turned to paddle back to the shore, the water was already up to her knees.

The water was rising.

Just like the evening of the party, the thought flashed through her mind: fingers crossed there won't be a storm today.

A lake – so far as Julia knew from geography lessons, at any rate – was a body of standing (therefore presumably motionless) water. They are fed by streams. In the case of Mirror Lake, the water came mainly from the Ghost's glacier. It was spring now, and the ice was melting. So it wasn't that odd for the level to rise.

But this quickly? How long had she had her feet in the

water? She hadn't looked at her watch. Only a few minutes, ten at most.

She hurried back to the shore, where she felt safer.

However, she didn't stay on the asphalt track but took the first opportunity to branch off on to a path leading off to the right and into the forest.

Julia was burning to open the envelope at long last, but for some reason she didn't want to do so anywhere near the college. She could see far too clearly the black roof with all its chimneys, the white balcony rails, and the bright dormers of the attic rooms – even though she doubted that anyone could see her from there. Unless they had a telescope.

The path ascended rapidly, and she was soon high up enough to see through the trees to the boathouse on the other side of the lake.

Here, the forest was lighter than on the opposite shore: along with the spruces and pines, there were deciduous trees every now and then. The ground was covered with moss and last autumn's foliage. She didn't come across even a single wooden bench. After half an hour she passed a clearing where the trees had only recently been dug up.

Eventually the path forked again. One of the trees bore a weather-beaten sign, but the writing had largely worn off and was now illegible.

Julia chose the path that led further upwards. The view became increasingly magnificent. The lake was still visible through the trees – but now the snow-capped peaks came gradually into view on Julia's right, all strung together.

Julia only noticed the fence when she was standing

directly in front of it. Her eye was caught by a little metal sign:

Electric fence.

It wasn't a dense, high wire-mesh fence like the one that cordoned off the restricted area on the other side of the lake. This fence was basically made of nothing but straight, taut wires between wooden uprights – like the fences around horse or cattle fields.

Julia stared across to the other side, where thick undergrowth and high ferns spread out beneath the pine trees. Why the fence? Maybe it was supposed to stop wildlife from getting into the valley?

The first piece of wire was a couple of hands off the ground; the second at chest height; and the third at head height. It was easy to climb through, as Julia did after a moment's hesitation.

She left the fence behind her with no problems, no injuries, no electric shocks – only to discover that the path on the other side didn't go anywhere. She turned left, where the trees weren't quite so dense, and struck out on her own path.

The long, spiky needles of the pine bushes were soon scratching her skin, but Julia carried on regardless. She couldn't understand why she didn't just stop, choose one of the tree trunks that were lying around everywhere, and finally read that wretched letter.

Why not, Julia?

Because you're scared.

It's the valley, she thought, that makes you act so crazy.

That compels you to run away. Further and further upwards, quite instinctively. She had done it on the day that she'd found Angela – and she was doing it again now.

What do you think, Julia? Should we run away together?

That was one of the first things that Chris had ever said to her.

The bushes suddenly came to an end. The forest became lighter, and ahead of her she saw a ramshackle hut. Completely out of breath, she sat down on the weather-beaten wooden bench in front of it. As she waited to get her breath back, she looked around.

The silence was unbelievable.

Julia felt as if she could hear the air humming. The intense smell of pine and resin had a narcotic effect.

Almost like drugs.

Drugs.

Something in her brain sprang into life, triggered a memory.

Drugs – a word that would send her into a panic for the whole of the rest of her life.

The envelope felt heavy. It was a letter to a dead person.

Did that mean it was still confidential?

No. Dead people had no right to secrets. And Angela Finder – who had been Loa.loa – most definitely didn't.

With trembling hands, Julia tore open the envelope. The first thing she saw was an invoice. It was written in German.

It was addressed to Angela Finder, and was for fifteen euros. It had been issued by the trading department of the *Tagesspiegel*.

Then she pulled out a copy of a newspaper article.
It took her several minutes to realise what it was about.
The cutting showed a photo.
Two boys sitting opposite one another at a table.
Between them was a chessboard.
Julia knew this photo.
Junior Chess Champions, said the headline.
She didn't need to read the text, but read it all the same.

Ralph de Vincenz is the new European champion. Fifteen-year-old Ralph de Vincenz won the title at the European Junior Championships, forcing his opponent, Ireland's Sam Dusket, into second place. The championships took place in Berlin in April amid much publicity.

Julia's heart was thudding faster than she thought possible.
How did Angela know Ralph?

CHAPTER 26

Angela Finder was the key to everything that was happening in the valley. Her death couldn't have been a coincidence. And it was definitely not an accident.

She had been editor in chief of the *Grace Chronicle*. That itself gave her access to information that others couldn't get their hands on. More importantly, though, she had been a well-known hacker and had been able to get into data systems on any network.

And it appeared that she had taken unlimited advantage of this fact.

She had found out Julia's mobile number and had been in possession of information about Katie. And even if her reasons and motives weren't clear, Julia and Katie might not be the only ones to have been investigated by Angela Finder.

Angela had been massively powerful. Lecturers, admin staff, students: it could have been any of them. Didn't pretty much everyone have skeletons in their closets?

Was that what had happened? And if so, why?

Why would Angela Finder have been so keen to exert power over other people?

Was it about money?

Maybe.

About her career as a journalist?

Definitely not.

Julia had repeatedly noticed that the *Grace Chronicle* was anything other than investigative journalism. Indeed, college life was venerated rather too much for Julia's taste in the *Chronicle*.

But in that case: what was it all about?

And why the text, which served only to tell Julia that her secret number had leaked out?

Julia would need to have known Angela better in order to work out the reasons for what she'd done. All she actually knew was that Angela had been self-confident and more than a little bit up herself. At any rate, that's the impression she'd given Julia during her interview for the *Chronicle*.

Was it revenge against everything and everyone?

Jealousy of other people?

Whatever: there could be any number of reasons for Angela's behaviour. She might even have just enjoyed tormenting other people.

Julia took a deep breath in and out. She could sense that she was getting to the heart of the matter. A whole host of different thoughts and feelings whirled around inside her, one of which kept pushing itself to the forefront of her mind: if anyone here in the valley could have been Angela's victim, then they were all suspects in her murder. Including Julia herself.

And Katie. A thought that Julia would dearly have liked to suppress. But it kept forcing itself stubbornly to the surface. Julia's flatmate had had a clear motive to murder

Angela. Not just because she had threatened Katie in her email; no, it was Katie who had in fact got wise to Angela. Again, the note she'd made on the email proved it. And she had had the opportunity to commit murder.

The only thing about the Angela Finder case that the police had officially confirmed to the media was the time of her death. According to the autopsy report, she had died sometime between 6 p.m. and 10 p.m. That, taken together with the fact that Julia had seen her before supper, had to mean that Angela had died sometime during the party and the storm afterwards.

Katie hadn't been at the party – which meant she had no alibi.

Along with hundreds of other college students and lecturers, Julia reminded herself.

She stretched and looked up at the sky. It was such a bright blue that it seemed to be mocking her dark thoughts.

Why hadn't the police discovered any of this?

Why not, Julia?

You're still wondering? You really trust them? Remember your father. Don't you know from experience that mistrust is the most important quality for survival? Isn't your and Robert's fate dependent on precisely the fact that the police make mistakes? Horrible mistakes?

Julia got up from the bench and paced up and down in front of the hut. The windows, blind with the filth of years gone by, prevented her from looking inside. The door was hanging from its hinges; the lock looked as if it had been forced at some point.

A chill ran down Julia's spine. It wasn't just because she had discovered that she was living in the valley with a cold-blooded murderer who had drowned a defenceless girl in the lake.

It was something else.

If she had learnt anything up here in the past few weeks, it was this: the valley was harbouring all kinds of secrets.

She turned round resolutely. While it was true that a fundamental mistrust ensured her own and Robert's survival, it was equally true that she couldn't solve her problem on her own. The fact became increasingly clear with every step she took back towards the college.

On the path following the shore of Mirror Lake, she washed her face in the water. In the smooth, still surface of the lake, Julia stared at the face that was looking back at her. But she didn't see herself – Little Miss Perfect – reflected on the water. Instead she saw her new self; the one that had decided to take her fate into her own hands.

A glance at the clock showed that it was 5.55 p.m.

One of the first things she had to do was finally make contact. The postcard that she had received was essentially a coded form of concern that she and Robert hadn't been in touch. Along with all the things she'd been thinking about on her way back from the hut, there was the question as to why Angela Finder, queen of hackers, had received the Berlin *Tagesspiegel* article through the post.

Why would someone bother with letters if they had access to any online archive they wanted? But wasn't that obvious?

Angela Finder was precisely the kind of person who would know that one's every movement on the internet could be traced. And Angela had come up with a startlingly simple answer: as slow as a snail, but reliable.

When Julia returned to her apartment, her flatmates were already at supper in the refectory along with most of their fellow students. Chris, Alex and Benjamin were presumably going to get something to eat in Fields, and wouldn't be back until late that evening; after all, the journey took almost two hours.

In the supermarket, Julia bought a postcard and retreated to Starbucks with it. It was practically empty at that time of day. She found herself a seat right by the window with a view of both the car park and the campus. She found the address in her diary.

William Gold
University of London
Lewisham Way
New Cross
London SE14 6NW
England, UK

She finally decided what to say.
Arrived safely! Seen lots of old friends – Julia & Robert
They would understand that message.

She posted the card in the box by the admin offices and went back to Starbucks. She had a long wait, and drank one cappuccino after another. She'd presumably spend the whole night sitting bolt upright in bed. Shortly after ten o'clock, however, she finally saw the Land Rover turning into the car park – and, shortly afterwards, Alex, Benjamin and Chris crossing the campus.

Julia ran out of the café, and only when the cashier called after her did she realise that she had forgotten to pay.

Chris waved when he saw her coming. He was smiling, as if their spat that afternoon had never happened.

'You should have come with us, Julia. It was so good being back in civilisation.'

'You call that civilisation?' Benjamin said scornfully. 'Fields is a miserable little dump. There are more people living up here than down there.'

'At least you could buy a new camera,' murmured Alex. 'Hand over your credit card, and get whatever you like.'

Benjamin ran his fingers guiltily through his hair. 'When my old man sees the statement, he'll be blocking the card.'

'But you have to admit, Alex, that the beer's got a lot going for it down there. And then there's the steak. Honestly, it tasted so good, it was like I slayed the buffalo myself.'

'It was only veal,' laughed Alex. 'And it's time I was in my office. Isabel will be mad at me for leaving her in the lurch for the consulting hour. I'd better at least go and deal with my paperwork.'

He waved at them and disappeared through the side entrance that led up to the apartments whilst Julia, Benjamin and Chris headed for the entrance foyer.

Before they went inside, Julia stopped. 'Hey, I've been waiting for you. I need your help, Benjamin.'

Chris looked at her sharply. 'Are you finally going to tell us what's happening? Something's up, isn't it? You were so weird this afternoon.'

'I need to see again what Benjamin recorded that evening at the boathouse.'

'Why?' Again, it was Chris who answered. 'You know what's on that video.'

Julia remembered the strange feeling she'd had the first time she saw the recording. 'I've thought of something.'

'What?'

'Not here. I need to show you.'

'Have you even still got the memory card from the old camera?' Chris turned to Benjamin.

'What do you think I am?' Benjamin shook his head. 'It'd be best to watch it in the media room. There's a big screen there.'

The lake was splashing against the stones on the shoreline that loomed up out of the water. They formed a regular pattern, almost as if someone had arranged them that way. But if the stones had been deposited there, it must have happened years ago, for they were covered in moss. Slimy looking aquatic plants slithered around between the gaps, and Julia imagined with a shudder how revolting they would feel on bare skin.

Such thoughts were, of course, absurd, and they only came into Julia's mind because Benjamin was inclined to follow jerky, wobbly sequences with long, lingering shots of insignificant detail until it was unbearable to look at whatever they were. It was unbearable in the way that silence can be. To drown it out, one's ears start hearing things that aren't there.

'Oh my God, Benjamin, how long's this going to go on for? I'm going to fall asleep if I have to look at this green muck any longer,' Chris protested.

'Anyone can take close-ups of landscapes. But it's all in the detail. Always in the detail.' All the same, Benjamin started fast-forwarding. First came the party scenes: their arrival, Alex at the mixing desk, Debbie, Chris disappearing into the forest, Julia and Robert on the jetty.

Then came the scene that Julia had been waiting for. The boathouse, Julia and David, the dance floor, people everywhere. Tom climbing on to the oil drum. Robert on his own. Trees. Trees. Trees. Water. Water. Water. The path to the college. Julia expected any minute to get to the bit that she'd noticed the first time. The bridge.

There was no wind, yet the lake was moving.

Julia stared at the images, following every tiny detail – and then she suddenly saw it. 'There. Stop!'

She jumped up.

Chris stared at the screen. 'What's the matter?'

'Can't you see? There, on the shore, behind the bridge! Can you enlarge that, Benjamin?'

'It's just water,' said Chris.

'Exactly,' said Julia. 'That's what it's all about.'

She strode forward three paces and pointed to little bubbles of air that were rising next to the shore.

'So?'

'Are you all blind? The surface was completely still before, wasn't it?'

'Yes.' Benjamin frowned.

'So where do those air bubbles come from? Why are there rings on the water all of a sudden? There's something wrong there.'

'Julia's right.' Chris looked up, startled. 'You realise, don't you, that that's where we found Angela?' he murmured. 'Play it again, Benjamin.'

'And look at the time,' said Julia.

The sequence re-started. The water was stirred up and slowly settled again. The clock was showing the time in seconds.

10:10, 10:11, 10:12, 10:13. All they could see was gradually diminishing circles.

Then the clock jumped forwards. 10:14, 10:16.

'Stop!' cried Julia. 'There's a second missing!'

There was a moment of silence.

'How can that happen, Benjamin?' asked Chris.

'Someone's cut a bit out.'

Chris and Julia stared at one another. 'Is it that easy?' Chris finally asked.

Benjamin nodded. 'If you know a bit about technology, it'd be easy enough,' he replied tersely.

Julia had an idea. 'Maybe it wasn't a coincidence that someone broke your camera.'

Benjamin shrugged. 'Why would they, if they'd already fiddled around with the memory card?'

Julia ran her hand through her hair. 'No idea.' She had the feeling that she was coming slightly closer to working out the secret. She began pacing the room agitatedly. 'But do you know what this means? It means there's proof. A clue as to Angela's death. There was something on that video that was so important that someone went to the bother of cutting one second – one second! – out of the film.'

She felt euphoric. The adrenalin in her body was practically having a party. But then her illusions were shattered with one blow.

'Yeah,' Chris said darkly, 'but the proof has disappeared.'

A babble of voices was coming from the boys' apartment.

Debbie was just wrenching the kitchen door open when Chris, Julia and Benjamin appeared in the hallway.

'Have you heard? It's all over. The police have closed the investigation and we'll have peace and quiet up here again. We were just going to give you a shout to come and celebrate!'

Julia glanced into the kitchen: Rose, David and Katie were there. Rose waved merrily at Julia. 'My parents were threatening to come and collect me after Angela's death was all over the news. We're the only ones who've been left in the dark for days on end.' Rose's blue eyes darkened. 'But I wouldn't have gone home in any case.'

Julia and Robert exchanged looks. He was the only one in the kitchen who wasn't in ebullient spirits. No doubt he was just as relieved as she was that the police were pulling out, but the fact that the mystery remained unsolved presumably bothered him just as much as it bothered her.

That blasted film. If only she'd been paying more attention the first time Benjamin had shown it to them.

Then she saw Benjamin coming into the kitchen. He was carrying his laptop, which he'd presumably just fetched from his bedroom.

Without paying any heed to the commotion around him, he sat down at the kitchen table, opened the laptop, and logged on.

At that moment, Alex stuck his head round the door inquisitively. 'Party?' he asked.

'Party!' Debbie cheered and pulled him inside. He thanked her with a warm smile, and Debbie blushed to the tips of her ears.

Julia had to force herself not to roll her eyes. Debbie so obviously fancied Alex that it was positively cringeworthy. And Alex didn't seem to find the adulation at all embarrassing.

David walked over to Benjamin. 'Hey,' he said, 'what's up with you?'

'You all think I'm all over the place, but don't forget I'm a complete control freak when it comes to my work,' Benjamin growled.

Julia bent over him. Chris, too, had sat up and was paying attention. 'What are you doing?' he asked.

'All my video files are stored on the internet in secure, encrypted form. The safe of the Royal Bank of Canada has nothing on this.'

'Meaning?'

'I've still got an old version, one that couldn't be tampered with because nobody had access to it.' He nodded proudly. 'Bingo! Here it is: May13Boathouse01.avi.'

'What on earth are you talking about?' asked David.

Benjamin just carried on prattling. 'I know why my camera was ruined and someone interfered with the memory card. Because Angela's death wasn't an accident. And I've got it all on video.'

Julia frowned. Why was Benjamin blurting this all out now? What if one of the others there had something to do with it?

She looked suspiciously at Katie. She was leaning against the windowsill, as if all this had nothing to do with her. It was impossible to tell if she was feigning a lack of interest, or if she was just being Katie.

Another thought flashed through Julia's mind. What about Benjamin himself? Was he being so over-eager because he was the guilty party? Hadn't he overreacted to the argument with Angela in the refectory? And hadn't she given him such a brush-off in the *Chronicle*'s editorial office that he'd gone storming out of the room in a rage? Then there was the business with the secure server: he was evidently not only a video geek, but knew all about computers too – just like Angela. Might there be some link between the two of them? On the other hand: who could have a better alibi than Benjamin? He'd been at the party the whole time. And the film that he'd taken was the ultimate proof. Benjamin couldn't have been responsible for Angela's death.

But then why wasn't he being more careful? Was it really a good idea to tell everyone what they knew?

'Julia worked it out,' he was just explaining as the others listened, open-mouthed. 'She was the only one who noticed that a bit of the party film had been deleted.'

'But why would anyone want to tamper with the film?' Rose's eyes opened wide.

'Ben hasn't finished yet,' Katie interrupted.

'Someone cut one detail out of the video,' Benjamin continued. 'According to the timer, there's a second missing from the current version. One second. You'd hardly notice it unless you knew. But ... ' Benjamin tapped the laptop, 'I've got the original here.'

'So what are you waiting for?' said Chris.

Nine heads bent over the computer.

And once again there came the fast-forwarding from the start of the party: Robert on the jetty; Alex behind the decks; Rose, David and Julia. Chris, heading towards the forest, Debbie coming towards him. Landscape scenes, lake, mountains. Alex on the phone. Chris looking grim. Ike panting at the camera.

The images were constantly changing and it was impossible to follow what was going on, although it was quite clear that something terrible had happened behind the scenes; something that they were now trying to work out.

'Watch closely now,' Benjamin murmured, and pressed a couple of buttons. The film was now playing at normal speed.

Nine heads stared, fascinated, at the screen. There were

just too many people there. Julia just didn't feel right about this.

She looked at the screen.

The water was churned up, and slowly settled down again. The timer counted 10:10, 10:11, 10:12, 10:13. All they could see were circles that were gradually becoming smaller. 10:14, 10:15.

'There it is,' Chris said in a low voice. 'Can you enlarge it?'

There was something inside the circle.

They all looked, horrified.

'It might be a branch,' Rose ventured. 'There are loads of trees, roots and branches right by the shore.'

'Can't you make it any bigger, for God's sake?' David snapped.

'No, that's as big as it will go,' replied Benjamin.

But it didn't in fact need to be any bigger. The longer they looked at the image, the more silent the room became.

On the screen – fuzzy, but unmistakable – was a hand sticking up out of the water.

A snow-white hand.

Five fingers.

It floated across the surface of the water. Julia thought she was going to be sick. It wasn't the hand of a dead person, it was the hand of someone who was dying.

CHAPTER 27

'You filmed it,' murmured Chris. 'You filmed Angela Finder's death.'

'I didn't know.' Benjamin sounded croaky. For a moment, Julia thought he was crying – but he then started to laugh in an odd, hysterical way, and didn't seem able to stop. 'I filmed a murder, and I didn't even notice.' Benjamin prattled on and on. It was evidently his way of coping with the shock.

'She's holding something,' Robert interrupted him soberly.

They all stared at the image again.

They could definitely see the hand. And, yes, it was holding something tightly.

'Can't we get a clearer picture?' asked Alex.

'We'd have to send it to a lab,' Robert said matter-of-factly.

'I wonder if the police found the object, whatever it was?' said Katie. 'Has anyone heard anything about it?' One after another, they shook their heads.

They finally turned to look at Alex, but he just shrugged too. 'Guys, I don't like it any more than you do,' he said helplessly. 'But the Dean's been quite clear about this. No information is being given to students, not even to student mentors.'

'In that case, we'll just have to go and look for it,' Katie said calmly.

'Where?' whispered Rose.

They all knew the answer before Katie gave it.

'On the bottom of the lake.'

'And who's going to be crazy enough to do that?' asked David. The question hung in the air.

'Me,' Katie declared.

Katie? Katie? Why? Was she looking for something? Was the thing – whatever it was – some kind of evidence that she wanted to find before anyone else did?

But while Julia was wondering about this, it occurred to her that the others could reasonably think the same of her. Someone who gave nothing away about herself was always going to seem suspicious.

'No.' David's voice was almost toneless. 'I almost died in the lake. You haven't got a clue what it's like.'

'What I do is none of your business,' Katie replied coolly.

'The lake's well over a hundred and fifty feet deep in some parts. You wouldn't stand a chance.'

'It's not that deep at the bit by the shore where we found Angela. Thirty feet at most. Otherwise we wouldn't have found her.'

'There's something wrong about the lake,' said Robert. 'The water level varies. And for every ten metres of immersion depth, the pressure rises by one bar. That's when it can become dangerous.'

'I know what I'm doing,' Katie replied stubbornly.

Julia could see from her eyes that nobody was going to be

able to stop her. It was something she admired in Katie. Something that she'd lost along with her former self.

'I'm coming too,' Julia said suddenly. 'I used to dive a lot.'

Robert looked at her in horror.

'I'm not taking any responsibility for this.' Alex had turned pale. 'I have to tell the Dean.'

'What about your famous code of silence?' Chris said sarcastically. 'We didn't drop you in it, so you'll keep your mouth shut about our plans.'

Julia's decision had been made on the spur of the moment. And she didn't just want to find whatever it was that Angela had been holding.

No: she suddenly felt an urgent need to do something extreme.

She wanted to do battle: to battle against life and death. And she wasn't lying when she'd said that she often used to dive. She had been in a diving club and had taken part in international competitions. She had mastered the pressure balance underwater – and, moreover, she had spent years training her lungs, even if she was now out of practice.

They met at six the following morning at the bridge where Angela had drowned. They could be certain that there wouldn't be anyone else around at that time of day.

Only once they had climbed down the embankment did Julia realise what diving here actually meant. Katie was right that the water was no more than thirty-five feet deep. But she had forgotten how steeply the shore sloped downwards.

There was no chance of gradually becoming used to the cold. They would have to plunge straight in. But the lake hadn't been that cold yesterday so perhaps she was worrying unnecessarily.

Julia glanced at Katie next to her. They both shivered in the fresh morning air. It was fifty degrees at most. The sky was grey and cloudy, but the sun was trying to break through the clouds. It was as if the day couldn't quite decide if it was going to be nice or not.

'Are you sure?' Chris asked quietly, putting his arm round Julia's shoulder.

She exchanged looks with him, and replied: 'Absolutely.' He nodded, and she was grateful that he hadn't tried to stop her.

'Off we go then!' Katie took a short run-up and dived head first into the water.

Julia's heart was pounding.

Then she followed Katie.

Despite her experience the previous day, Julia was prepared for the water to be freezing cold. Now, though, she could hardly feel it. Or was that because her body had become impervious to pain in recent months? Like it had grown a protective layer.

She took one more deep breath on the surface, then shut her eyes and dived downwards.

She was surrounded by silence and cold, which she was becoming increasingly aware of. At first when she opened her eyes, she couldn't make anything out.

With fluid movements, she began to swim further down –

until someone grabbed her by the shoulder. Katie was looking at her, obviously frightened.

Julia nodded to her. Everything's fine, she signalled, and wanted to add: I'm happy!

That's precisely what she was. Here underwater, everything was different – familiar, almost. It was a bit like coming home.

Julia's diving record was two minutes forty-three seconds. Now, though, she felt she could stay under this water for much longer.

She looked around. The shore fell steeply away, ending with a concrete reinforcement. If someone had pushed Angela into the water, she would have sunk like a stone.

The thought of it made Julia feel faint. Or was that already a lack of oxygen?

Concentrate, Julia.

She started swimming again, and after a couple of strokes she could already see the bottom. No plants, no fish. But lots of stones instead. It all felt desolate, forlorn, barren. She had read on online diving forums about mountain lakes that resembled a desert at the bottom – this seemed to be one of them. Or this part of it, at any rate.

Julia could feel her breath slowly running out. Well, what could she expect? She hadn't dived for months, and was completely out of practice. She hastily scanned the bed of the lake, simultaneously counting the seconds until she would have to go back up again.

An ancient plastic bottle.

A bit of old tarpaulin.

Where was Katie?

Had she already gone up for air?

Julia carried on looking. There had to be something there. Some trace of Angela. She could feel her chest tightening and it was becoming harder not to breathe, but she didn't want to give up.

She suddenly felt someone pulling her arm upwards. Julia shook the hand off. She was there to get to the bottom of things. To find the truth.

She ran her hands over the stones, felt in all the gaps.

Then her fingers felt something.

Something rough.

A chain?

She pulled it out. It was jammed. Julia gave it another jerk. The chain was stuck somewhere. Using all her strength, she pulled again – and then she was holding the object that Angela must have dropped. Without thinking, she slipped the chain down the neck of her swimsuit.

Again Katie grabbed Julia by the shoulder, and again Julia shook her off.

Why?

Julia didn't understand it herself. It was beyond her control. It was as if she'd found what she'd wanted. Down there, she didn't have to lie; she didn't have to deceive; she didn't have to look into the eyes of other people who wanted something from her. As if that tortuous time had gone and she could now just let go.

Perhaps dying there hadn't been all that bad for Angela?

Maybe there were worse ways to die than by drowning?

Maybe death wasn't in the slightest bit gruesome in the way that everyone said it was, but instead was the kind of peace that she was experiencing now?

She could feel her limbs losing strength. Her body floating. She let go of something that she'd been clinging on to with all her might for the past few months. Something that would never return.

Her past.

Mum.

Dad.

Then a jolt.

Julia felt someone tugging at her. Cries. Shouting. Felt herself being pulled upwards. She let herself be pulled. And when her shut eyes were blinded by the sun, she thought she had dreamed the whole thing.

Frantic voices.

'Breathe! For God's sake, breathe, Julia!'

Someone was crushing Julia's body. Her ribs hurt as if they were snapping one after another.

'You have to breathe!'

Why?

Julia's head was forced backwards, her mouth pushed open, and then strange lips were on hers. They felt hard, determined. And then air was streaming into her body, and she opened her eyes and looked into a face that turned out to be David's.

And he looked absolutely furious.

'Are you crazy?'

Voices, faces – Julia couldn't quite put them together. 'What do you think you're doing? Four minutes! Four minutes under-water. Were you trying to kill yourself?'

Robert's white face and big eyes behind his glasses appeared in her line of vision. His expression of misery and horror shocked Julia. As did something else.

He knew.

He knew why she had stayed under so long, why she had hoped for a moment, just a moment, to dissolve and find peace on the bottom of the lake.

'I'm fine,' she stammered. She gasped for air, unable to stop either her teeth chattering or her body shivering. 'It's fine, really. I didn't have a problem down there. None at all.'

She could see the mistrust in Robert's face, but he didn't say a word as David carried on cursing to himself. 'This damn valley and its effing lake', as if it were nature's fault that Julia had played roulette with her life for one short moment.

'So how did it go?' Debbie seemed to be the only one unmoved by events. 'Did you find anything down there?'

Still concentrating on pumping air into her lungs, Julia shook her head and thought of the chain down the front of her swimsuit. A chain with a locket attached to it.

'Just this,' she heard Katie murmur. She was holding two jagged metal objects.

'What's that?'

'Crampons,' Katie beamed. She seemed happy – for the first time since Julia had known her.

Chris was the only one who hadn't moved until now. He was sitting slightly away from the others, his hands covering his face. Julia stared across at him. At that moment he raised his head and his eyes were dark, almost black.

Later on – she had no real recollection of how she got back to the college – Julia sought sanctuary in the toilets near the entrance foyer. She couldn't tell anyone what had happened or how she'd felt in the water. She tried to act as normal as possible, hoping that nobody would notice what an effort it was. It was all the harder as people kept on being astonished by the fact that she'd stayed under the water for more than four minutes.

She stared at the chain.

The silver locket felt heavy in her hand.

There was nothing to suggest that it had been in the lake for almost a week.

Julia couldn't explain even to herself why she wasn't showing it to anyone. No, she did actually know. Apart from Robert, she didn't know anyone here at the college. Not properly.

Not her flatmates or the others in her year, and definitely not the students in the years above. Before she'd left, it had been drilled into her that she mustn't trust anyone.

Not Chris?

No, not even Chris.

She'd already got too close to him as it was.

Much too close.

She took a deep breath and opened the locket. By some

miracle, the water hadn't got inside, and it was completely dry. She reached for the black object inside that was still intact despite having spent days underwater in its silver hiding place.

At first, she had no idea what it was. But then it dawned on her. She was holding the smallest USB stick that she'd ever seen in her life. And there was more. The black metal casing was embellished with tiny diamantés.

CHAPTER 28

Julia didn't escape unscathed from diving to the bottom of Mirror Lake. When she was in bed on Sunday evening, her throat was already feeling horribly scratchy. She felt cold, and she was bound to wake up with a splitting headache thanks to the pressure on her temples.

Things aren't looking good, she thought.

Just before eight, there was a knock on the door and Chris came in. He didn't sit down, but stood at the side of her bed. His grey eyes scrutinised her grimly.

'Are you coming to the cinema?'

'No, I'm tired,' she replied. 'I want to stay in bed. I've had an exhausting day.'

She actually managed to laugh.

Chris, though, didn't join in. Instead, he muttered through clenched teeth: 'Don't ever do that again.'

It sounded like a threat.

'What?' asked Julia, though she knew exactly what he was talking about.

'Put your life at risk.'

'No,' she replied. 'I won't. I'm not stupid.'

'I'm not so sure about that.'

'Thanks a lot.' She was aiming again for a light-hearted,

sarcastic tone – but completely failed. Instead she just sounded pathetic – and all the more so for her croaky voice.

'What did you do down there for so long?' He rubbed his hand across his unshaven chin.

'I didn't have a watch. And by the way ... you need a shave.'

'That's not what we're talking about.'

His face was saying: don't change the subject.

At this point Julia's former self couldn't help but re-emerge. Never in a million years would she have allowed another person to spot her insecurity.

'Do you think that suddenly growing stubble is a sign of stress? Like spots? Are you having a sudden burst of testosterone?' she mocked.

'Shut up, Julia!' Chris clenched his fists; his knuckles were white. 'Just shut up and stop playing games!'

The anger that suddenly arose in him shocked Julia to the core. As if he had read her thoughts, he hissed between clenched teeth: 'You lie every time you open your mouth. You lie because you're hiding something. And you show me with every word, every gesture, every look, that you don't trust me.'

She stared at him. Her heart felt all knotted up. She tried to convey her feelings in her look, in her face.

I do want to trust you, she wanted to scream. But it's not a question of what I want. If I trust you, you have to have reason to trust me! But how can that work if my whole life consists of lies?

Could he tell what she was thinking?

Could he sense her desperation?

Could he feel how much she longed to unburden herself?

There was a moment of silence. Waiting, as if the ticking clock were deciding what would happen next.

'Please,' he suddenly whispered. 'Talk to me.'

She could feel the tears welling up as she turned her face to the wall and shook her head.

She heard him getting up.

'Okay, then there's no reason for me to stay any longer.'

She heard his footsteps nearing the door, then stopping as if he were expecting her to relent.

'Chris,' she said in a choky voice, turning to him.

'Yes?' He looked at her full of expectation. Had she reconsidered?

She was going to disappoint him. 'Can I borrow your laptop?' she asked.

He was going to run away and never speak to her again. And she wouldn't blame him either.

'It's in my room,' he said. Every trace of emotion was carefully banished from his voice.

Maybe, Julia thought, love is trusting someone even when you know they're lying.

She looked at him. Chris was looking at her.

'Thank you,' she whispered.

'Don't you want to know my password, Julia?' he asked.

It was one of those still nights in the valley. The moon hung over the mountains, bathing the landscape in an unreal, dark blue light. Julia could smell the night. It tasted of forests and earth and water – and of Angela Finder's death.

Julia shivered.

This was the deepest darkness that Julia had ever experienced, but also the most beautiful starry sky that she'd ever seen. The mountains were reflected in the still water of the nocturnal glacial lake. There was a new moon, and the stars were twinkling: tiny diamonds in the total darkness. Above the Ghost, the Milky Way stretched out with the constellations of Cassiopeia and, to its right, Perseus. In this constellation, Robert had explained to her, was the star Algol, also known as the Devil Star or Demon of the Desert because it changed in brightness at particular intervals.

Maybe someone somewhere up there could foresee her fate. Could determine it. But her past belonged to her, and she had to protect it.

Here in the valley, Julia had come to know this kind of silence for the very first time. She had spent her childhood in a city filled with high-rises, traffic jams, crazy dossers hanging around outside, fire engines racing through the streets, police sirens, the loud parties held by her parents. Booming seventies rock music. Virtually no plants – well, apart from a few trees out in the street. They somehow looked as if they could have been made of plastic. At any rate, they barely changed over the course of the years that they lived there.

Maybe they'd been made of plastic too.

Oh yes! She'd forgotten the animals. Neutered dogs and stray cats.

And now that Julia came to think about it, the cars had really been the secret rulers over her home city.

Had been.

Thinking is a process that people have to learn to control. Dad had always said: *You're far too emotional.*

Mum's words: *Take care of Robert.*

Mum and Dad were both dead. And neither she nor Robert had had any idea of what their father had been involved in. People said he'd risked his life for justice. Yes, but he'd risked his whole family's lives too. And he hadn't even bloody well asked if they were okay with it.

Julia burst into tears.

How short the past felt in retrospect, and how long it would take for the glacier to melt into the darkness.

Julia shook herself. She went back into her room and shut out the darkness by closing the balcony door.

Just to make sure that they really had all gone down to watch the film, she went out into the hallway. There was no sound coming from any of the rooms – yet the tension in the apartment was tangible. On the way to the first floor, Julia could feel the draught in the old corridors. The brown floors with the worn carpets seemed shabbier than ever; there was something about the whole block that made it look as if it had turned its back on time.

She grabbed Chris's laptop and scurried as quickly as possible back to her own room, where she decided not to turn on the light. Then she opened the laptop and switched it on.

She wasn't like Robert.

She didn't derive enormous pleasure from hoovering up the contents of all thirty volumes of the Encyclopaedia Britannica, just to get to the bottom of things. No, Julia had always been ace at avoiding and repressing things. And now, too, she would have far preferred to run away rather than wait for this stupid bloody laptop to boot up.

Thousands of thoughts were spinning round in her mind.

Why she was doing what she was doing.

Why she wasn't telling anyone what she'd found on the bottom of the lake.

Next moment, the pale light of the screen lit up the room. Julia shivered in the face of the silent, dumb lifelessness of technology.

Her hands were trembling and drenched in sweat. Finding the USB port cost her several moments; and putting the memory stick in cost her several more.

And then, finally, the operating system opened up.

After just a few seconds, she was asked for Chris's password. It was: Julia Frost.

CHAPTER 29

Julia's eyes were glued to the laptop screen. And it only took her a few seconds to work out what was stored on the diamanté-encrusted USB stick.

Angela Finder had been better than any secret service in the universe; more proficient than any detective; more meticulous than the Stasi; smarter than the CIA.

The USB stick contained a complete data bank of the entire college. Every teacher, every employee, every student included. Even Mr Walden, the Dean, had his own file.

The directory was clearly organised. Bungalow 17: Sayaka Kitube, Angela Finder, Eliza Wood.

Apartment 231: Katie West, Debbie Wilder, Rose Gardner. And although she'd been expecting it, Julia's heart seemed to freeze inside her chest as she read her own name: Julia Frost.

Julia sat there for a while, staring at the screen. Then she watched herself slowly reaching out, moving the cursor on to her name as if in slow motion, and her right middle finger pressing the Enter button. It seemed like an eternity before the programme loaded and a file opened. As if paralysed, she stared at the page.

It was a photo album of her past that was now on the screen. Julia's parents' house. Their photos. Photos of the whole family. Then Julia on her own. Robert. Photos of her old school in Berlin. Newspaper articles about the diving competitions she'd taken part in. Her reports.

She had been certain that all this information had been completely destroyed – but here it was. The police had promised her that nobody would ever have access to it.

But hadn't Dad always warned her? He'd kept on saying that anything you put on the internet can never be completely destroyed. And she'd just laughed.

She felt a wave of nausea. Her stomach was rebelling. Everything swam before her eyes. Just in time, she managed to run through the hallway to the toilet, where she knelt by the loo and was repeatedly sick.

Puking her guts out. Whoever had come up with that expression had bloody well known how Julia felt at that moment. Everything that had overcome her when she'd seen those pictures – her fears, her suppressed memories, her feelings – they were being regurgitated from deep within her until, at some point, there was nothing left but bitter bile.

Julia leaned against the tiled wall, trembling and exhausted, and for one peaceful, wonderful, unspeakably precious moment, she thought about nothing at all.

But then it all came back to her. She remembered about the laptop and about what was stored on that USB stick. She pulled herself together, washed her face in the basin, gave her teeth a quick brush and, her knees trembling, made her way back to the kitchen, where she took some water from the fridge.

And then she heard it. It was a soft, gentle sound – but

Julia instantly knew that it was the sound of the door on to the landing being cautiously opened.

With one bound, she was out of the kitchen. The hallway was empty. She wrenched the door open. The long corridor was in darkness. There was nobody to be seen.

There was a faint pinging noise. The lift! Julia raced off, but was too late. The door was shutting just as she turned the corner. Then the big numbers of the individual floors lit up. 2, 1, G, –1, –2.

Julia raced back into her room. The only sound was the humming of Chris's laptop. She pressed the space bar. The screen sprang into life.

Her hands flew across the keyboard.

She clicked frenziedly on the list of files.

Nothing!

G drive device not available.

Her hands felt for the USB stick at the side of the machine.

The slot was empty.

The files had vanished.

And so had Angela Finder's locket.

CHAPTER 30

Robert was sitting in the stuffy cinema, which was near to the computer department and media rooms in the basement of the college. The basement extended far into the cliff. There were no windows down there. The corridors were lit by lurid neon strip lights and whenever Robert went down to the basement he always felt as if he were going to suffocate. He could hear all around him the rustling of popcorn containers and constant whispering.

The Lord of the Rings was showing on the screen, and Robert was wondering why the film held such fascination for so many people. There was nothing in it that was real, was there? The whole thing was a fairy tale, a fantasy. Of course Tolkien had been a genius and had even invented an entire language, which Robert had spent a long time learning. Today, though, he was finding both the images and words irritating and creepy.

These woods are perilous.

You can't turn back.

They say that a great sorceress lives in these woods.

These sentences whirled around non-stop in his head, joining up in a nightmarish way with reality.

Why did he find the valley so creepy?

What dangers were lying in the forest around him? Why couldn't he get rid of the feeling that there was something wrong with the lake?

The lake.

It was the lake that had been bothering him above all since the night of the boathouse party. There was something down there. Something that was causing the weird currents and dangerous whirlpools.

Maybe a subterranean stream, he thought for what must have been the hundredth time. Subterranean streams that supplied Mirror Lake with water.

And he had never found any record of how deep the lake actually was. Hadn't he discovered that for himself? That night in the swirling water it had felt as if there was nothing but unfathomable depths below him.

And all the misfortunes that seemed to be piling up. Was there a reason for that too? Or was it all just coincidence?

The policeman who had looked after Julia and him – it felt to Robert as if it was years ago – had said: *Your father was a hero.* Maybe he was, Robert didn't know.

Robert derived no consolation at all from viewing his father as a hero. What would have been a consolation was if someone had told him the truth, all the details that . . .

He was jerked out of his reverie as Rose suddenly stood up next to him to let Benjamin pass. 'D'you want me to get you a Coke?' he whispered.

Robert shook his head and tried to concentrate on the screen once more.

Just minutes later, though, there was more rustling. This

time someone further forward had stood up and was disappearing through the door curtains. If he wasn't mistaken, it was Debbie.

Then peace was finally restored. The Black Riders appeared on the flickering screen. They were chasing Frodo and Sam. Robert shut his eyes.

Why did death automatically turn you into a hero? So the Dean, Richard Walden, hadn't arranged a funeral, as Robert had expected him to do, but he had ordered that the flags be flown at half-mast and had had Angela Finder's picture put up in the reception foyer. There was a book of condolence too. Robert hadn't looked at which students and lecturers had signed it. All he knew was that Angela was someone few would mourn for.

He had heard that one of the older students had called her 'the bug', and Isabel had even described her as a sewer rat. And Benjamin had had it in for Angela. Okay, maybe that was the other way round, but Robert had himself seen them together down here in the basement on the evening of the party. Angela had been going on at Benjamin about something. And Julia had told him later that Angela had sent Benjamin packing from the *Grace Chronicle* office not long before that.

And then there was Debbie. There wasn't a day that passed without her starting some new rumour about Angela that generally tended to contradict the last one. Like she had confided all her secrets to Debbie and Debbie alone.

If anyone asked for the details, though, Debbie just shook her head and shrugged her shoulders.

A chill ran down Robert's spine when he recalled Debbie

fixing him with her false-looking eyes, as if she were afraid that he might really be able to read her thoughts.

Although – and now Robert had to grin – this naive way of thinking went well with Debbie. As if he really could predict the future. Not even he himself believed that. It was more the case that he had more faith in his own feelings and intuition than he did in others'. And he sometimes wished he had more control over what was going on inside him. Yes, he longed for his brain to develop some kind of missile defence system that would arrest all the signals sent out by his fellow humans.

Instead, he felt the familiar racing in his heart. It corresponded to the sudden fear he had felt that night when his father had been found in the boot of his Mercedes.

Robert sat up in his chair.

And two things suddenly sprang to mind. Julia wasn't in the cinema, although *The Lord of the Rings* had once been her favourite film. And secondly: he hadn't seen Chris anywhere in the cinema either.

CHAPTER 31

Julia spent the next couple of minutes sitting in front of the empty screen, listening.

She wanted it to stop.

She wanted everything to stop: the silence in the apartment, the whirring of the computer, the fear, the questions, the headaches, the heat in her body, the trembling. She didn't want to do anything any more; she didn't want to be brave, didn't want to have to protect Robert. She didn't want to have to think about whether to trust people or not.

At that moment, she wanted to be nothing.

She was tired.

Empty.

Everything hurt.

Her eyes hurt.

But although she wanted to feel nothing, she didn't want anyone else to have the power to make her feel that way.

She wanted to decide for herself when she was going to give up.

The lift had stopped on the lower basement level. Down there were the cinema, media rooms and computer department, and also the server room, where all the files on Grace and its students were stored.

And was the person who had taken Julia's past down there as well?

Julia squared her shoulders and got up. No, she wouldn't allow anyone to find out her real name. And nobody was going to find out that Robert had been christened Ralph.

Julia didn't encounter anyone as she made her way down in the lift. The lift doors opened with a gentle hum, and she stepped out into the long corridor.

The corridors in the basement weren't much different from those in the seminar rooms, apart from the fact that there weren't any windows here and the floor was made of parquet rather than unpleasant grey lino. The greenish glow of the energy-saving lights gave the long passageways a cold, eerie atmosphere. It was like being in one of those horror films where you find yourself wandering around the long corridors of a morgue, expecting some kind of gruesome zombie to come round the corner at any moment.

As Julia reached out for the light-switch, she would have put money on the light flickering, but the corridor was immediately bathed in bright light. But there was nothing reassuring about it. It seemed as if the builders had deliberately designed the basement to be creepy.

The film music to *The Lord of the Rings* was resounding through the basement. She could tell which scene it was by the music.

Julia's head was pounding, but it was nothing to do with the noises coming from the cinema.

Two red-hot needles were pressing into her left and right temples. She put her hand on her forehead. She felt hot.

She quickly set off and ran down the corridor. Ahead of her was the computer department. The door was ajar.

She could still hear the music to the Battle for Middle-earth. She could be grateful that it wasn't a different film; a comedy or some kind of romance. She'd presumably never have found the courage with that kind of musical accompaniment.

She slowly opened the door to the computer department.

And although she'd tried to prepare herself for whom she might encounter, she couldn't believe it when she saw who it actually was.

It was Katie.

Katie West was sitting at one of the PCs. Julia instantly recognised the list of files up on the screen.

Katie looked at her. 'So there you are,' she said, as cool as a cucumber.

Julia cleared her throat. Something was stuck in her throat, making it hard to swallow. 'What are you doing here?' She couldn't recognise her own voice.

'Do you really need to ask?' Katie shook her head. 'I'd have thought you were more intelligent than that.'

Julia didn't reply. She couldn't think of the words – no, she had too many words swirling around her head. And so she remained doggedly silent and didn't speak even when Katie said, 'You got the chain out of the lake, didn't you? And you found the locket.'

Julia glanced across at the USB port. The diamanté-encrusted stick looked so tiny, so harmless. And yet it had the power to cause so much misery.

'What did Angela know about you?' she finally asked.

'Nothing,' replied Katie, twisting her face into that odd, sphinx-like smile. 'Absolutely nothing.'

'You're lying! Angela was blackmailing you.'

'Why would she have done that?' Irritation, surprise, threat? Julia couldn't quite define Katie's tone.

'What did you do to her?'

'What did I do to her?' Katie looked at the screen again. 'Nothing. You're crazy.'

'"I know what happened",' Julia quoted at her. 'That's what it said in Angela's email to you.'

For the first time, there was a visible reaction. Katie turned white.

'So what did Angela know, then?' Julia persisted.

'I didn't do anything!' Katie clenched her fists. 'And nobody's blackmailing me. It's not me!' The expression on her face scared Julia. Katie stood up slowly, turned to look at Julia, and adopted a threatening stance. 'It's got nothing to do with anyone else, do you hear me?' Her dark, narrow eyes were blazing. 'And I swear to you, if you tell anyone, then I'll . . .'

Katie didn't finish, but suddenly grabbed Julia's arm and pulled her down. 'Down. Now!' she hissed. 'And if you even so much as breathe, I'll make you regret it!'

With these words, she pulled Julia down the aisle, through the rows of computer work stations. Once they were right at the back, she pushed Julia behind one of the partitions and forced her to the ground.

Julia's teeth were chattering loudly and her whole body was shaking. It seemed as if Katie were changing. From one second to the next, her eyes were becoming even narrower than they already were. Her high cheekbones seemed to be rising even higher; her mouth was broadening until all Julia could see was a grimace.

Now she raised her hand, and Julia shut her eyes. She was expecting a blow, but it didn't come. When she opened her eyes once more, she saw Katie crouching beside her, holding a finger to her lips.

A door banged.

Then she heard footsteps.

Then came the Windows jingle. Someone was starting up one of the computers.

The clack of a keyboard.

Next to her, Katie didn't move a muscle. Had she actually taken out the memory stick, or was it still in the PC?

The door opened again.

'Have you still got to work?' Unmistakably Debbie.

No reaction.

'Or didn't you fancy coming to the film?'

'Didn't fancy it,' came the short reply. Julia recognised that voice too.

'Hey, nor did I. Why would I want Orlando Bloom if I've got you?' Debbie laughed in her characteristically shrill way.

Still crouching next to Julia, Katie moved slightly forward in order to peep out from behind the partition. Julia seized the opportunity to shift from her uncomfortable position. Katie immediately grabbed her arm, looked angrily at her, and put her finger on her mouth.

What was going on here? Julia still didn't get it. What was Katie up to?

'As it happens, I was looking for you,' said Debbie.

'Oh yeah?' the voice growled.

'I wanted to talk to you about Angela.'

No reply.

'She helped you, didn't she?' Debbie persisted. 'Well, she was clever, pretty clever, but believe me, she wasn't the only one.'

'Why don't you just go and watch the film like everyone else?'

'I've never been able to stand fantasies.' Debbie relapsed into her usual, apparently oh-so-harmless, chatty tone. 'And I prefer to make up my own stories.' She giggled. 'But let's get back to the matter in hand. You know who my dad is, don't you? He's pretty well connected. He might be able to help you.'

Everything started spinning in Julia's thudding head. What was this stuff about 'well connected' all about? And why was Katie still holding on to her?

'Why don't you just get lost?' she heard from further forward. 'I don't need your father's connections any more than I need your stupid prattle about Angela. If you don't want to watch the film, just go to bed.'

'Alone?' Debbie was presumably trying to sound seductive, but she sounded like something from a bad film. 'You can't really mean that. You know how much I like you.'

'Hey – what are you doing? Leave me alone!'

'I know you like me. I can tell!'

'Are you crazy?'

'But you said at the lake that I could come to you any time.'

'Because you were moaning about how you couldn't cope with your course.'

The idea arose unbidden in Julia's mind that Debbie might be about to start stripping off. And as if on cue, she heard an angry exclamation.

'Stop it!'

'But you want it too,' wailed Debbie. 'Why else did you bother with me that night?'

'Are you out of your mind? I'd rather sleep with Ike than you!' Then came a laugh, and a noise came from Debbie's throat that Julia couldn't identify. A cross between a sob and a growl.

'You're horrible,' Debbie whispered. 'You're just horrible.'

A noise that sounded like a chair turning over. Something bumped against a table.

'I'd do anything for you.' A short pause, then a tone that didn't sound like Debbie's:

'Like Angela did.'

Silence. Next to Julia, Katie didn't stir. Her eyes were wide open.

'I love you – don't you understand?' Debbie cried. 'I really love you!'

Another chair moved, then the voice again. Sober. Cold. Icy cold in a way that Julia had never heard it. 'Just get lost, Debbie. I've had enough. Have a nice evening; have a nice life – without me!'

Suddenly all the whining and desperation in Debbie's voice vanished. 'If I were you, I wouldn't be telling me to go away,' she said as calmly as if she were talking about the weather. 'I know that Angela gave you the exam questions.'

'I have no idea what you're talking about.'

'Angela could get into the computers of even the biggest banks. The entrance exam questions – that must have been a complete cinch for her.'

Julia saw Katie flinch.

And now she gradually started to realise what had happened. Angela had been blackmailing him too.

Loud noises were coming from the front of the room.

'Ow – that hurts!'

'It's supposed to hurt, and it'll hurt even more if you don't keep your mouth shut.'

'Is that what you said to Angela when you pushed her into the lake?'

Julia held her breath. Him? No, that was impossible!

'Debbie, just take my word for it. You're skating on thin ice – extremely thin ice!' There was no doubting that this was a threat.

'Oh really?' The sarcasm was obvious. 'I don't think so. Because it just so happens that I know what you're doing here. You're looking for Angela's secret files, aren't you? So that you can save your precious ass. But how do you think you're going to find them when they're so encrypted and hidden? They can only be tracked down by someone who knew as much as Angela.' Debbie's voice now had a ring of triumph. 'Someone like me!'

CHAPTER 32

There was an angry exclamation, and then a gasping sound. Katie stuck her head out and Julia, too, couldn't help but try to see what was happening.

The partition wall largely hid Debbie's body, but Julia recognised the hands that were clamped around her neck. For a moment it seemed as if just her head were floating in mid-air, only then to be flung with full force against the metal leg of the desk.

Debbie had stopped moving.

Her face was even paler than normal, if that was possible. A clearly visible trickle of blood was running down her cheek.

Feeling hot, so hot, Julia watched – as though from far away – as Katie was removing her shoes and creeping off, keeping her body close to the ground. Cautiously, oh so cautiously, always keeping in the shadow of the partition.

Julia herself couldn't move. The memories had all come suddenly flooding back, suppressing all rational thought, destroying all the protective mechanisms in her brain.

The gasping.

The scraping sound.

That's how Robert had described it.

But Julia had seen Mum's hand behind the desk for herself when she'd come home that fateful night.

The ghastly red on her fingernails that Julia had thought was nail varnish until it turned out to be blood.

Her first night with Kristian – and her last.

Why? Why hadn't she stayed in that night? Why had she crept out of the house after that dreadful row with her father? Why had she cleared off?

Why hadn't anyone warned her?

Julia's father had been a policeman.

A run-of-the-mill policeman.

Or, at any rate, that's what Julia had thought. And then it had transpired that Mark de Vincenz had been an under-cover agent. He had posed as a drug dealer and had pretended to deal in heroin in order to track down a Chinese Mafia gang who were running their European operation from Berlin.

But it had gone wrong. Someone had blown Julia's father's cover and betrayed him to his enemies. The men had got into her parents' bungalow, shot her mother, ransacked her father's study, tied him up, and dragged him right through the house. Then they'd bundled him into the boot of his Mercedes and pumped him full of heroin – so full that he had died right there in the boot. They had parked the car containing his body outside the police headquarters in Potsdamer Platz. It was more than a day before the body was discovered.

One betrayal leads to another.

One lie leads to another.

Every secret creates new secrets.

Robert had been at home that night and, hidden in his room, had had to hear it all happening. He was the only witness. And it was little short of a miracle that the men hadn't found him.

Julia couldn't move, although she was aware that Debbie was still lying motionless on the ground, barely ten yards away. The little trickle of blood was growing. It was streaming from a head wound and down her face.

She watched Katie's lithe movements. There wasn't a sound as she flitted from one partition to the next until she was just a few metres away from Debbie. Julia had no idea what she was doing, but she trusted her. She had no choice but to trust her.

It was Julia who made the mistake. As she now tried to follow Katie, she bumped into a chair. It tipped over with a crash.

Then she could already hear footsteps making their way quickly across the room.

Trainers.

Black Nikes, to be more precise.

She didn't dare look up.

He was standing directly behind her, staring down at her.

Alex.

No, it wasn't Alex any longer.

He might look like Alex, but he wasn't Alex.

His eyes were dark and narrow. And the silhouette of his

face looked white against the bright neon lights in the computer room. Julia had never seen anything like this. Alex's expression was so wildly angry that his face looked eerily deformed.

Before she could say or do anything, his hands were already pressing her head on to the floor. Julia's lips were touching the dirty lino.

She was in turmoil. An insistent voice in her head was whispering: Do something! Defend yourself! Don't let it happen like Mum and Dad did!

'Why didn't they defend themselves?' Chief Inspector Peter Bauer had asked Julia – no, she'd been Laura then.

'Because they didn't get chance to.'

But wasn't there always a chance?

Katie? Where was Katie?

Julia hated feeling like a helpless victim. She hated lying on the ground with her lips touching the filthy floor.

Alex suddenly let go of her shoulder. She could feel his grasp loosening as he quickly looked round.

Her body tensed up and she raised her head slightly.

It took all Julia's might to tense up her muscles and sinews and concentrate on her legs.

But she managed to summon up the strength. And she kicked out with full force.

A deep voice. A dark yell. A croaky curse.

But the next moment the heavy, sweat-drenched hands were pressing her face back on to the floor. Her teeth banged against the foot of a desk. She could taste metal. One of her lips split with the pressure. Her mouth tasted of blood.

Debbie groaned loudly somewhere.

Julia couldn't think. She couldn't speak.

Couldn't breathe.

Fear of suffocating.

Panicky choking.

Loss of consciousness.

She must have been unconscious for several seconds. Julia only started to come round when she heard a rattling sound. Someone was hammering away like mad at a PC keyboard, breathing heavily and cursing quietly as he did so.

Julia couldn't feel her body any more. She felt strangely weak, almost as if she were floating, weightless, like an astronaut. And she was no longer lying at the back of the room. Alex must have dragged her further forwards.

With difficulty, she turned her head to one side. Debbie was lying next to her. She was so pale, she looked as if someone had splashed white paint all over her face. A white infused with bloody lines, making Debbie look hideously disfigured.

And Katie? Katie had vanished into thin air.

Julia moved, raised her head, tried to sit up.

'Damn it,' she could hear Alex's voice above her.

A chair was pushed backwards, then he was kneeling down beside her, scrutinising her. His face was immobile, cold, rigid.

'What . . . ?' croaked Julia. It was the only word she could manage, and it sounded pathetic.

'You little bitches and your stupid nosiness,' the voice

whispered right into her ear. 'People watching me, spying on me, running around after me, pursuing me. Trying to destroy everything I've built up for myself.'

Julia guessed what he was talking about.

'Knowledge is power,' the detective in Berlin had told Julia and her brother. 'If anyone finds out where you are, then you're in danger. So don't trust anyone, you hear? Nobody. You're the only two who can keep your secret.'

'But I don't know anything.' Julia could barely speak, as Alex's hands were now pressing on her larynx.

'You think I don't know why you're here? Why you were rummaging around in my office in the middle of the night? First that stupid Debbie, and now you. Thought I wouldn't notice, eh? Well, you're both wrong. I see everything, and I can see through you. It was all just about one thing for you, wasn't it? That's why you risked your life in the lake and didn't say anything about the locket, isn't it? You want to do the same as all the other little bitches.' Alex's voice was now just a hoarse whisper. 'You want to blackmail me.'

'No, none of it had anything to do with you,' Julia croaked. But Alex wasn't listening.

'And then Angela thought she could take away my future, but she was wrong.' He laughed briefly. 'You're all wrong. My life is my own, d'you hear me? It belongs to me.' He paused for a fraction of a second. 'Why couldn't you just leave me alone? Now it's too late.' It suddenly sounded as if Alex were close to tears. At any rate, he loosened his grip. Julia could move again.

'Debbie,' she murmured. 'We have to help her.' She tried to turn round.

Alex's hands closed around her neck once more. 'Don't you move an inch,' he hissed.

'I'm good at keeping secrets,' Julia said desperately. 'And I'll make sure Debbie keeps her mouth shut. I swear it.' She tried to make her voice sound as though she were making a promise. *You can trust me.*

'Ah, so this is the psychological ploy, is it?' Alex laughed, and it sounded as if his mood had changed yet again; as if he were genuinely amused now. 'So you think I've gone mad, do you? You don't have a clue. But that's the problem with you freshmen. It takes you too long to realise what's going on here. The joke isn't what's going on in me, but what's going on all around us. You haven't understood the valley, have you?'

Understood the valley?

'What are you talking about . . . '

Alex laughed shortly, then whispered: 'Can't you feel it? We all change up here. The valley does something to us. When I came here, I was a completely different person. I thought I could do anything. Absolutely anything. But as time's gone by, I've realised: you leave the past behind here, and become your true self.'

Julia could feel herself struggling for air as Alex carried on talking. 'Nobody understands. Not in the way I do. It's about saying goodbye, goodbye to whatever is outside the valley. This here is a laboratory, a laboratory in the wilderness, and anyone who wants to escape has to find their own way to do so.'

He had gone crazy. Angela may have been intelligent – but obviously she hadn't noticed that she was trying to black-mail a madman.

'The laws of the outside world all fall apart here, don't you see? That's the whole point! We're all in the valley for our own reasons.'

For a while an odd silence prevailed, as if someone were stopping the world from turning. Julia was mulling over what Alex had said. Then the moment had passed. She returned to the orbit of reality.

The hand on her windpipe was trembling. Should she dare to move?

No. Too soon. She had to let Alex feel that he was in total control.

Let him talk. Just talk. Get him to talk to you, then he might not do you any harm.

'Was it all really so important that Angela had to die because of it?'

'You didn't know her! She spent her whole time trying to court sympathy, disguising herself in that wheelchair, but she was a parasite. A parasite in my life.' He kicked Debbie. 'Just like her! They wanted to bore their way into my life like parasites. I was nice to Angela, you know? I'm always nice and friendly. But she wanted to eat me alive.'

Julia had a strange feeling that she wasn't the one with a fever, but Alex, who carried on whispering incessantly. 'She didn't want to let me go. And just because she did me one tiny little favour. That made her think she had some kind of claim on me, did it? That it would earn her my love? It was a complete cinch for her, getting hold of the entrance exam questions. Not even worth mentioning.'

Everything was clattering around inside Julia's head.

'What questions?' she whispered. Surely not the questions to the Grace entrance exam? That didn't make any kind of sense.

Then it suddenly dawned on her.

The full grant for Yale! Alex was on the list of recommended candidates. And he hadn't got there on his own merits, but because of Angela. Why hadn't she worked that one out?

The fingers had loosened more, but Julia still didn't dare try to escape.

'Do you know where I come from?' whispered Alex. 'From a ranch in Nowheresville. I was a nobody. But that all changed here in the valley.'

Now.

This was her moment.

Julia tensed up all her muscles, drew back her legs, aimed her right knee at his crotch – and then came . . .

Bang!

It sounded like a shot.

Someone screamed.

Was it her?

One of the overhead neon strip lights smashed and shards of glass fell down like a shower of sparks, no, like thousands of shooting stars that they could wish on.

Someone commanded: 'Let go. Now!'

A cut-glass voice that sent shivers down the spine.

And then the shooting stars faded and Julia saw Katie standing in the middle of the room. She was holding a gun in her hand, as small and inconspicuous as a child's toy, but Julia didn't doubt its lethal power for a second. And she believed every word when Katie, looking completely impassive, said: 'Next time, I'll aim for you rather than the light.'

It didn't come to that. Katie didn't have to prove what she was capable of, as two men came racing in through the door. They too were armed, and were closely followed by Robert.

Julia looked Alex in the eye. He initially looked shocked, but his expression turned to disorientation, bewilderment, hopelessness, until there was nothing left in his eyes but blank despair.

And then everything around Julia turned black.

CHAPTER 33

Robert couldn't put his finger on the feeling that had led him to leave the cinema. As always, he called it an equation that wouldn't balance, for which he could simply find no solution. All he could say was that he'd suddenly felt very close to Julia and had simultaneously felt as if she was moving further away from him. This had told him that she was in danger, and he'd alerted Security.

'And that's all?' asked Benjamin, who was videoing Robert's explanation. 'I need some proper material, y'know, Rob? I need something really good to go on. I'm trying to make a film here. And you're my hero!'

'Honestly, Benjamin,' Robert replied, shaking his head. 'I can't tell you any more than that. I don't know myself what goes on inside me.'

'It's because of you that I'm up to my neck in it.' Katie joined in. 'If I'd saved Julia's life, nobody would be going on about illegal possession of weapons. I'd be the hero, wouldn't I? Instead, I'm facing police charges and I might get chucked out of college.'

The group had gathered in the sick bay, where Julia was recovering from pneumonia.

The infection had already penetrated her bones that

terrible evening, now almost two weeks ago. It had pre-sumably been an after-effect of her dive into the lake. While Julia had been treated at the college, though, Debbie had had to be helicoptered to hospital. By the time the doctor appeared, Debbie was so hysterical that even an injection of tranquillisers hadn't helped. However, her injuries had looked worse than they actually were. She was diag-nosed by the hospital with severe concussion and a head wound.

However, Debbie had meanwhile turned it into a fractured skull, according to Rose, who went with David to visit her in hospital. Debbie's version of events sounded completely different from Julia's. She said she'd only gone into the computer room to rescue Julia because she'd had a premo-nition – before Robert's – that her best friend was in danger.

Katie and Julia had both been questioned by the police, but they hadn't mentioned the part that Debbie had played, along with several other details.

And anyway, it seemed that further investigation wouldn't be necessary as Alex Cooper hadn't stopped talking since his arrest. He didn't deny murdering Angela, but told so many crazy stories about the valley that he had to be held in a psychiatric ward to await trial.

'Let's be honest,' Benjamin was saying now. He put his camera down and stretched. 'There was always something a bit creepy about Alex, wasn't there? He was like one of those film psychopaths who act super nice, but are really serial killers.'

Julia adjusted her pillows so that she could sit up more

comfortably. It still hurt to breathe, but it was a great improvement on just a few days ago.

'To tell the truth,' she said, looking sheepishly at Benjamin, 'I thought for a while you had something to do with it.'

'Me?'

'Yeah, well, your row with Angela in the refectory. And then you not getting a job at the *Grace Chronicle*.' She shook her head. 'I'm really sorry.'

Benjamin bit his lip. 'You don't need to be,' he said slowly, and without his customary ironic tone. 'Actually I was kind of involved.'

Julia wasn't the only one who was staring at him wide-eyed.

'No, no, it's not what you're thinking,' he said indignantly. 'But that film – the idea of filming on the jetty at the party while Tom was putting on his show – that was Angela's idea, you see. Or, rather, Angela commissioned it.'

'Angela commissioned it?' Chris shook his head in disbelief. 'Why would she do that?'

Benjamin rubbed his chin. 'She knew about the murder mystery party. I only realised afterwards what she wanted the film for. She wanted more material that she could use to blackmail Alex. And maybe a couple of other people too.' He paused briefly. 'That evening, before she died, she offered me a deal. I was to film the party; she even wrote down when I was to aim the camera at Solomon Cliff.'

'And you didn't ask why?' said Julia.

'I didn't care why if it meant I got to make a film for the *Grace Chronicle*.' Benjamin shrugged. 'Well, anyway, it all went wrong. If that girl hadn't bumped into me at the critical moment, I'd have caught Isabel's jump from Solomon Cliff on camera – live and in full Technicolor.'

For a while there was silence. Chris finally cleared his throat. 'Do you know what that actually means?' he asked. His voice sounded even hoarser than ever.

'Without realising it, Angela Finder commissioned a film of her own murder.'

For a moment, Julia shut her eyes. Her fingers clasped the chain around her neck. Her parents' wedding rings were on the chain.

She couldn't believe what she was hearing. She was suddenly desperate for them all to go, to leave her alone. All except Chris.

But nobody seemed to hear her silent plea.

'Guys, there's still one thing I don't understand,' said Rose agitatedly. She was sitting on the windowsill. 'Alex was at the party, everyone saw him. And as soon as Robert jumped into the water, he ran off to tell Security.'

'Wrong.' Robert's serious voice cut through the room.

'Why, wrong?'

'For one thing . . . ' Although Julia had her eyes shut, she could clearly see Robert adopting a stance as if he were already a lecturer in Advanced Maths. 'Alex never told Security. Allegedly so that the party wouldn't be busted. And secondly – secondly, did anyone really see him at the party at precisely the moment I jumped into the water?'

'But Tom told me himself that Alex had gone to fetch help!' objected Rose.

'Oh, that!' Now there was a note of triumph in Robert's voice. 'But I asked Tom. Alex just rang on his mobile to say he was going to let Security know. Don't you see? Alex had it all worked out. He knew when Isabel was going to jump! He'd agreed on the time with Angela, who was blackmailing him with the Yale business. He pushed her to the edge of the water. She'd never have managed that on her own. Then he pushed her into the water, and she was under within a matter of seconds.'

Julia squeezed her eyes even more tightly shut. She wished she could shut her ears too. Why couldn't they go? Why couldn't they stop talking about it? Even Robert was talking about Angela's death as if he were offering some kind of mathematical proof. As if he weren't talking about someone's life, but a simple arithmetic exercise.

Or, it flashed through Julia's mind, was it a reaction to his own trauma? Was he simply relieved to have found whodunnit? Proof? Precisely because this was impossible in the case of their parents? Because the culprits were still somewhere at large?

It was David who diverted her from this train of thought. 'Do you think that's why Alex came up with this murder mystery party in the first place?'

Julia opened her eyes and looked at Chris. He was sitting right beside her bed, as he had done so often in recent days. She felt for his hand.

He returned the look, and she could tell that he understood.

'I don't suppose we'll ever find out,' he said briskly. 'And

307

to be honest, I don't think it matters much. Anyway, this visit should have been over ages ago.'

'But of course you're going to stay and play the devoted nurse.' Benjamin grinned suggestively – but, along with all the others, he dutifully got up. Robert and Katie were the last ones to say goodbye to Julia and Chris.

In the doorway, Katie stopped once more and looked at Julia. She smiled, and Julia smiled back.

Neither of them had told anyone what had actually happened in the last few minutes in the computer department. That Debbie had declared her undying love for Alex and that he'd treated her like dirt.

Julia couldn't have brought herself to say anything, but she didn't know why Katie had kept quiet.

Her former self, Laura de Vincenz, might have told – but a part of Julia had actually turned into Little Miss Perfect, and this part of her knew that there was nothing worse than loving and not being loved in return.

She thought back to the moment in the computer department when she had come round, just after Robert and Security had come storming in. Within the shortest possible time, the room had filled with people, as if it were rush hour at the Kurfürstendamm Underground or – as Julia Frost would say – Charing Cross Station.

It had only taken a couple of seconds.

One step.

Nobody had been watching her then.

Julia was the only one who had seen Katie pull the USB stick out of the PC and put it into her trousers pocket. And nobody apart from the pair of them knew anything about it.

Julia had no idea what Katie was hiding, and Katie didn't ask Julia for her story either. Without actually saying so, they had agreed that they would keep their secrets to themselves.

Nobody else in the college knew about the locket.

Nobody knew about the USB stick, apart from Alex.

And nobody had yet found the files that Angela Finder had hidden somewhere on the server.

It was an unsolved mystery, but Julia knew all about mysteries.

Katie gave her a last wave, then gently pulled the door behind her. The silence in the room spread out over Julia like a blanket.

Chris took his shoes off, lay down next to her on the bed, and put his arm under hers.

'Thanks,' she whispered. 'I needed that.'

He grinned at her. 'How are you, Julia Frost?'

'My lungs are rattling as if I'd swallowed a tambourine.'

He laughed, his fingers played with her hair, and he looked again at her with those wonderful, fascinating eyes.

Julia couldn't help herself. She simply had to keep diving into them. But she knew about diving, didn't she?

And as his mouth neared hers and his lips met hers, ready to open, Chris Bishop whispered: 'One day, Julia Frost, I'll find out the truth about you.'

The truth, thought Julia, as she crept out of bed later that night to meet Katie. The truth is just as incomprehensible as everything else.

They met at the place where Julia had thrown her mobile into the water.

It was Katie who was holding the black memory stick. They stared for a while at the diamantés glittering in the darkness. Only now did Julia realise that they were arranged in such a way that they formed the initials AF for Angela Finder.

'Are you sure?' Julia asked Katie.

'Aren't you?'

'Absolutely.'

'Here we go then. After all, it's not a funeral, and it's just zeros and ones that are stored on here really. No more than that.'

The next moment Katie raised her hand and threw the USB stick into the water.

It vanished within less than a second.

And Julia's past vanished with it.

She would now have to accept that she was no longer Laura de Vincenz. She hadn't in fact been Laura for a long while now. Alex had been right on one score. Until she'd arrived in the valley, Julia had only existed on paper. The valley, though, changed people – and it had turned Laura de Vincenz into Julia Frost.

She hadn't wanted it, but after the media coverage in the *Tagesspiegel*, anyone could sit at the breakfast table reading about how her brother had been in the house while his mother was being murdered. He had seen the culprit; he was the only witness. Since then, they'd both been in the most serious danger. And as of that moment, Laura and Ralph de Vincenz ceased to exist.

Witness protection programme, it was called. All it meant was that you had to leave behind everything that you had once been. The German police had given Laura de Vincenz the birth certificate, the brilliant credentials: in short, the life of another girl. A girl who was born on the 24th of December in London and who, together with her brother Robert, was killed in a car crash a year ago. This girl had been called Julia Frost, and she'd been chosen because the Vincenz children spoke fluent English, thanks to their mother.

Julia had been told that it was rather like an organ transplant. Someone died, and someone else carried on living with the dead person's kidneys, lungs, heart, so long as ... yes, so long as nothing unexpected happens. Security was a word that Julia no longer recognised.

The decision to come to Canada, though, had been Julia's. Her liaison officer had agreed to it; indeed, had thought it a good idea. The further away the better, he had said.

He, however, knew nothing about the letter welcoming Julia and her brother Robert as new students to Grace College.

And he had no idea that Julia and Robert Frost had ever applied to the college.

Katie's hand brushed her shoulder, then she turned and headed back for the college without another word. A short while later, Julia also crept back to the sick bay.

Only once she was back in bed did she realise that she hadn't struggled for breath once during her secret escapade, and that the pains in her chest had gone.

EPILOGUE

Three weeks later.

It was just after midnight, and the dark forest was lit with flickering torches. It had been Julia's idea.

'What are you up to?' asked Chris, who was tramping alongside her through the forest.

'You'll see,' replied Julia, turning and calling to Benjamin. 'Have you got your camera?'

'Yes.'

'Is the battery charged?'

'I've already told you it is, and I've got a spare one too.'

'Hey,' called Rose. 'How much further is it? I don't fancy getting lost in the middle of nowhere.'

'Nearly there.'

Pine needles rustled beneath their feet. Branches crackled in the darkness; a breath of wind blew through Julia's torch flame and for a moment she feared that it might go out.

But up in the sky, there was still a full moon which mag-icked its pale light into the night.

'It must be here, Katie, what do you think?'

'What must?'

'The clearing. And the stone.'

In the light of the torch, Julia could see Katie's sudden realisation.

'The memorial stone!'

'That's the one.'

'What are you talking about?' Debbie grumbled. She was her old self again. Or, rather, even worse.

'That.' Julia stretched out her hand. The moonlight fell directly on to the clearing ahead of them, where the memorial stone was gleaming white in the darkness. The hollow in the ivy-clad stone and the flowers inside it were clearly visible in the light of the torches.

'What's that?' asked Rose, bewildered.

'You know the story,' Julia began, 'the story of the students who disappeared without trace in the seventies.'

'I'd always thought that was just a legend.' Rose's hair was now almost half an inch long.

'No, really, it did actually happen.' Debbie's eyes gleamed excitedly. 'I've seen old newspaper cuttings.'

'Maybe they didn't disappear; maybe they just managed to escape from the valley,' laughed Benjamin.

'Have you ever thought about it?' asked Julia.

'About what?' David looked at her attentively.

'There are eight of us,' said Robert, moving to stand next to Julia.

'Eight?' repeated Rose.

'Eight students disappeared then,' Katie explained.

They stood there for a while, watching the curious patterns made by the torches on the memorial stone.

'Someone's brought flowers,' David said in surprise.

'I did,' replied Julia.

'Why?' asked Benjamin.

'Because it's a grave, and we ought to take care of it.'

The only one who hadn't spoken until now was Chris.

Benjamin held his torch right up to the stone and said, disappointed: 'But you can hardly see anything. The writing's been all weathered and washed away.'

'Where's your camera?' Julia asked.

Benjamin took off his rucksack and pulled the camera out.

'Focus on the stone.'

The camera whirred in the darkness.

'Do you think we could enlarge it and doctor it up so that we can read what it says?' Julia asked.

'Yes, with a bit of luck.'

'X-rays would be better,' interposed Robert.

'Exactly. Our little Hercules here can put the stone on his shoulders, carry it down to Fields, charter a plane at his own expense, and take it to the FBI.' Benjamin was practically wetting himself with laughter.

'No, but if you give me your film, I can send it to an institute that knows how to do it,' Robert explained calmly. He never responded to provocation.

'No way, I'm not letting go of my film.'

'But there are lots of other ways,' said Rose. 'I could copy the inscription. It wouldn't be a problem in daylight. A rubbing would be even more precise.'

'Good idea,' said Julia.

'But why are you so interested in this, Julia?' This was David again.

She didn't reply.

'Here's another idea.' David pulled a torch out of his

pocket. 'Move back a bit with those torches. The artificial light of my torch might make the contours show up a bit better.'

Julia went right up to the stone, and immediately saw that she could indeed read the writing more easily.

'What are you trying to do?' asked Chris. The tension in his voice was audible. 'They're just names of dead people.'

Julia felt as if her heart were trying to jump out of her chest.

'Right at the bottom,' she said. 'The last name.'

And Benjamin called: 'I think I can make it out. Though I'm not quite sure. It sounds a bit odd.'

'Go on,' said Julia impatiently.

'Well, if you ask me, the first bit is Mark. That must be the first name, then there's a D, an E and ... De Vin ... De Vincens or de Vincenz.' Benjamin stood up. 'Yes, Mark de Vincenz. Unusual name, isn't it?'

The torches flickered in the wind.

Robert's face was lit up for a moment. He was as white as a sheet.

And a voice inside Julia was screaming: it's him. It's really him! My father's name.

She had been wrong. You couldn't just leave the past behind; you couldn't just close the door behind you. For at some point, fate would return and open that door again with full force.

To be continued . . .